Grace stood before him, wearing only a slip of silk

"It's called a bra-slip," Grace explained. Logan tried to listen, but he couldn't focus on anything but the movement of her hands. She cupped the sides of her breasts and pushed them forward, nearly spilling out of the filmy undergarment. "The top doesn't give me much support though," Grace continued blithely.

Logan stood, fatigue and frustration and a sudden rigid strain in his jeans overriding his patience and good intentions. Grace needed to have that piece of lingerie. She very definitely *needed* to have it.

But Harris Mitchell, the city's worst crime lord, didn't need to see it. And no man who accidentally wandered past the dressing room's waiting area needed to see it, either.

Logan snatched Grace's arm and turned her back to the dressing room. "Don't you have any instinct for survival, Agent Lockhart?" he asked, pushing her into the closet-sized area and pulling the door shut behind him. "You can't go parading around half-dressed."

Because he couldn't ████████ to his sides, trying to ████████ his partner, not his ██ teach her, not take ██

But God help him, he desperately wanted to do both....

Dear Reader,

They say it's the quiet ones you have to watch out for. And I guess I've just proven that to be true. I've entertained myself for years, writing stories in my head—paranormal, action adventure, mystery, intrigue and, of course, romance. But I never dreamed that one day I'd be writing for Harlequin's sexiest series!

I started out writing for Harlequin Intrigue, and it will always be my first love. But when one of the Harlequin editors approached me about the new Blaze line, how could I refuse the chance to explore my naughty side? A planner by nature, I frantically started making a list. What did I consider sexy? How could I mix the thrill of danger, an irresistible hero, a laugh or two, and all of those titillating situations that kept overheating my imagination?

As my list grew, *Intimate Knowledge* was born. Like me, my heroine, Grace Lockhart, needs to think things through—and then she flies by the seat of her pants. Pairing up with a hero as hot as Logan Pierce, she doesn't have any other choice.

I'd love to know what you think of Grace's "education." You can contact me at P.O. Box 5162, Grand Island, NE 68802-5162.

Enjoy,

Julie Miller

P.S. Don't forget to check out tryblaze.com!

Books by Julie Miller

HARLEQUIN INTRIGUE
588—ONE GOOD MAN
619—SUDDEN ENGAGEMENT
642—SECRET AGENT HEIRESS
651—IN THE BLINK OF AN EYE
666—THE DUKE'S COVERT MISSION

INTIMATE KNOWLEDGE

Julie Miller

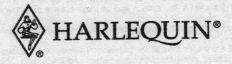

TORONTO • NEW YORK • LONDON
AMSTERDAM • PARIS • SYDNEY • HAMBURG
STOCKHOLM • ATHENS • TOKYO • MILAN • MADRID
PRAGUE • WARSAW • BUDAPEST • AUCKLAND

For my agent, Pattie Steele-Perkins.
Thank you for sharing your business savvy, your wisdom
about planning a writing career around real life,
and your enthusiastic support.

ISBN 0-373-79049-X

INTIMATE KNOWLEDGE

1

"I WANT YOU to teach Miss Lockhart about working undercover. I'm reassigning you to the organized crime division to work as her partner. We intend to take down Harris Mitchell."

"What?" Logan Pierce glared at the silver-haired FBI chief, Commander Sam Carmody. "Harris Mitchell?"

Thief. Money launderer. Murderer.

Logan had never worked a case against Mitchell, but when the crimes you committed were big enough and bad enough, every agent knew your name.

Stunned disbelief carried his gaze across the room to the stone-faced young woman sitting on the couch writing down in her stenographer's notebook every word being said. She'd dressed herself to appear older than she was, pulling her hair back into a tight bun, donning an unflattering pair of seriously thick glasses and wearing no makeup.

Grace Lockhart looked all of twenty-three—twenty-five, tops. She needed to work a few kiddie assignments before tackling something as dangerous and unpredictable as a major undercover case.

Logan shook his head and turned back to Carmody. "I work solo—you know that."

He hadn't had a partner for two years, two months and eleven days. Roy Silverton had been fresh out of the

academy on that first mission, too. Quick to learn, eager
to please.

Too young to die.

Logan could watch his own back. He'd learned to do
that long before the FBI had recruited him. It had been
a matter of survival back in downtown Chicago with no
mother and a father steeped in terminal grief.

Larry Pierce had been devastated when his wife had
been held hostage and then murdered during a botched
robbery at the bank where she'd worked. He'd found his
solace in a bottle. But six-year-old Logan had been devastated, too. And without a father's guidance, he'd raised
himself. He hadn't always made the best choices, but
he'd found a way to survive, a way to stay on top of the
game.

Eventually he'd straightened out enough to become a
cop, and was discovered by the Bureau on a joint undercover investigation. Discovered by Carmody himself,
who sent him to college and recommended him for the
Federal Bureau of Investigation's training academy here
in Quantico, Virginia.

Logan had taken a vow from the moment he'd earned
that first badge. He'd sworn to protect innocents like his
mother.

Like Roy Silverton.

To be responsible for another life...for another
rookie...

He didn't need that kind of grief.

An age-old pain tightened in Logan's chest, threaten-
ing to squeeze the breath right out of him. He covered
the vulnerability with a cocky smile and took a shot at
reasoning with his boss. "I'm good at this job."

"That goes without saying."

"You recruited me personally because I knew how life on the streets worked."

"Your skills have proved most invaluable."

"The Bureau has been my home for thirteen years."

Carmody sat back in his chair and narrowed his gaze the way a wise old father would. "Get to the point, Logan."

Logan hooked his leg over the corner of the desk and sat, leaning in toward the commander. "Commander—Sam," he began, using the gentlest, most rational voice he possessed. "I don't deserve to be saddled with a newbie. I've earned the right to pick and choose my assignments."

"She has experience."

"Experience?" *Doing what? Typing memos?*

Logan glanced over his shoulder. The instant Grace Lockhart realized she was the focus of his attention, her fingers moved to her face and adjusted her glasses. Then she busied herself writing something in her notebook while her cheeks flooded with color.

Interesting, he thought. So quick to blush. He wondered if anything else about her reacted as quickly.

Logan blinked and mentally shook off the speculation. She radiated virginal innocence in a way that piqued his jaded, world-weary curiosity. Nothing more.

He stared at the shapeless bag of femininity and absently wondered if Grace Lockhart had ever been laid. If she even knew what the words meant. If she had any idea what he was thinking right now. She looked so clueless. Full of theory and stratagems learned in a classroom, without a day of real-world experience, much less experience working undercover with real criminals.

Had she ever ventured out of her shell? Let her hair down? Smiled? Why would an obviously mature woman in her twenties get up in the morning and deliberately put on a bulky suit that made her figure look like a sack of potatoes?

Didn't she know that a man liked to see a woman's curves? That she could look professional without resorting to the two-sizes-too-big routine? Whether she was skinny or chunky or somewhere in between, there were tricks to dressing that most women knew.

But obviously not Grace Lockhart.

As the color in her cheeks crept down to her neck, she cleared her throat and looked up at him, finally responding to his scrutiny. "Is there something I can help you with, Agent Pierce?"

The tone of her voice pulled him up short, dashed water on his original assessment of her sexual experience.

Her voice was deep, husky. Sultry as sin. With that voice, she could call men on the phone, read something as unerotic as a grocery list, and still make all their fantasies come true.

"How much field experience do you have?" he asked her.

"None. I've been working in research. This is my first assignment."

Logan swore. He got up off the desk, jammed his hands into the pockets of his jeans and stalked to the far end of the room before turning back to her. She was serious!

How could she stand up to a notorious crime lord if she didn't even know how to dress?

"Oh, this just gets better and better."

Her fingers flew up to adjust her glasses, a nervous gesture brought on by his rich sarcasm, no doubt.

Maybe he could teach her a thing or two about making herself attractive to a man. That would be the place to start with Grace Lockhart. Yeah. Teach her a few of the basics about her sexuality before she tackled anything like threats and guns and people dying.

Logan swept his gaze from the top of her bun to the soles of her sensible black shoes and was surprised to discover that the idea actually intrigued him. Maybe he *had* seen too much of the world's darker side. Why else would he be contemplating the notion of investigating whether she might be hiding any more delightful secrets like her voice beneath her dowdy appearance?

How long had it been since he'd made love to an inexperienced woman? Had he ever?

"Agent Pierce." Her soft voice trickled down his spine like a lover's caress, commanding his attention. "Why do you keep staring at me? Is it that my appearance has something to do with whether or not you plan to accept this assignment?"

"Hell no." He turned his anger on Carmody. "You have no business putting her in the line of fire."

The commander refused to budge. "She's been studying Harris Mitchell for almost a year. She came up with the plan herself. I think it's brilliant."

"Book smarts and street smarts are two different things. I won't be her partner."

He could almost visualize her body, lying battered and bleeding on the docks of New York. He could see the life draining out of her before she ever really had a chance to live it.

Just like Roy. Logan squeezed his eyes shut as imagination turned into memory. He should have saved him. He should have saved the kid.

No, he wasn't about to partner up with any neophyte agent who wanted to mix it up with the big boys and get herself killed.

He opened his eyes and drilled Carmody with his final offer. "I'll go after Harris Mitchell myself, if you want me to. But I won't be her partner."

Logan strode to the door, putting an end to this ludicrous conversation.

"Pierce, there's no use making this unpleasant." Commander Carmody stood. Logan paused, respecting the rank, and the man himself, even if he didn't agree with his current ideas. "We're working on a narrow time frame with this case. Mitchell's about to go bicoastal with his operation. He has contacts in Los Angeles already. I want to stop him in New York before that happens and bring in every connection he has."

Logan puffed out a frustrated sigh. Carmody had planned this takedown on a grand scale. "Then you want your best agents on the case. Men with experience in the field. It shouldn't be a training mission."

"I want you to work with Lockhart because you *are* my best agent. You know all the ins and outs of undercover work. You can handle that end of the assignment, and Lockhart will handle the technical aspects. Together, I know you can get the job done."

"I appreciate your confidence in me, Sam. And I know I owe you for saving my butt and bringing me to the Bureau in the first place." Logan spared one more glance at the mysterious, myopic Miss Lockhart. "But I work alone."

He pulled his keys out of his pocket and doffed a salute to Carmody. "My report's on your desk. Get McCallister or Anderson to work with her. I'm gettin' some shut-eye." Then he headed through the door.

"Pierce! Get your butt back—"

"Excuse me, sir. Let me have a word with him."

LOGAN WAS A GOOD TEN paces down the hall before Grace was out the door. "Agent Pierce?"

He didn't answer.

She'd spotted him immediately. He didn't look like anybody else milling through the administrative end of the FBI training center. He seemed an anachronism to the tradition of discipline and routine radiating from the walls around her.

Exactly what she needed. Someone different. Someone who could teach her to be a different person.

She pushed her way through men in three-piece suits and women dressed in similar fashion and called his name again. Either he was going deaf or purposely ignoring her. She had a feeling it wasn't the former.

Logan Pierce was tall, with broad shoulders emphasized by the bulk of his black leather jacket. His lean hips and long legs seemed naturally built for clinging to hardware-heavy motorcycles. He wore his dark brown hair short, like most of the other agents he passed. But the day-old scruff of beard clinging to the jut of his jaw and angular planes of his face altered any air of respectability.

He rounded the corner and headed toward the elevator, pausing to wink at the leggy blonde who passed by. Grace opened her steno pad and jotted down the woman's reaction to his flirtation. The woman's eyelids dropped a fraction as she watched Logan pass by. Her bottom lip pouted out into a smile. No, not really a smile. Not exactly a pout, either. More of an upward tilt at the corners, a pressing of the lips—oh, hell.

Grace scratched out the observation. If she couldn't even explain how it was done, how could she ever hope to do it herself?

But Logan, too, had slowed his pace to study the

woman, and Grace seized the advantage by dashing ahead and falling into step beside him. "Is it your usual practice to walk out on a superior officer?" she asked.

His easy stride stuttered a fraction, as if her appearance at his elbow surprised him. He stopped and sucked in a deep breath, stretching the black T-shirt material across his chest and momentarily distracting her from her purpose.

He was such a big man. Even bigger up close like this. So tall. So broad.

So bad.

Oh, God, what had she been thinking? A quick catch of breath filled her nose with the rich scent of leather and spice and man. Foreign smells to her untrained senses. Enticing smells.

"Nope. But I've done it before." He pointed to the steno pad tucked under her arm. "Be sure you write that down, too."

He turned and marched on down the corridor. Grace swallowed the impulse to run back to Carmody's office. That would mean accepting defeat. And the thought of failure frightened her more than the idea of harnessing the overwhelming power Logan possessed over women.

Commander Carmody had agreed to her plan only if she went in with a seasoned veteran at her side. And only if she could prove she had what it took to work undercover.

Logan Pierce could help her on both counts.

She tapped the corner of her glasses with her fingertips, pushing them up to the bridge of her nose. She could do this. She had to do this.

Instead of retreating, she doubled her pace.

"You're living up to your reputation, Agent Pierce. I've heard that your arrogance has gotten you into trouble on more than one occasion. But I've also heard that you have more citations of merit in your file than any agent in the drug enforcement division."

Logan halted in his tracks. She took an extra two steps past him before pulling up. There was no mistaking the warning glare in his gray eyes.

"Your research should also show you that I work alone."

Then Logan went and did the one thing sure to move her past her insecurities about herself, past her trepidation about asking a living legend at the Bureau for his help.

He patted her on the head.

"Now be a good girl and run along."

He brushed past her and headed for the elevator. Grace stood rooted to the spot, feeling the resentment well up inside her, overtaking her, making her curse the day she'd ever been born the daughter of Mimsey Lockhart.

She squeezed her eyes shut and gritted her teeth.

Logan Pierce was just like any other man.

Her chest began to move up and down with heavy breaths as she struggled to control the anger.

Of course, Logan wasn't exactly like the men her mother had known. And he certainly wasn't anything like the men—make that *man*—she'd known.

She'd come a long way from Joel Vitek and his groping hands and drooling lips. A long way from hearing her mother's name instead of her own as he'd found his completion within her. As he'd lived out his fantasy at her expense.

She'd thought Joel was different. But men were all alike.

Patronizing, self-serving sex machines who talked to a woman's breasts instead of her eyes, who winked at a woman only if he thought she was pretty...who patted her on the head and set her aside as if she was unimportant.

The hot breaths hissed between her teeth now as resentment began to win the battle inside her.

Grace had come a long way from Hollywood, California, to Quantico, Virginia. But she hadn't come for the snatches of verdant hills or the history of the area. She hadn't come for the eligible marines stationed nearby. She hadn't even come for the chance to get away from the painful memories of her childhood.

She'd come to prove she was more than the sum of her parts. That she had a brain inside her body.

She'd come to prove she was nothing like her mother.

Her breath seeped out in one cleansing breath, leaving her feeling weak. She tapped into the logic and common sense that had gotten her thus far. That logic would give her strength.

No man would take advantage of her the way they'd used her mother. The way they'd wanted to use her.

Lusty old men who had tried to catch her mother's eye and failed sometimes turned to her. She hadn't known there were laws then about grown men hitting on fifteen-year-old girls.

But she knew now. Now she was twenty-six and educated. Now she carried a gun and a badge.

The perverts and the users of the world had better watch their backs. Agent Grace Lockhart was out to get them.

And Harris Mitchell was the man who topped her list. She had him in her sights, with every intention of bringing the exploitative thief, murderer and racketeer to justice.

But, first, she had to learn all those feminine secrets she'd worked so long and hard to deny.

She had to get Logan Pierce to help her.

He hadn't listened to a direct order.

He hadn't listened to reason.

Time to play her best hand.

Grace hurried after him. She saw a length of well-worn denim stepping onto the elevator. When he turned around, she rushed forward, her desperation replaced by a self-righteous anger. "I don't care what kind of agent you are, Pierce. I don't care if you think you failed Roy Silverton. Despite what Commander Carmody said, those aren't the skills I want from you."

His cheeks flushed at the mention of his deceased partner's name, and his fingers curled into a fist at his side. Grace flinched when he raised that fist. But his hand shot over her shoulder to brace the door open. "What skills are you talking about?"

His size and proximity didn't matter right now, even as he towered over her. The heat in her own cheeks fueled her anger. She tilted her chin and stated her case.

"I've devised a plan to bring down Harris Mitchell. From the inside. I can handle the computers once I'm in, but I need your help to get there."

"What skills, Miss Lockhart?" he repeated, moving a step closer, forcing her to tip her head back farther.

"*Agent* Lockhart." She corrected him and continued on without taking a breath. "Harris Mitchell is eccentric. He hires only women for his inner circle. His bodyguards, chauffeur, housekeeper, hit men—hit women, I suppose—"

"What skills do you want from me?" He articulated each word with probing finesse. His warm breath fanned across her lips, shocking her into silence.

Her anger vanished in an instant and she became acutely aware of just how close he stood to her. How his arm stretched beside her cheek, close enough for her to turn her head and bury her nose in the leathery smell of his jacket. How his chest rose and fell in steady rhythm just inches away. How she could feel his heat at the tip of her chin, at the tips of her breasts, even at the tips of her toes.

"I do need you to keep me safe. But..."

What was she doing? What was she thinking?

Her glasses fogged as her skin rapidly chilled with a sense of foreboding. Without thinking, she reached up to adjust them on her face and inadvertently brushed her fingers against his stomach. He sucked in his breath and she snatched her hand away, hugging it close to her chest as if she'd been singed.

"But what?" His low voice vibrated through her.

What did she have to lose? She'd already tossed away most of her pride by chasing him so relentlessly.

She had to have his help. There was only one way to get to Harris Mitchell. Carmody would reassign the case if she couldn't learn what she needed to. And she knew Logan Pierce, legendary field agent, undercover expert, and love-'em-and-leave-'em ladies' man was the best choice to teach her.

She lowered her gaze to his scuffed boots and followed a hesitant path up the tantalizing length of his legs and chest before meeting him eye-to-eye.

"I need you to teach me how to seduce a man."

2

GRACE TWISTED AGAINST the soft steel grip on her elbow as Logan steered her down the hall to the first empty office he could find. He shoved her inside, locked the door behind him, and closed the outside blinds before turning to face her.

"What did you just say to me?"

She stood in the center of the room, clutching her steno pad to her chest while he circled her, eyeing her like a hawk with a delectable bit of prey in his sights.

"I need you to turn me into a femme fatale."

"A femme fatale?" He plowed his fingers through his hair, standing it up on end in spiky disorder. "Who talks like that anymore?"

Okay. So maybe she had no clue what she was doing. But, damn it all, she'd done her research. Logan Pierce's way with women was standard gossip around the break room.

If one liked the dangerous, smooth-talking, bad-boy type.

And judging by her uncontrolled reactions to Logan— the shallow breathing, that naughty feeling that had tingled in her fingertips when she'd accidentally touched him, the way she kept turning her head now to keep him in her line of vision—she *did* like that type. A little. Well, maybe more than a little. Okay, probably too much for her own good.

He reminded her of those handsome backstage bums and one-night stands who had chased after her mother all those years.

The kind of man who promised nothing but heartache. The kind of man she needed right now.

"As I said earlier, Harris Mitchell will only work with women. Directly, that is." She fought to keep the businesslike detachment in her voice. "Word on the street is that as he gets ready to expand his enterprise, he'll be hiring a new personal accountant. I intend to be that woman."

"Word on the street?" Was that a swearword that hissed between his teeth? "What do you know about 'word on the street'? How many times have you even been out of your cubicle?"

"If you'll kindly watch your mouth, Agent Pierce." Grace's fingers trembled in their grip on the steno pad. "I've done my research—"

"I'll bet you have." He stopped circling and closed the distance between them. She felt the heat of him at her shoulder as he leaned in behind her, felt his hot, moist breath like a caress down the side of her neck. "But can you think on your feet? Be creative? Dodge bullets? Forget who you really are and become someone else?"

When she realized that the tempo of her own short breaths matched his, she took a step away and turned. She would not let this man distract her from her purpose.

"Commander Carmody gave me the green light for this project. I intend to go forward, with or without your help."

As that hawk who had circled her earlier, Logan snatched her glasses from her face, plunging her world into a blur of smeared colors and lights and shadows.

"What are you doing?"

She reached out blindly, groping the air.

"Seeing if you have what it takes to go forward."

"I can't see a damn thing right now."

"If you'll kindly watch your mouth, Agent Lockhart." He clicked his tongue behind his teeth in admonishment.

Embarrassed by the instinctive panic in her reaction, she hugged her steno pad to her chest, calming her fluttering heart and giving her shaking fingers something to do. "I am an excellent student, Agent Pierce. If this is some sort of test..." Her nose detected the smell of well-worn leather, and she guessed he'd circled behind her again. Pleased with her detection skills, she actually smiled. "I graduated top of my class. I'm a Phi Beta Kappa. I had personal recommendations from two senators for my appointment—"

"Yeah, yeah. But can you kiss a man and make him forget what he was thinking?"

With a magical snap of invisible fingers, he zapped her confidence and took her into uncharted territory. "I beg your pardon?"

"When it comes down to it, can you turn all that brain power into a seductive smile that Harris Mitchell will find irresistible?"

"I—"

She felt the heat of his lips brushing against her ear. "Can you do this...?" A vise clamped around her waist—Logan's arm. She snatched at his leather sleeve to free herself, but froze as he pulled her back against him. Shoulders to chest. Hips to belt buckle. Bottom to... Grace squirmed at the vee of pure masculine heat that cupped her buttocks, not yet understanding the lesson he was teaching her. The long, strong fingers of his free hand seized her hip and stilled her struggle. "Without flinching?"

His lips moved to the column of nerves that ran down the side of her neck. "Can you let a man do this to you...?" She tilted her head to the side, straining away from his hot, moist assault on her senses. His tongue joined the foray, supping at an undiscovered indention where her neck met her shoulder. The electric current that had tingled beside her ear now shot out to the tips of her breasts, hardening her nipples, making the tender globes feel heavy above the restricting band of his arm. "And pretend you enjoy it?"

Pretend?

A damp mix of pleasure and pain gathered between her legs. Her hand, which had once tried to push him away, now tugged at his arm, unconsciously begging him to ease the friction gathering in the breasts it cradled.

Grace turned her jaw to his mouth, struggling to speak, fighting through the current of unaccustomed electric heat consuming her. He was making a point, she tried to remind herself, teaching her about working undercover.

"I should—" she stuck out the tip of her tongue and licked the circle of her parched lips, trying to regain control of the conversation—and her traitorous body "—be taking notes."

He shifted his attention to the movement of her tongue and traced the same circle around her lips with an erotic rasp of his own tongue. The electric current humming through her transformed into an outright jolt. Her thighs clenched together and she lifted her bottom, rubbing herself against his bulging heat.

"Logan?" The sensation was too much. *He* was too much.

She was drowning. Falling. Building. Rushing.

She was alone.

Logan had released her and stepped far beyond her line

of vision. He left her cold and exposed and swaying in the center of the room, counting silently to herself as she retrained her lungs to breathe in, then out, all over again.

As she gathered her senses, she could hear his measured breathing across the room. Was he sneering at her inexperience? Laughing at her combustible reaction to a simple embrace? Shaking his head over just how ill-suited she was for this task? His voice, which had rumbled in such a seductive pitch beside her ear, now clipped with all the command of a military officer. "That's what you'll have to do. If Mitchell suspects for one moment that you're not sincere, you'll be dead."

Logan's first lesson had bordered on virtual heaven. But the reality of his harsh words chased away the haze of sensual awareness and reminded her that he had yet to agree to work with her on the case.

"I'm aware of the danger, Agent Pierce. I'm not so naive as to believe there's no risk involved in this assignment. That's why I asked for your help."

Reaching over her shoulder, he plucked the steno pad from her fingers.

"Hey!" She heard it land on something soft as he tossed it aside. The bombardment of man and lingering sex and unexpected actions made her jump when she felt his hands at her nape. "What are you doing now?"

"Seeing if I can help you."

Logan's deft fingers seemed to have had plenty of practice unfastening pins and rubber bands. He loosened her hair from its constrictive wrap and it fell around her shoulders down to the middle of her back. It had grown long and untamable, so she never wore it free. Even at night, she wove it into a braid to sleep.

But there was something...distracting...in the way he sifted the long strands through his fingers. Lifting it to test its weight, easing the pressure on her scalp. Something...soothing...in the way he draped it along her shoulder blades.

She should write this down. This feeling of being tended. This...

"It has a natural wave in it. Lots of potential—if you do something with it. We'll cut it so the weight doesn't pull it straight."

His impersonal tone snapped her out of her foolish observations. It seemed he was doing his job. At last. She should remember her job, as well. "I'm prepared to alter my appearance."

"I hope so." He released her hair and stepped away. "The only way you'll turn any man's eye with that outfit is if you take it off. Let me have the jacket."

"Agent Pierce, I hardly think—"

He was already tugging at the shoulders. Grace quickly unhooked the buttons before it ripped and he pulled it off.

"You want me for my expertise. I need to see what I have to work with."

A whisper of wool gabardine landed in the corner somewhere. "This is a two-hundred-dollar suit, Agent Pierce."

"You'll have to cut the 'agent' crap. Call a man by his name."

She felt the tug on the top button of her blouse before she saw his hand there. Grace swatted it away. "What do you think you're doing—" she swallowed hard and forced herself to say his name "—Logan?"

"That's better." His hands returned, resuming their path down to her waist. "All of this has to go so I can assess what you're asking of me. I'm all for getting Mitchell, but I don't like impossible missions."

"Impossible?"

Plain white cotton seemed no barrier for the man, either. He pushed the blouse down her arms and pulled it free of her waistband. It joined the jacket. In a self-conscious habit learned by the age of fourteen, she crossed her arms in front of her, laying her left hand on her right shoulder, her right hand at her waist, forming a shield of armor to mask every plump inch from an unkind word or critical eye.

His fingers moved to the zipper on her skirt.

Impossible, he'd said. That hurt. She had never flaunted her body. Not intentionally at any rate. Not once. She forced her mind away from the taunts and teasing of her adolescent peers. She shut down the memory of grown men leering at her, speaking to other parts of her anatomy instead of making eye contact.

At least Logan was denigrating her for the right reasons, not casting her aside as inconsequential because she'd managed to inherit one inescapable thing from her mother.

Make that two.

She was down to bra, half-slip, panties and hose before he pried her hands from their protective positions and spread her arms wide to either side of her.

Grace knew the exact moment when his gaze lit on her breasts. Though she couldn't see his expression, she could imagine the surprise, maybe even admiration, and certainly interest that would cross his face.

Attached to a five-foot, five-inch body, a 40DD seemed to have that dumbing-down effect on a man.

Maybe he even noticed the ample hips, rounded to match, giving her body that out-of-date, out-of-place hourglass shape that had served her mother so well in the string of B-movies she'd starred in back in the 1970s.

That same shape that Grace had fought for years.

"I know I'm fat—"

"Fat?"

"—but there's no way I can lose ten or twenty pounds in a week's time. You'll have to work with what's here. If you're willing to take the job, that is."

Logan released her arms and she hugged herself again, praying the room's rise in temperature was due to a faulty thermostat and not her own blushing skin.

"You're worried about seducing a man with a body like that?"

"Yes! Why the hell else would I..."

The husky timbre of his voice registered. The low-pitched rumble skittered along her skin, raising goose bumps. His voice alone triggered the same electric switch that had left her body humming from his touch just moments earlier. Damn, she wished she could see his face. Was he calling her an idiot for not knowing how to use her mother's gifts to full advantage? Or was there a note of promise in his tone that meant he was considering working with her?

"Does this mean you'll be my partner?"

Above her own pounding heartbeat, his long-winded sigh was the only sound in the room. Grace squinted, trying to read his expression, trying to find out if that was a yes or a no. Though she could see his silhouette, he was just a big, broad blur to her eyesight.

"There are ten things I find sexy in a woman, Miss Lockhart—Grace. The first is when she looks me straight in the eye. You should write that down as rule number one in your little notebook."

Grace began to hope. "Well, since you've conveniently taken my glasses and my notebook from me, there's no way I can. And I asked you to call me Agent—"

Her words caught in a strangled gulp in her throat as Logan suddenly stepped into focus. That meant he was close enough to... The temperature went up another ten degrees. He was close enough...she could feel his measured breath stirring the tendrils of hair along her forehead. He was close... She was standing in her underwear and he was fully dressed. For decorum's sake, she should move away.

And yet those steel-gray eyes ensnared her as if she was a helpless bird caught in his trap.

"Eye contact?" Oh, God, that quavering, wispy voice sounded so like her mother's. "What are the other nine rules?"

He didn't touch her, yet she could feel him. Their breaths mingled in a strangled heat. And she did her research. Up close like this, she could see the individual whiskers on his cheeks and jaw, dark little pinpricks that made her palms itch with curiosity to touch them.

Rule number one. Look a man in the eye.

She ran her gaze past the flat, flexing plateau of his lips and up beyond the slightly bent angle of his nose to those eyes. This close, she could see the silvery sunburst of color around his pupils, bewitching irises of dove-gray and steel and flint, rimmed by a darker shade of charcoal.

She'd never seen such beautiful eyes.

"Just like that," he whispered, his words stirring a caress of air against her cheek.

Grace's lungs expanded, as if just now remembering to breathe. The sudden intake of oxygen seemed to stir some coherent thought inside her brain.

"Does that mean you're taking the assignment?"

"You're going after Mitchell no matter what I say, aren't you?"

Trapped by the unexpected warmth in those beautiful gray eyes, she could only nod.

"You're clueless enough that somebody needs to watch your back."

His shoulders shifted in her peripheral vision, and a moment later she felt the weight of silk-lined leather settling around her, enveloping her in Logan's warmth and scent. She clutched his jacket together at her neck, but wondered if the tender gesture was the equivalent of another dismissive pat on the head.

"Will *you* be the one watching my back?"

He raked his gaze down along the swell of her breasts, giving her the distinct impression that he might be willing to watch even more. She pressed her lips together to quell the anticipation that raced through her, not trusting her ability to read a man's thoughts.

"You have the raw materials to get the job done. But a rookie like you needs the best in the business to pull this off. You need me."

There was less cocky arrogance in his statement than there was a reluctant acceptance of fact.

"So you'll have me ready to go undercover by the end of the week...partner?"

"I won't promise miracles. You still have nine rules to learn." He pushed her glasses back onto her nose, plunging her back into plain-Jane obscurity and reminding her of the enormity of his task. "And don't call me partner."

WHO'D HAVE THOUGHT? The stunned question played through Logan's mind again as he unpacked a second helmet from the back of his Harley-Davidson.

His body still ached from that torrid encounter back in

the administration building with Grace. He thought he could scare her off from her foolish notion of going after Harris Mitchell. Knock some sense into that virginal determination of hers. But she'd been so soft to the touch, so responsive to his hands and mouth.

Teach her how to seduce a man?

She'd damn near seduced him.

And she didn't even know it.

Grace Lockhart was deliberately disguising a national treasure. She was plain as a bucket until she lost her temper. But a little bit of makeup would get her noticed no matter her state of mind. She was blind as a bat, but contacts would help. She had soft hair with a tendency to curl that she controlled in an unflattering bun. A reputable salon would know what to do there.

But beneath that gray, shapeless suit—

Who'd have thought?

She might be the brainy strategist Carmody claimed, but she had inexperience written all over her. Sexual and professional. He had to make her smarter. Teach her survival skills. Teach her to mentally detach herself from a man's touch when she was working undercover, to look at him with those liquid green orbs and make him think he had just given her the best sexual rush of her life.

A look like that could make a man think the cuddling and fondling and kissing they shared was the real thing.

Logan raked his fingers through his hair and struggled to find a similar detachment. He had five days to mold Grace Lockhart into a savvy, sexy field agent who could bring Harris Mitchell to his knees, and then walk away unscathed. Did he really think he could pull this off? Or was he just too afraid that nobody else understood the consequences of failure?

A sobering image of Roy Silverton's bullet-ridden body blipped into his mind and reaffirmed his decision to take this assignment. He had to do this right. He hadn't prepared Roy for every contingency. But he'd make double sure Grace knew how to take care of herself. How to think on her feet.

And what he couldn't teach her, he'd take care of himself. He'd keep her alive.

To do that, he couldn't let himself be distracted by the temptation of that goddesslike figure. He had to play this like a pro. Keep his mind focused on the mission. Keep Grace in one piece, not take her to his bed.

The scuff of her flat-heeled oxfords on the asphalt pavement announced her arrival long before she said a word.

"You're joking, right?"

He watched her look down at the slim fit of her skirt and up at the back seat of his Harley. She thumbed over her shoulder toward the center of the parking lot. "My car's just over there. We could take it to lunch, instead."

"Sensible sedan, right?"

She nodded. "Safe. Good mileage—"

"We'll requisition a new car for you. Something sporty. Red, I think." Lustful thoughts of long blond hair blowing across the back seat of a red convertible eased the doom and gloom that had consumed him. A nice roomy back seat where...

"I would prefer blue. Or green."

Logan opened his eyes and shook his head at her earnest expression. She'd rebuttoned her gray-suited armor up to her neck, and fastened her hair back into that tight little bun. She hadn't even left any curling wisps free to soften her face. Instead, she'd added a functional black shoulder attaché to the outfit. Probably where she carried that ever-present notebook.

She just didn't get it, did she? Men would salute that body of hers. Harris Mitchell would voluntarily go to prison for that body. He, personally, would sacrifice a well-earned vacation for the opportunity to know that body better—once he got her through this assignment.

He had to teach her to get comfortable with her fantasy-proportioned figure. To use it to her advantage.

Oh, yeah.

"Definitely red."

Logan reached into his jeans and pulled out his pocketknife. Confused, distrusting perhaps, Grace took a step back when he knelt in front of her. "What are you—?" With a grasp and a twist, he slit the seam of her skirt. "Hey!"

He preferred that flash of fire in her cheeks to her usual pasty-faced demeanor.

"If you want to work undercover, you have to be willing to take risks. Willing to do what you don't normally do. Willing to do whatever's necessary to get the job done." He punctuated his first bit of advice by ripping the seam of her skirt up to the hemline of her jacket.

"Oh, my God. You ruined it."

Logan stood, smiled, put away his pocketknife, and enjoyed the twists and turns of her body as she struggled first to assess the damage, and then to tuck her slip up beneath the thigh-high slit. "Don't worry, just make a note of it. The agency will reimburse you. C'mon."

He put on his helmet, buckled the second one around the flushed fury of her face and climbed onto the Harley. When he had the engine purring smoothly beneath him, he extended his hand for Grace.

"I've never been on a motorcycle before."

He'd guessed as much. He steadied her while she tested one foothold and then another, finally climbing aboard as if it were a horse waiting to buck her off. She settled astride the seat, behind him, leaving a good five inches of space between them. "What do I do?"

Logan grinned. "Hold on, sweetheart."

He could barely feel the pressure of her fingertips at his waist. Definitely not the way a sexy woman held on to her man. Time to teach her another lesson.

"Just hold on."

He revved the engine and kicked it into gear, pulling the bike up to forty miles per hour before even reaching the security gate. By the time he had her on the highway cruising toward New York City, Grace had become a second skin to him, her face buried in the middle of his back and her arms cinched around his middle. He glanced down at her white-knuckled grasp on his belt buckle.

Oh, yeah.

Between her body and his guilty conscience, the next five days were going to be one hell of a ride.

have to look like you're at home in this sort of thing. His way of well note. There at her clothes. So you're not going in looking like this.

She stiffened at his insult. Mitchell doesn't say re-

3

GRACE WATCHED Logan slip twenty dollars to the maître d'. "Is the agency going to pick up the tab for that, too?"

Logan smiled at her sarcasm and urged her along in front of him.

Despite his casual attire and her torn skirt, they were seated in the center of the plush Willingham Hotel restaurant, amid tables filled with businessmen and women dressed more appropriately and impeccably in suits. Keenly conscious of several curious stares, Grace opened her menu and hid her face behind it.

Once their arrival became old news and the patrons returned to their own conversations, she slapped the menu shut and leaned forward. "What the hell are we doing here?"

Logan had unzipped his jacket and sprawled back in his chair. With his long legs hidden beneath the white linen tablecloth, he sipped on a glass of water topped with a twist of lime. "I believe it's called lunch."

"I said I was happy to eat at the hot dog vendor's down on the corner."

At the snap of her whisper, Logan set down his glass and leaned forward, as annoyingly relaxed in their posh surroundings as she was self-conscious. "Hot dogs are a whole other lesson. You want to seduce a big-time crime lord. So we have to learn the big-time lessons first. Mitchell's got money out the wazoo. You're going to have to look like you're at home in places like this.'' His eyes lit with amusement at her expense. "So far you're not doing very well, Gracie."

She stiffened at the nickname, hearing the cutesy, belittling appellation like a hundred bad memories slapping her in the face. "Never call me Gracie. I am a twenty-six-year-old professional law enforcement officer. Grace or Agent Lockhart will do just fine."

He patted the air with his hands, placating her. "Don't be so eager to defend yourself. Keep your temper. Grace, it is."

At least he'd allow her that one smidgen of respect. She had a feeling she'd have to swallow plenty of pride before this mission was accomplished. She pulled out her steno pad and opened it to the page where she'd listed ten numbers.

"Is that one of your rules?" She clicked her mechanical pencil and prepared to write. "Play it cool? I can do that."

He reached across the table and stilled her hand. Sensing her instinct to jerk away from the personal contact, his long, calloused fingers wrapped around hers, pencil and all, trapping her in a vise of velvet and steel. Short of stabbing him with a fork or screaming her head off, she was his prisoner.

She shot him as damning a glance as she could muster through her glasses.

"Control, Grace." Logan shook his finger at her like the recalcitrant pupil she was. "I'm talking about control. A man likes the challenge of breaking that control. You want to be his match, not easy pickings. He wants to earn his reward."

Something about the softly articulated movement of his lips distracted her from the need to assert herself. The husky pitch of his voice, whispered for her ears alone, seeped inside her like a promise.

She heard her voice in the same soft whisper. "What's your reward in all this?"

"Walking away from this assignment with you in one piece."

"I can handle myself."

Without blinking, those silvery eyes fixed on hers, capturing her curiosity, demanding her attention. Logan pulled her hand to his lips and pressed a kiss to the inside of her wrist. Grace jumped in her chair, shocked by the bubbling heat that simmered beneath the firm, warm pressure of his lips against her pulse. The whiskers on his chin abraded an apparently sensitive patch of skin there, sending out thousands of tiny little aftershocks in the kiss's wake.

What surprised her more though, was the lingering, languid warmth that seemed to turn her arm into molten putty, rendering it useless. Rendering *her* useless for the time being.

"If you can't handle *this,* you can't handle Mitchell."

"What? Oh." Grace pulled her hand away and tucked it beneath her napkin in her lap, subconsciously hiding the betraying appendage until she could gather the good sense to compensate for such a mind-numbing reaction to a simple kiss.

Logan settled back and nodded toward her notebook. "You'd better write that down, too. Rule number three. Know your erogenous zones. But don't tell a man where all of them are. He likes the thrill of discovering some for himself."

The discovery part hadn't been all that bad for her, either. She was honest enough to chart that bit of research in her memory. But, good God, it was just a kiss! The world hadn't shattered beneath her feet. She'd seen no fireworks. After all, men and women had been kissing for centuries, eons, in fact. No need to make a big deal of it. He hadn't even touched her mouth, just a silly little nibble on her wrist.

She quickly jotted down seduction rules numbers two and three—stay in control; know erogenous zones—embarrassed to admit that, though the earth hadn't swallowed her up whole, she had, for a few moments, lost all capacity for rational thought. Logan had a point. If she couldn't stay focused in Harris Mitchell's company, she wouldn't be able to plant the computer virus that would expose all his contacts. And she'd be endangering both her and Logan's cover.

In an act of self-preservation, she quickly turned to the front of her steno pad and wrote a word at the top of the first page.

Research.

Only, she went back to add, in capital letters. No sense getting confused by the education process. Logan was teaching her what she needed to know about working undercover. She was the student who needed to know about catching Harris Mitchell's eye, winning his trust, and becoming part of his organization. This was research.

This wasn't real.

Getting trapped in those silvery eyes, collapsing after a kiss on the wrist or a sweep of Logan's tongue against her neck—none of that was real.

She caught a glimpse of her torn skirt. What was left of her self-righteous anger deflated in a heartbeat. She was Grace Lockhart, frumpy computer nerd. She'd spent her formative years developing her brain and a defensive suit of armor to compensate for the developing shape of her body and a fear of repeating her mother's mistakes.

Logan Pierce was a secret-agent hero. A handsome, dangerous man who could have any woman he wanted around the world.

She was a curiosity, perhaps. One of those *challenges* he said men liked. He might even be intrigued by the outrageous proposal to turn her into a seductress. But no way could she be on his list of desirable women. No way.

She went back to the Research Only note and added five exclamation points and a handful of stars.

GRACE HAD JUST POLISHED off her grilled chicken and mushroom pasta when she heard the *voice.*

"Gracie!" That high-pitched, whispery voice managed to carry across the entire restaurant. "Gracie, darling!"

Her fork clattered on her plate and she scanned the room for the nearest exit.

"Friend of yours?" Logan set his napkin on the table beside his coffee.

"Not exactly."

Though she'd already been spotted, she nevertheless tried to shield her face behind her hand.

But the woman would have found her one way or the other. Something about a special bond she claimed they shared.

She felt a hug around her shoulders and a kiss on her cheek. Automatically, Grace wiped the spot with her napkin, knowing there would be a splotch of crimson lipstick.

Odd, she thought, when she looked at her napkin. Pale pink.

"Honey. Aren't you going to get up and give me a hug?"

The different shade of lipstick had thrown her enough

to respond without thinking—the way she had when she was a child.

"Mother." She stood and hugged the woman she matched physically, inch for inch, although the outside trappings were considerably different.

Mimsey Lockhart leaned back and held Grace's hands. "I never thought I'd run into you in the city today. What a glorious coincidence."

"May I get an introduction?" Grace recognized a touch of more-than-polite interest in Logan's husky voice.

"Mother. This is Agent Logan Pierce. My mother— Mimsey Lockhart."

"Delighted to meet you." His dangerous charm turned on to full magnetism was practically blinding. He clasped Mimsey's hand between his and lifted it to his lips. Grace caught her breath.

He kissed her mother's hand! Not quite the way he had kissed her wrist, but still... Grace averted her face, ashamed to recognize a stab of jealousy. She quickly derailed the emotion by remembering two things. Logan was a natural charmer. If he didn't have the ability to please all the ladies, she wouldn't have requested him for this assignment.

And, second, she knew that beaming smile on her mother's face could have been achieved with considerably less than a kiss on the hand.

"Won't you sit down?" Oh, God, had Logan really invited her mother to join them?

Grace shot him a look across the table. "We were just leaving."

"No, we weren't." Logan absorbed her subtle plea for help with a smile of feigned innocence. "We haven't finished our coffee."

"Who needs coffee?" she muttered between clenched teeth. "The caffeine's bad for us."

Ignoring her not-so-subtle hint, he pulled out a chair and Mimsey perched on the edge. "I can't stay long, anyway. Grant's checking into the hotel and then he's taking me down to his new theater."

Logan sat, angling his body toward Mimsey, a gesture of interest and acceptance that irked Grace. "Grant?" he asked.

"Grant Stewart." Mimsey patted her platinum coiffure and turned to Grace. "You remember him from our California days, don't you, dear?"

What had he been, paramour two? Seven? Twenty?

But Mimsey hadn't really been expecting an answer, so she turned back to Logan. "Grant's a producer, mostly Hollywood stuff. But he's expanding into the New York theater scene now. He's putting together an off-Broadway play, and is thinking about casting me in the role of the aunt." She reached for Grace's hand and squeezed it. The excitement playing over Mimsey's painted features was contagious. Almost.

"Congratulations," Grace offered, but couldn't help remembering all the other promises made to her mother and broken over the years. "I hope it works out for you."

"Imagine." Mimsey's green eyes lit with the sparkle of hope. "A legitimate stage play, after all these years. That's how I started my career, you know. Long before you were born."

"That's where I know you." Logan snapped his fingers and diverted Mimsey's attention. "*The Ants That Ate Metropolis. The Beast from Beneath the Sea.* You're *that* Mimsey Lockhart."

Seriously? He knew her mother's movies?

Grace watched in horror as her mother's fan-club personality emerged.

"Is there any other?" Mimsey laughed, her beautiful smile undimmed by fifty years of flamboyant living. She clutched a modest hand to the plunging décolletage of her pink suit. "I'm flattered you remember those old flicks."

"Are you kidding?" Was Logan's enthusiasm for real? Or was this all part of the act that made him irresistible to women? "Sci-fi Sundays were a staple in the old neighborhood. I grew up thinking I could save the world, too. Maybe that's part of why I went into law enforcement."

"That's so sweet."

Grace had to give her mother credit. She'd never become the actress she'd aspired to be, but she was always proud of the work she'd done. Those monster flicks had put food on the table and given her a place to go when one lover after another abandoned her for younger, easier—childless—fare.

"Mimsey?"

A tall, polished man with jet-black hair touched by gray at the temples joined them at the table.

Did Grace detect a subtle change in her mother's smile? "Grant, darling, you remember my daughter, Gracie."

"Of course." He took her hand and offered a slight bow. "It's been too many years. You're looking well."

Not pretty, not sexy. Well.

Ah, yes, Mimsey stirred hormones, turned heads. Grace looked…well. Like a healthy horse or a well-seeded lawn. Maybe Logan's mission was impossible, after all. Maybe she had no business trying to prove herself as a competent agent by taking on an eccentric crime lord.

It required every bit of strength she had to look him in the eye and dredge up a smile. "Mr. Stewart. It's good to see you again."

"I'm taking Mimsey down to the theater to introduce her to the director personally. Then I have a meeting with some financial backers. Perhaps you could join us for dinner later?"

"Uh, no. Thank you." She had to take her mother in short spurts, and allow herself plenty of time to recover for the next encounter. She excused herself on an easy white lie. "Agent Pierce and I are working together on a special project."

"'Round the clock," Logan added. Her gaze shot across the table and clashed with the terminal amusement in his soft gray eyes. Grace's cheeks blazed with heat. After all these years in her mother's company, she should have picked up a few tricks on how to handle a man's teasing. But no, she'd been busy learning calculus and studying the history of modern warfare instead.

"Another time, perhaps. Pierce." The two men shook hands. "Grace." He nodded politely and pulled out Mimsey's chair.

Before Grace could stand, Mimsey had leaned over her and wrapped her in a tight, maternal hug. Grace gave in to the urge to return the hug, missing those days of innocence when she hadn't worried about her mother being taken advantage of by men interested more in her breast size than her heart or career.

But Mimsey was independent as ever. Her conspiratorial whisper tickled Grace's ear. "That Logan's a keeper, honey. Maybe this FBI gig is working out better than we thought."

"Mother—"

But Mimsey was gone in a whirl of drama before Grace could launch a proper protest.

Lost between dazed and fuming, she didn't notice that Logan had moved to the chair beside her until his hand covered hers where it fisted in her lap.

"At ease, Agent Lockhart." Unwittingly her fingers turned and clutched at his supportive hand. "Embarrassed by Mimsey, are we?"

"Worried about her. She doesn't always make the best choices. I hope Grant's sincere in wanting to help her."

He leaned closer, close enough for the scent of the tangy gel he used in his hair to tease her nose. "You don't have to live in her shadow, you know."

He was close enough that she could have seen him without her glasses. But, for once, she was very grateful to have that barrier between them. "What are you talking about?"

"You could learn a lesson from your mother."

Grace frowned. "What lesson?"

"Rule number four. Sex appeal is all about attitude."

"What does that mean?"

"Decide that you're sexy. Once you believe it, everyone around you will, too."

Without a doubt her mother was sexy. The woman knew what she had and she used it to her advantage. Mimsey Lockhart had learned all about being sexy.

But all Grace had ever wanted was for Mimsey to learn how to be her mother.

LOGAN CLOSED the fashion magazine and slumped on the couch of the department store fitting room, wondering how much more of this Pygmalion stuff he could take. The store could at least provide some male reading while he waited. Anything with fishing rods or pitching stats would be appreciated. He needed something to distract his overworked imagination from creating images of Grace behind the closed door at the end of the hallway, stripping naked and trying on the wardrobe of clothes the salesclerk had selected for her.

He'd been intrigued by Grace's request to turn her into a seductress. But it had taken those big green eyes of hers, staring up at him with trust and innocence, to trigger a protective impulse and make him say yes to working as her partner.

He'd tried scaring her away from this suicide mission with some crass behavior—the kind Mitchell might throw her way. But it had backfired on him. Badly. She'd responded to his forward touches as if they'd been lovers. As if she'd known exactly the way he liked a woman to respond to him.

She'd battled words with him, proving that intellectual moxie she kept bragging about.

He'd met her mother, saw the potential for the beautiful woman Grace could become.

He'd tortured himself all afternoon and into the evening, watching the transformation take place.

After fitting her for contact lenses, they'd taken a trip to a salon where a man named Miguel had cut her hair into a riot of sexy, chin-length curls, and then highlighted the whole beckoning array to bring out bright gold and soft strawberry shades. Miguel's friend Bruce had made up her face in a palette of soft colors that emphasized the emerald richness of her eyes and the sensuous pout of her lips.

And now—Logan inhaled deeply and silently cursed the partial arousal that had been with him on and off throughout the day—she'd been parading past him in a variety of outfits that reflected every mood from professional to fun to provocative.

"Logan? Do you think I'll really need something like this?"

Grace's sinfully seductive voice interrupted his thoughts and wound into his fantasies. When he looked up at this latest in a long line of outfits, he wished he still had that magazine to pull over his lap.

The woman had the survival skills of a turnip.

She stood in front of him, wearing nothing more than some sort of slip thing and a doubtful expression.

"It's called a bra-slip. The clerk suggested I wear it with that evening gown I tried on earlier. I could save some money, though, and wear one of my own slips with a strapless bra." Though he heard her explanation, he paid more attention to the movements of her hands. She cupped the sides of her breasts and pushed them forward, nearly spilling the satiny globes over the tiny strips of ivory silk and lace that cradled them. "The top doesn't give me much support, anyway."

Logan stood, fatigue and frustration and a sudden rigid strain in his jeans overriding patience and good intentions.

She needed to have that piece of lingerie. She very definitely needed to have it.

But Harris Mitchell didn't need to see it.

And no man who accidentally wandered past the dressing room's waiting area needed to see it, either.

Logan snatched Grace's arms above the elbows and turned her back to her dressing room.

"Don't you have a lick of common sense?" he asked, pushing her into the closet-size area and pulling the door shut behind him. "You can't go parading around in something like this."

"I thought you wanted to approve all the changes I've made. I'm sorry. Did I embarrass you?"

Logan sputtered. Was she really that naive? "It's perfect. It's sexy. It's gorgeous."

She folded her arms across her chest, hiding her bounty in self-conscious shame as she had that morning. "It's just a piece of underwear—"

"No." He pressed a finger over her lips, silencing her apology. "Rule number five. Never explain away a man's compliment."

"But—"

"Say thank you," he ordered, trying not to react to the brush of her lips on his sensitive fingertip. "You've turned into a real knockout, Agent Lockhart." Her shoulders lifted and her eyes swelled with protest, but he shushed her again. "What do you say?"

"Fank oo?" He pulled his finger back and let her try again. That same vulnerability that had sucker punched him into taking this assignment in the first place darkened her eyes. "You really think I'm a knockout?"

He let his gaze sweep the three mirrors in the dressing room, catching her in that slip from every delectable angle. He'd seen garments that showed less of a woman— garter belts, bustiers, thongs. But there was something incredibly appealing about the demure silk molding to her curves, stopping at her thighs and creating a shadowy cleft between her legs. Something wonderfully enticing about a swath of lace barely hiding the pink areolae at the tips of her breasts. Something about that creamy expanse of bare skin across her shoulders just a shade darker than the ivory silk straps that held the whole confection up.

"Oh, yeah. So much so that I'm going to treat myself to one of my favorite lessons. I'm going to kiss you."

He touched her with just his lips, bending down and capturing her startled "Oh" with his mouth. She tasted sweet and potent, just like the creamy coffee she'd had on their dinner break. It was a gentle mating, and he held back the urge to plunder her mouth. Her lips moved shyly, as if testing the whole idea of kissing. A true researcher, Logan observed in heady amusement.

He clenched his hands into fists at his sides, trying to remember that this woman was his job partner, not his bedmate. He was supposed to teach her, not take her. Her hesitant, though willing, response should remind him of that fact.

But he couldn't resist. A lock of her hair got caught between their mouths and he had to brush it away. Then he tunneled his fingers into the springy softness of her hair and stepped closer, angling her head back to receive the full advantage of his kiss.

"Just a second." Grace's hips backed away. His fingers were still tangled in her hair as she reached for something behind her. She came up with that damn notebook, flipped it open to a blank page, and clicked her mechanical pencil. Twice. "I want to know how to do this just right."

"Grace—"

She tipped her face back to his and puckered her lips. "Okay. Go ahead."

Damn the woman. Maybe she could frustrate Harris Mitchell into surrendering to the authorities.

Logan tightened his grip at the nape of her neck and pulled her up onto her toes. He kissed her again, harder this time, plunging in and stroking the soft skin inside her mouth with his tongue. He kept his eyes open, demanding she look at him. When he touched his tongue to hers, she did. Green eyes snapped at gray. He circled her tongue…suckled…angled his mouth to do any number of delightful things to hers.

When he came up for air, she ran her tongue along her lips and then pressed them together, tasting and savoring the new sensations they'd created together.

Or so he thought.

"Hold on." This damn research was hard on a man's ego. At least she had the decency to be short of breath. Her hand shook as she tried to write.

Logan smiled. Maybe this kiss wasn't just about research anymore.

He nuzzled the side of her neck, ran his tongue down to that exquisite nerve bundle along her collarbone until he found the spot that made her shiver. "Put down the notebook."

Grace pushed at his chin, turning his gaze up to meet hers. "I want to learn how to kiss."

"I want to teach you."

The steno pad hit the floor with a thunk as Logan lifted her hands around his neck. She arched into him as he skimmed his palms down her sides, cupped her ripe, round bottom and lifted her up to his mouth and his heat. She opened her mouth, giving all that he asked of her and more, and he seized her offering.

He came back to fill his hands with her generous breasts. He pushed them together the way she had earlier and buried his face between them. He tasted the salty tang of sweat deep in her cleavage, inhaled the delicate scent of the rare fragrance she wore.

"Touch me, Grace," he commanded on a breathless whisper, capturing a beaded peak in his mouth through lace and silk. She groaned in her throat, and as he laved the responsive bud with his tongue, the groan became a purr that vibrated through him, that teased his loins and made him impossibly hard with want. "Touch me."

"I've only done this kind of thing once." Her fingers flailed against the collar of his jacket, even as her lips scudded across his temple and found the sensitive shell of his ear. "I don't know how."

"Any way you want."

He was drunk with passion by the time she'd pushed his jacket off his shoulders and worked his shirt free of his jeans. She bunched up the material in her hands, tugged it behind the holster that hung from his shoulder, exposing his chest and torso to her curious quest. Her hands scorched him with their searching. A delicate brush of a fingertip here. An outright grab there.

He ground his hips into hers, amazed at how quickly, how thoroughly, this prude-turned-seductress had aroused him. She didn't need any lessons on how to seduce a man. She was a natural. A prodigy.

"Miss Lockhart?" Three sharp raps on the dressing-room door brought Logan up short. "The store is closing in fifteen minutes. If you like, I could start ringing up your selections."

The salesclerk's friendly voice intruded from the outside world. Logan tore his mouth from Grace's. He breathed silently through pursed lips so as not to reveal his presence, and pressed the palm of his hand against Grace's mouth, keeping her ragged breathing from giving them away.

He tried to collect his thoughts, but the image looking back at him from three different angles made him wonder just how far he would have gone before he realized he had completely botched this mission. His knee was wedged between Grace's thighs. He had the ivory slip hiked up to the waistband of her panties. The straps dan-

gled loosely in the crook of her elbows, leaving her
breasts bare and beautiful from every conceivable view.
Her hands were lost inside his shirt, her mouth red and
swollen with his kisses—and the whole scene was reflected in the dressing-room mirrors.

"Is everything all right?" Now the clerk sounded
vaguely concerned.

Logan slowly pulled his hand away and mouthed the
words, "Say something to get rid of her."

"What should I say?" she mouthed back.

He tilted his head and glared at her.

Grace shrank away from the hard look. She pulled the
slip straps back over her shoulders and covered herself,
but finally responded to the message. "I'm fine," she
said in a loud, surprisingly clear voice. "I'll be out in
just a minute. Thank you."

After the clerk left, Logan shook his head. "That's the
fastest you can think on your feet?"

Her unshielded eyes swelled with something more than
embarrassment at being caught in a compromising position. "Is that what this was? A test?"

"No." He was too honest to tell her otherwise. He
swiped his fingers through his hair, literally and figura-
tively trying to straighten the mess he'd made of their
professional relationship. "But there's a hell of a lot
more to working undercover than just looking the part."

"I know that. I might be naive, but I'm not an idiot."

He tucked in his clothes and backed himself up to the
door. No. He was the only idiot here. She'd crossed her
arms in front of her, but stood straight in that proud yet
vulnerable stance he'd gotten to know so well today.

"Tomorrow I'll fill you in on covert weaponry. And
we'll work on some self-defense tactics."

His aching groin and shredded sense of self-preservation

mocked the cool authority in his voice. He'd known this assignment would be trouble from the start, and he'd already blown it big time by losing his objectivity to a case of carnal lust.

"Fine. Would you step out so I can get dressed, please?"

He closed the door and headed back to his lonesome spot on the couch.

"Definitely need to work on self-defense."

4

AUTUMN IN NEW YORK be damned. The September humidity was wreaking havoc on both her hairdo and her mood.

For the umpteenth time, Grace pushed an annoying curl out of her eyes. Useless. Absolutely useless. Just what was the advantage of this new hairstyle, anyway?

Surrendering to the forces of nature, she let the curls fall where they may and knocked on the door of the town house. She'd come all the way to New Jersey by subway and cab, thinking the trip would be less wearing than sitting in morning traffic for two hours.

Ha!

She pulled out her steno pad and made an entry reminding herself that unless she had proof the public transport's air-conditioning systems were working, she would rely solely on herself for transportation.

Her watch already registered 9:15 a.m. She was late, to boot. She leaned back and double-checked that she did, indeed, have the right address before knocking again. Then she used those few moments of time to bemoan that she had natural curl in her hair, and that no matter how many products Miguel recommended she use, it was going to kink up into an unruly mess until the humidity dropped below fifty percent.

If only she hadn't spent so much time on her hair this

morning. If only she'd gotten up sooner. If only she'd been able to get a decent night's sleep.

But no, images of Logan's steely-gray eyes had haunted her dreams, laughing at her at first, then looking at her in ways she didn't fully understand. She'd woken up more than once with her mouth open, panting hard, remembering the feel of his mouth on hers. The unique taste of his lips, hard and soft, hot and sweet, all at once.

And once, near three o'clock in the morning, she found herself wrapped around her pillow, rubbing against it, squeezing it tight between her thighs, her body straining for the memory of something it had never found.

She'd gotten up and showered then, but quickly discovered that the warm pinpricks of water reminded her too much of the fiery scrape of Logan's whiskers across her skin. Sensitizing her, seducing her.

His body seemed to be hard wherever hers was soft. And the shape of him had been completely different from hers. Enticingly male, while she'd felt, oh, so terribly, wonderfully female.

But she hadn't known what to do. She hadn't known what he wanted from her. She scarcely knew what she wanted for herself.

Only that she shouldn't want it.

This distracting, confusing, consuming obsession with Logan had to stop. Or she'd never get any work done.

That meant she'd never capture Harris Mitchell. She'd never earn the respect she deserved. She'd never get a second chance to bring down a user who was so much like those men who had abused her mother's trusting heart.

As a child, she hadn't been able to help Mimsey. But she could now. She could help all the innocents who'd been taken advantage of by greedy, self-serving egomaniacs. If she didn't do this, she'd always be frumpy Grace Lockhart, spinster computer geek, second-rate shadow of her halfway-famous mother.

It was a mighty sad epitaph.

But ten life-changing lessons from Logan could turn her into a knowledgeable woman of the world who understood how to use her body as well as her brain to lure Harris Mitchell into her clutches, and straight to prison.

She hated depending on anyone else though. Any other project, she could take a class or read a book, make herself the expert she needed to be. But not this sexy thing.

She needed a man to learn that.

She needed Logan.

But, oh, Lord, she didn't want to need him. For her work *or* her fantasies.

Fantasies?

Rule number five in the ladies' dressing room last night had nearly undone her.

"Oh, God," she whispered out loud as her body heated all over again at the very thought of what lessons six through ten on Logan's list might entail.

Grace breathed in deeply, desperate now to regain some semblance of decorum. The hot, moist air didn't help cool the frustration broiling within her.

She raised her fist to pound at the door once more. "Damn you, Logan Pierce."

Her fist never hit the wood. Instead, she got caught in the quick reflexes of Logan's hand, mere inches from his naked chest. "Good morning to you, too."

"I might have known you'd oversleep." There. She sounded justifiably ticked off. Dignified even.

If only she'd quit staring at the broad expanse of skin lightly dusted with coffee-dark hair that curled over well-defined muscles and faded into a narrow vee before veering in a straight line down beneath the unhooked snap of his jeans.

Maybe then she could manage to *look* a little dignified, too.

Grace tugged her hand away, more angry with herself for her adolescent gawking than for any tardiness on his part. But anger was an easy emotion to latch on to. Far easier than trying to decipher the tightening of unseen muscles low in her belly.

"We're down to four days of training. I thought we'd agreed to an early start."

"I'm coming off forty-eight hours without any sleep. I needed to catch up." He turned away and walked on into the house, expecting her to follow. "If your highness can spare me another fifteen minutes, I'll hit the shower and grab some breakfast."

As he walked away from her, she noticed he had a shape remarkably similar to that of a lean, muscular T-bone steak. Broad shoulders, tapered waist, narrow hips.

Men and women were so utterly different, she observed.

And Logan was different from any man she'd known.

Maybe only because he was giving her a chance to do research with him, to study those differences in details. Straight lines and rounded curves...

"Coming?"

Fine-tuning her powers of observation, she also noted that his deep voice lacked any trace of the indulgent patience and charm he'd had in such abundant supply yesterday.

Grace shut the door and hurried after him. "Is everything all right?"

She backpedaled to avoid plowing into him when he suddenly stopped and spun around.

"First, no conversation before coffee in the morning."

He turned and headed up a half flight of stairs, leaving Grace standing at the bottom. "What's the second thing?" she called after him.

He disappeared around the corner and a door slammed shut.

"Logan?"

The sound of running water provided her only answer.

So where was the irresistible lady-killer who had kissed her senseless and haunted her dreams? Where was the legendary agent who brought down smuggling rings almost single-handedly?

Who was this sexy, rumpled grumpy-butt who refused to even talk to her?

Four days and counting. Maybe infiltrating Harris Mitchell's ladies-only workforce was an impossible mission, after all.

Left alone without any direction, Grace gave herself a tour of the main floor of the town house. As far as housekeeping went, Logan was the one who could use some training. And the place was sparsely furnished to the point of being ascetic. A leather couch and maple entertainment center with a TV and VCR were the only furniture in the main room. He didn't even have a lamp to read by.

She dropped her attaché onto the couch beside a pile of laundry and, needing something to do to pass the time, began to fold. The towels were easy. Then came the jeans.

It felt almost naughty to straighten and fold the soft denim. Smoothing the wrinkles out of the considerable length of leg. Pressing her hand over the rear pockets and running her fingers along the same material that cupped his buttocks. Zipping up the front where...

Grace cleared her throat and snatched her hands away, feeling as embarrassed as if she'd been caught snooping through his things. She set the last pair on top of the pile and moved on to the safer territory of the kitchen.

"Yeesh." Apparently secret-agent school didn't include any classes on health codes. Stacks of takeout trash, from flat pizza boxes to folding Chinese food cartons, littered the countertops.

She went to the first box and pried a fork from the graying contents. Hadn't Logan said he'd been away on an assignment? Surely he hadn't left these things sitting here all that time. And wouldn't a man who had as many conquests as he reportedly did have at least one woman willing to clean up after him?

Scrounging a garbage bag from under the sink, Grace made quick work of all the trash. She had coffee brewing in a freshly scrubbed pot, and utensils running in the dishwasher by the time Logan walked into the kitchen.

She rinsed her hands in the sink and was drying them with a towel before either of them spoke.

"What are you doing?" he asked.

"Just cleaning up a bit. I didn't know how long you'd be. I waited until your shower was done before turning on the dishwasher." She noted his clean-shaven jaw, exposing an angular stretch of tanned, smooth skin. Idly she wondered how it would feel against her cheek compared to yesterday's more dangerous look.

"This is all a little too domestic for me." He already had his black leather holster strapped across his shoulders. He tucked in his New York Yankees T-shirt and scanned the kitchen. "Is that real coffee there?"

Grace nodded. "I found some in the cabinet. It's past its expiration date, but I don't think—"

Any explanation proved superfluous. Logan pulled a mug from the cupboard and poured himself a cup, even before it finished brewing. The dripping coffee popped and sizzled as it hit the hot plate and spattered onto the counter.

She picked up the dishcloth and moved toward the mess. "I just cleaned that—"

"Not a word." He carried the mug to his lips and savored the first sip.

"I was just helping out. You don't mind, do you?"

"Are you here to catch a crook or to play house?"

Grace absorbed his rudeness by transforming it into sarcasm. "Sor-ry. I thought you might appreciate some civilized behavior since you seem to be in such short supply yourself." She slapped the dishcloth in the sink and left the room. In a way, she was glad he'd been so curt with her. It made it a hell of a lot easier to knock him off that obsessive fantasy pedestal she'd elevated him to last night.

Some sexy man-god. He could be as rude and ungrateful as any of her mother's lovers had been.

She picked up her attaché and slung the strap over her shoulder. Grumpy, she could handle. She'd even forgive him for not appreciating her help.

But to question her commitment to this case?

Grace was fuming by the time she reached the door. She flung it open, eager to welcome the heat and humidity outside. It would be a damn sight cooler than the resentment building up inside her right now.

A vise clamped around her wrist. Logan pulled her back inside and slammed the door shut. She whipped around, fist raised, her heel aimed at the instep of his foot. He shuffled his feet and avoided her punch, pinning her to the door in a deft move that made her feel like an amateur.

His big hands pressed her shoulders into the wood behind her as he threw her off balance by wedging one leg between both of hers—a mockery of the embrace they'd shared last night.

Trapped in this position, with her breasts thrusting out toward his chest, and that ultrasensitive feminine spot at the juncture of her thighs balanced like a fulcrum atop his knee, she felt exposed and vulnerable. The layers of blouse and suit she wore didn't help. His heated gaze swept across her breasts like the caress of his hands, and that feminine spot tingled in response.

But his moody silence demanded she ignore both her self-conscious fears and her body's unexpected reaction to their brief struggle. She looked up into those deep gray eyes, darkened now to the color of fierce summer storm clouds. "Let's start this conversation again. Only this time, you tell me why you're so upset."

"Upset?" He laughed. But it was an unpleasant sound that rasped deep in his throat. "'Teach me how to seduce a man.' Do you have any idea what you're getting into?"

The crisp line of his mouth moved with damning precision. But his soft, dark voice caused her more confusion than fear.

She kept her own voice hushed and even when she answered. "I'm going after Harris Mitchell. You tried to change my mind yesterday and it didn't work. It won't work today, either."

"We'll see."

He eyed her a moment longer, held her prisoner in the same arms that had held her so tenderly the night before. And then he released her. Her heels hit the floor. She adjusted her clothes against her sensitized skin before following his determined stride at a more cautious pace.

On the way to the kitchen, Logan pulled a large envelope from the entertainment console and plunked it down on the table. "This was delivered earlier this morning."

She recognized the courier's logo, and the return address of Commander Carmody's office. So she hadn't been the first to awaken him. "What is it?" she asked.

"What the hell are you thinking, going after this guy? He's a freak."

Grace reached for her glasses in an unconscious habit. But her nervous fingers brushed against an unadorned cheek. "Excuse me?"

"Harris Mitchell." He thumbed through the dossier on Mitchell's background. Pages and pages of allegations. Eye-witness testimony that had been tossed out of court because the eye witnesses kept disappearing or recanting their stories. It had taken her weeks to pull all that information together. He'd read through it in a single morning?

She dropped her attaché into a chair and stood straight, defending her hard work. "If you've read his file, then you can see why he has to be stopped. He runs a multimillion-dollar money-laundering business. He's strengthening the positions of several different mob factions and bypassing the entire Internal Revenue system. You understand why we have to do this, don't you?"

"Understand?" He jabbed the stack of papers, then he pointed that same finger at her. "Look, Gracie, I thought we were playing a game here. Teaching you a few tricks so you could go after a standard-issue hoodlum. But Mitchell's serious business."

"I know that. Don't call me Gracie—"

"The man's nickname is Mr. Clean. And it's not because he showers twice a day. His loose ends wind up in the city dump, which is where you'll be if he even suspects you're an undercover agent. And I haven't even started on all the kinky stuff in his file."

Grace planted her hands on her hips and swelled with indignant fury. She wasn't an idiot. She had no delusions about Harris Mitchell being an easy case. "So he's a dangerous man. The FBI doesn't put pool hustlers on their Most Wanted list. I'll be careful."

"You'll be dead. You're a rookie. A walking disaster waiting to happen. This guy is slick and smart and expecting trouble. Carmody must be out of his mind to send you after him."

"Disaster?" Defensive anger swelled inside her, pushing its way past the self-doubts, past the need to prove herself to a world that refused to take her seriously. "I earned this assignment. I came up with the plan. It's *my* computer program that's going to find his second set of books and flush out all his contacts. It's *my* strategy. I've done my homework."

"On paper." He plowed his fingers through his short-cropped hair and paced the kitchen, shaking his head as if the idea of her succeeding was incomprehensible. "Sure, your numbers look good. You can download his files and corrupt his system so all his little minions come out of the woodwork to find him. Well guess what, sweetheart? He doesn't want that to happen." He stopped abruptly and faced off over the table, leaning toward her in a way that made her curl her toes inside her pumps to keep from retreating.

"If he finds out you're a Fed, you're dead."

Grace resisted the self-preserving need to look away

from the accusatory gleam in those piercing silver eyes. "Then it's up to you to make sure I don't screw up."

"You're not going."

"I'm not Roy Silverton. And sticking me behind a desk won't bring him back."

Logan froze as if she had slapped him. His cheeks flushed with color. It was a cruel reminder, she knew, but she had enough obstacles of her own to overcome without having to compete with the memory of a dead man.

She gentled her voice to reason with Logan. "It didn't matter that Roy was on his first field assignment. You couldn't have foreseen what was waiting for him on that dock. I'm sorry. But a seasoned agent would have been slain, too."

"And that's supposed to reassure me?" Logan stood straight and tall again, dismissing her argument. And her compassion. "I'll take this up with Carmody. If anyone's going after Mitchell, it's going to be me."

Logan strode from the kitchen. He pulled on his leather jacket, expecting her to obey his pronouncement like a good little girl.

Grace did one better. She grabbed her bag and circled the room, blocking his path before he reached the door. The man couldn't argue with cold, hard logic.

"Afraid you can't do that, Agent Pierce. You lack the necessary credentials for the job."

"Credentials? Like what?"

She looked down at her chest, which he had studied so thoroughly only minutes ago, then back up at him. "Forty, twenty-eight, thirty-eight."

"Take your forty, twenty-eight, thirty-eight and get in the damn car."

NOT FOR THE FIRST TIME in his life, Logan wished he'd spent more time practicing his diplomacy skills. Sam Carmody held up his hand like some magic talisman and demanded the room be still. Then he lined himself up at a forty-five-degree angle to his putter and knocked the tiny golf ball across the plush carpet into a green mechanical cup.

Logan bit down on his protest, grinding his teeth on the silence until his jaw ached. A red light blinked on the cup, signaling victory. When the ball spit back out, Logan was released from the spell.

He marched up to Carmody's elbow. "Look, I'll admit I thought this was doable at first. But now I'm up to speed on the particulars of this case. You don't send an untested agent out on an assignment this big to bring down a creep like Mitchell."

Grace approached from the other side. Though her cheeks blazed with suppressed emotion, her tone held the same bureaucratic detachment as Carmody's. *Suckup.* "I deserve this break. I worked hard for it. You yourself said you'd never seen a program like mine."

The commander tilted his putter toward the ceiling and examined his grip. "It *is* pretty ingenious. Have you seen it, Pierce?"

"She'll never get a chance to use it." The very idea of sending this novice into a den of murdering thieves who dealt with traitors as casually as they dealt with annoying insects violated his sense of justice. It violated common sense. He thought he'd been training her to catch the eye of some computer hack, not to become the right-hand woman of a man wanted for capital crimes in fourteen different states. "Mitchell's got too many weird hang-ups to guard against. If she blows her cover, he'll blow her head off."

"Agent Lockhart, are you going to blow your cover?"

"No, sir."

"See, Pierce? Everything will be all right."

Logan grabbed the putter and pulled it away from Carmody's line of vision.

"Commander—"

Too late he realized his tactical error. The absolute stillness on Carmody's face as he turned to him told him the discussion was finished. As if he'd ever really considered changing his mind. He'd picked the agents he wanted on this case, and now he expected them to do their job.

"Your concerns are duly noted. But I'm confident that between her brains and your experience, you can complete the assigned task in record time." He pulled the putter from Logan's unresisting grasp and returned to his practice stance. "I believe the clock is ticking."

Dismissed without another word, Logan followed the smug sway of Grace's butt down the hallway to the elevator. Her shoulders were thrown back in proud triumph at having the boss side with her. She wore a gray suit today, too. But the softer charcoal color, shorter hem length and belted waist had subtly transformed her appearance from a shapeless box into a confident, professional—sexy—woman.

Maybe that was part of his problem. Guilt. He'd been so busy trying to dress her up and have some fun with her that he hadn't seen the real problem.

She might be half good at this assignment. But half good was worse than no good. If she thought she had some skills—such as her eye for details, her thorough research on Mitchell, her way around a computer—she'd take risks.

And for an agent with no covert experience, taking

risks could be suicide. She'd panic or lose her temper or pull that soft and vulnerable act the way she had when her mother had stopped by yesterday. Any one of those mistakes would clue in a smart guy like Mitchell to the fact she wasn't who she claimed to be.

All that would change now. If he had to train her for deep cover work, he would train her hard. No time for flirtations and fun. He had four days to make her as tough and savvy about the business as he was.

Four days of sheer torture.

There were just the two of them on the elevator. Still, Grace stood by the button panel while he leaned against the rail on the opposite side. Not once had she turned to look at him since leaving Carmody's office.

"Don't think you've won anything here," he said.

"I'm not trying to win anything. I'm trying to do my job."

"Your job?" As if she knew what this job was about. Logan bristled at the same naiveté he'd found so intriguing at their first meeting.

He reached in front of her and punched the stop button, triggering a high-pitched buzzer and stalling the elevator between the sixth and seventh floors.

"Lie to me."

"Are you crazy?" As any cubicle-trained technician would, she immediately searched for the right button to push to silence the alarm and get them moving again. "What are you doing?"

"Tell me a lie and make me believe it." Logan grabbed her by the shoulders and pushed her to the back wall. He released her, but blocked her way to the doors, the buttons, and any chance of freedom. "You may catch Mitchell's eye with your new look, but you won't last two minutes if you can't convince him that every word you're saying is the truth. So tell me a lie.''

Her big emerald eyes clouded over with thought. The emergency buzzer might as well have been her own death knell.

Her eyes brightened the instant before she spoke. ''I appreciate your...'' she paused—a dead giveaway ''...Unorthodox training techniques.''

''You lose. Try again.'' He leaned in a fraction, upping the stakes in this little dare. ''Rule number six is surprise a man. Show him the unexpected. If I can read you like a book, then so can Mitchell. I don't think you can do it. I don't think you can tell a convincing lie.''

This time she had the good sense to look down and fiddle with her bag while she tried to think of what to say. A classic gambit that Mitchell might recognize, though it was a step in the right direction.

But when she looked up at him, her cheeks flamed with color, a sure sign of distress. ''I resent the hell out of you taking my fitness for this assignment up with Carmody.''

''That's not a lie.''

''What do you want me to say?''

He bombarded her with questions, purposefully inciting her temper, forcing her to fight for logic and control and credibility. She failed on every count.

''Damn it, Logan, what do you want me to do?''

A sheen of perspiration glowed on her skin. The elevator filled with the heat of her frustration, which was multiplied by the heat of his body's unbidden response to her fire. Without touching, he was breathing as hard as he'd been last night when he'd nearly stripped her naked inside that dressing room.

Logan pushed out a cleansing breath as he turned

Intimate Knowledge

away. One of these times he'd get smart and do this battle-of-wills thing with her someplace wide open. Well-ventilated. Air-conditioned, even.

He punched the start button and felt the elevator lurch deep in his bones. He absorbed the sudden jolt of movement as easily as he absorbed the brunt of her accusatory silence.

"I want you to resign from this case."

5

RESIGN FROM THIS CASE.

As if!

Grace removed the heavy earphones that muffled the sounds of the firing range and hung them around her neck while she reloaded blanks into the Smith & Wesson .38 Logan had given her. She brought the paper target into view and cringed with embarrassment.

"Damn it." She'd missed all five shots.

She never claimed to be any kind of marksman, but at least with her company-issue Sig Sauer she could meet the basic proficiency requirements.

"Time to go back to your cubicle, Gracie."

The hated nickname rippled along her spine, and her self-appointed sentinel unfolded himself from the shadows of the booth behind her.

"The weight of the gun is so light." She refused to give him the satisfaction of getting defensive again. But she had to argue the logic. "The barrel is shorter. It's hard to get used to the kick of this."

Tall and dark and oozing superiority in his spare movements, Logan came up behind her and peered down the lane that separated them from anyone else who might be practicing. "It's smaller so that it's easier to conceal. That's why it's called an Undercover .38."

She'd asked him to teach her about being sexy, not categorize her as some helpless female or incompetent rookie. Yet here he was, patronizing her, just like her co-workers who thought she was crazy for wanting to trade in her safe, predictable computer job to become a field agent. Patronizing her just like the men who had paraded through her life growing up, abusing her mother's trusting nature for a shot at making it with a starlet.

Using Grace herself as a poor substitute. Until she'd learned to hide her attributes behind bulky clothes and thick glasses. Until she'd decided to play the role of responsible adult and tried to teach Mimsey the difference between taking in someone in need and simply being taken in.

"You need to be as smooth with the gun as you are with a lie. If you have to defend yourself, you won't get a second chance to shoot."

There he went with the lie thing again. How many times did she have to prove herself before Logan would take her seriously? Before he'd trust that she actually had more brain cells than boobs?

For a while yesterday she'd thought Logan was different from the other men she'd met. Sure, he'd noticed her ample breasts and hips. But she thought he'd seen beyond them. That maybe he'd actually listened when she'd talked about her fears and hurts.

But no. He was turning out to be like every other man on the planet.

Commander Carmody was giving her a chance to do something important, something meaningful. Something only *she* could do. Grace suspected that if she failed, she wouldn't get another chance.

Logan Pierce and his sexy eyes and shadowed past weren't going to ruin this opportunity for her.

Resign from the case, indeed! She had a thing or two to show Logan Pierce.

She hoped.

Grace put the earphones back on and adjusted her goggles. Logan slid his left hand along her arm, leaving a trail of goose bumps in its wake. His larger hand covered hers where it rested on the butt of the gun.

He lifted the right ear cup and whispered a command. "Compensate for the lighter weight like this."

By the time he had his chest pressed against her back, with both hands holding hers around the gun, an idea had taken root.

The man wanted surprises?

Well, she was about to give him one—and teach him a lesson in the process.

Maybe there *were* advantages to being an actress's daughter.

Thinking back to her mother's heyday on the big screen, Grace pursed her lips in a studious pout and squinted as she concentrated on sighting the target. She adjusted her shoulders so that they nestled snugly beneath Logan's outstretched arms, and wriggled her bottom against the juncture of his thighs.

Though words would be impossible to hear, the warm hiss of his breath at her temple told her she had made contact with her intended target.

Wrapped like a cocoon in the cradle of Logan's body, Grace hid her triumphant smile and squeezed the trigger. Her shoulders recoiled into his chest. Her shot went wide of the target.

She adjusted herself again, this time angling the crown of her hair along his solid jaw. She dragged her tongue along the arc of her lips, and with his hands guiding hers, she pulled the trigger a second time.

She made a hole in the shoulder of the paper target.

But, more importantly, Logan's arms tightened around her to steady her next shot.

Think like Mimsey, she coached herself, ignoring her body's softening response to the hard contact of Logan's body. What Grace didn't possess herself, she'd borrow from her mother. Play a part. Mimsey Lockhart had played seductresses and lusty innocents in all her movies, always winding up in a passionate embrace just as the monster or alien or scientific creation-gone-wrong was about to attack and destroy the world.

The only thing Grace wanted to destroy was Logan's superior attitude. She could work undercover. She could lie if she had to.

She could stay in control and surprise a man. Rules number two and six, if memory served her correctly.

She'd beat Logan at his own game. Use his list of what he found sexy against him.

Just think like Mimsey.

Think sexy.

While she prepared to shoot again, she spread her feet a half step apart, putting one foot on either side of Logan's. Her lower regions grew mysteriously heavy. Moistened with thoughts of the game she was playing.

She retreated another fraction of a step and felt the solid trunk of Logan's thigh pressing along the seam of her buttocks. Every muscle between her waist and thighs jumped at the contact, then tightened involuntarily. Anticipating. Waiting. He adjusted his position, rubbing his hard thigh into the natural space between her curves. The hidden muscles clenched again. Her new silk panties dampened with heat.

Denying her body's flagrant response, Grace peered through the lenses of her protective goggles and focused on the target.

But Logan was having some trouble concentrating, too. His nose stirred the hair at her temple in a nuzzling caress. Seizing the advantage of his distraction, she squeezed the trigger a third time. Momentum threw her backward, but the unbending wall of Logan's body refused to budge. She would have stumbled forward, but his left hand snaked around her waist, catching her, trapping her in the deliciously hot vise of his body.

If he spoke, either tutoring her aim or condemning her little tease, she never heard him.

His forearm drifted upward, catching beneath the weight of her breasts. The size and heat and hardness of him surrounding her, splitting her, shielding her, distracted her from the carefully calculated role she was playing.

She tried to form a picture of her mother playing out a similarly breathless scene with a heroic sheriff in *Mutant Rat Attack.*

But the only image that would come to mind was the memory of herself, half-naked, mounted on Logan's knee in the cramped confines of the dressing room last night. Her bare, damp breasts flattened in the crisp, curling hair on his chest as the erotically masculine reflection of broad shoulders and big hands and his long, sleek, leather-holstered gun tantalized her from every angle.

Her palms tingled with remembered heat around the grip of her pistol.

Think like Mimsey! She practically screamed the words inside her head, begging her mind to seize on the painful memories from her childhood and stifle her body's helpless reaction to this calculated seduction.

Without even trying, Logan was claiming the upper hand in this latest tutoring session.

Again.

She wouldn't let him.

Grace opened her mouth and breathed slowly, in and out, consciously dragging cool air into her feverish body. *Stay in control.* Rule number two.

Almost as if guided by instinct, his fingers curled around hers on the gun. She lifted it and fired.

She was inside the target outline now.

And then his lips grazed her neck, moist and hot, pushing aside the curls at her nape. An unfamiliar ache throbbed at her center, changing dampness into a little gush of honey. She shifted her stance to ease the pressure, and inadvertently gave him access to a tiny dimple behind her ear.

Erogenous zones. Rule three. She made the observation through instinct as a blaze of molten rapture pulsed to the spot. He touched it with his tongue and her teeth nearly chattered as waves of sheer pleasure shivered through her.

In the aftermath she became aware of something new, something firm and strong pressing against her bottom. He was aroused.

Okay, technically, so was she. But intellectual triumph gave her the control she needed for that last shot at the target.

Stretching herself like a cat, priming the tension in her own body, she backed every inch of herself against Logan that she could. His hand moved up inside her jacket and palmed her breast. Through her blouse and bra he squeezed. Grace gasped at the exquisite tingle of pleasure-coated pain. She struggled to stay in control. She had something to prove. She could lie. She could do this.

His fingers glided along the silky material, rubbing at the tender peak until the vibration she felt in her chest could have been his moan...could have been her own.

Grace inhaled deeply, fighting for oxygen and coherent thought. Logan took advantage and found his way inside her bra to bare skin. He pushed the strap aside and seized its full, straining weight. His thumb and forefinger rolled the aching tip until she cried out at the delicate agony of his touch.

He pulled his other hand from hers, dragging it with a teasing, deliberate friction along the length of her arm, over the thrust of her breast, into the nip of her waist, and then farther down. His fingers splayed at her abdomen, pushing it flat. His long fingers reached farther to dance across her inner thighs, bunching up her skirt in his hand. And then, through her panties and hose he cupped her raw, swollen heat.

Instinctively her crotch gyrated against the pressure. Her low, keening moan rang in her ears until she could hear nothing more, think nothing more, but the snare of Logan's hands and mouth and body in which she was trapped.

"What are you doing to me, Grace?" His voice was a ragged whisper against her skin.

What are you doing to me, Miss Nancy?

Grace's eyes shot open as a snippet of rational thought crept into her mind once more. That was the line the sheriff had said to her mother's character in the movie. Logan's words were almost identical.

Mimsey. Of course. Remember Mimsey.

Stay in control. This was all a lie. She was playing a part.

Grace sought the survivor's strength that had seen her through her childhood.

She raised the gun, clutching it in both hands now, needing something—anything—to hold on to, to concentrate on, besides the unfamiliar tension nearing its snapping point inside her body. She narrowed her gaze and focused on the circle drawn around the target's heart.

Logan's hands squeezed.

She pulled the trigger.

Something keen and unexpected exploded inside her, in rhythm with the gun's report.

Orgasm.

Oh, my God. Was that...? Did she...? Without...?

Grace never got the chance to analyze the rapturous sensation that drained her, released her, leaving her stunned and shaking.

In one fluid motion, Logan pried the pistol from her unresisting fingers and turned her in his arms. Goggles and earphones clattered to the floor as he swept her into his kiss. His hands were on her breasts, grabbing, stripping, squeezing. He backed her against the booth counter and lifted her up, hiking her skirt to her thighs and walking between her legs. He speared his fingers into her hair, catching her and holding her beneath his mouth as he plundered and took what he wanted.

She surrendered to his demands, letting her tongue mate with his, letting her hands find their way around his waist where they dipped lower, past the pockets of those very jeans she had folded that morning. She squeezed him tight and held him, wantonly rubbing herself against the ridge in his pants. He groaned into her mouth and she repeated the action, reveling in her newfound femininity, delighting in her power over him as his hips rocked against hers.

"Grace. Damn it. Grace." His words were a low-pitched rasp against her lips. "Someone might see—"

That was enough to break the spell. Enough to give her an opportunity to think. To remember how this had all started.

She moved her hands to his chest and pushed away. She pressed her knuckles to her ravaged mouth and concentrated on breathing at an even tempo. Despite legs that supported her like twin sticks of jelly, she dropped her feet back to the floor and summoned all the prim dignity of the Grace of old. She straightened the front of her blouse and tugged down the hem of her skirt.

Logan himself seemed to be working on his own recovery. He shoved his fingers through his spiky hair, wiped his hand over his mouth and jaw. Once. Twice. Again. "Grace. Sweetheart. I'm not sure how that got out of hand, but— We can't—"

His hands settled lightly on her hips as Grace turned and pressed the button that would bring the paper target down the rail toward the booth. When it was close enough, she released the button and smiled with almost giddy relief.

"I hit the target. Bull's-eye."

"What?"

She looked at the hole in the middle of the paper heart and wondered if the symbolism of achieving her goal would be lost on Logan. She'd lied. Not in words, perhaps, but with her body. She'd led him to think there was something between them. That she saw something *personal* in this teacher-student relationship.

Of course there wasn't.

Logan Pierce was a man who could set off her temper and her body with equal finesse. But there was no emotional attachment involved. She wasn't developing feelings for the man.

Grace cringed inwardly. With her body still thrumming with the aftershocks of that "training" session, she was turning into a bigger liar than she could have ever imagined herself to be.

But she had wanted to show him she could play a part. Just like Mimsey.

She'd shown him, all right.

Though victory seemed shallow, she fixed a self-satisfied smile on her face and turned to Logan. She placed her hands on top of his where they rested with comfortable possession on her hips.

"Surprise. My mother's not the only actress in the family," she gloated with perfect suavity, forcing her brain to take charge of her traitorous body.

Logan snatched his hands away and retreated a step. The stunned look of betrayal on his face shouldn't have bothered her as much as it did. But she ignored her immediate inclination to apologize and thumped him once in the chest with her forefinger.

"Pretty convincing, wasn't I? Put that in your rule book and smoke it. I am *not* resigning from this case. If you want to get rid of me, you'll have to find another way."

She waltzed out of the booth with her head held high, her body still throbbing as it carried her away on a very shaky tide of victory.

LOGAN COULDN'T DECIDE whether to strangle Grace or to kiss her into submission. He opted for the former since the latter choice would surely get him into trouble again.

He unlocked the driver's side door of the red 1966 Mustang convertible he'd leased for the job and opened it for her to climb in behind the wheel. Once she had her short skirt adjusted around her thighs, he handed her the keys. "You ever pull a stunt like that again and I'll tan your hide."

Her cheeks flooded with color. "You mean you'd spank me?"

Now there was a picture. One that threatened to tie him in knots all over again.

Logan swore at his body's instantaneous reaction to her innocent question. Or maybe it wasn't so innocent. In that phone-sex voice of hers, even a stunned question sounded like a come-on.

"Get out your notebook, Gracie. You still have a lot left to learn about men." Logan slammed the door and forced his brain back to rational reality. He took his time circling the car before settling onto the passenger seat.

His reputedly virginal partner had pulled a fast one and he'd fallen for her teasing game like a lust-starved rookie. She was headed into one hell of an assignment and she wanted to play games!

The really scary part was that he'd played right along with her. He was the veteran on this team, the one who was supposed to have the common sense. The one who knew that staying focused on the case could be a matter of life and death.

He'd lost focus with Roy. Gotten cocky. Thought he'd seen it all and knew it all. He hadn't sensed the waiting danger until it was too late to save his partner.

He refused to repeat the same mistake with Grace.

He looked over and watched her twist in the driver's seat as she backed the Mustang out of the parking space. The white silk of her blouse stretched and gaped at her cleavage, giving him a clear glimpse of the lacy bra she wore underneath. Logan swallowed hard as she inched a bit further, pushing a mound of pure womanly flesh up over the edge of the bra as if it was trying to escape. As if it was reaching out to him.

Lace and silk and a few straps of elastic weren't nearly enough to contain and support those beauties.

They needed a man's hand. A man's mouth. His—

Logan swore and turned away from the provocative display. He had to get this unexpected lust for her out of his system so he could do the damn job.

He caught a glimpse of his own dilated pupils in the side-view mirror, a visible hint of his body's response to hers.

"Son of a bitch," he muttered, disgusted by his body's reaction. He could control this!

Blotting out that pitiful look in his eyes, Logan jammed on his reflective sunglasses and concentrated on what he considered justifiable anger.

Twenty-four hours ago Grace had been a shy, shapeless cubicle nerd. Just because he'd discovered the incredible body beneath her clothes and the fire in her eyes and the stubborn spirit that forced him into hyper-alert mode whenever she was around didn't mean she'd truly become that femme fatale she aspired to be. "You're playing out of your league, Grace."

Her knuckles turned white around the gearshift, foretelling her protest. "I did what you told me to do, didn't I? I made you think what I was doing was real. I pretended like I was a B-movie seductress and you fell for it. I stayed in control—"

"You lost it just like I did."

"I did not."

"You're blushing now, just talking about it."

Her hand flew to her cheek to gauge the heat rising there. He watched the darting focus of her eyes as she fumbled for an excuse. "My cheeks are flushed because I'm angry at you."

"And losing your temper is going to help you convince Harris Mitchell you're on the up and up with him?"

That stunned her into silence.

Logan softened his tone. A little. He understood that she was still myopic, insecure, Grace Lockhart, a little lady who needed to prove something. But that sexy, determined Agent Grace with the damn gun and the dynamite body showed some potential for working undercover. Too much damn potential for her own good. A couple of years of on-the-job training and then, yeah, she'd be ready to take on the likes of organized crime bosses.

But in five days?

Make that four, and counting.

If only miracles still happened.

And ever since Roy Silverton's death, miracles had been in short supply for Logan.

Grace was like a comic-book hero with newly discovered superpowers. She could save mankind from the scummy likes of Harris Mitchell if she learned how to harness her talents. But those same talents—her drive, her brains, her sensual instincts—could just as easily destroy her if she wasn't trained correctly.

Logan finally, fully, accepted that the mentor role had fallen to him.

Leaning back into the white bucket seat he reached across the console and brushed a fingertip across her flushed, hot cheek. He wasn't surprised when she jerked away from his touch.

Typical reaction for an amateur. Logan shook his head at the enormity of his task. "You've got a few lessons left to learn, sweetheart, before you're ready to play with the big boys."

"Are you going to be the one to teach me?"

"As long as you can remember rule number seven."

"What's that?" Like the straight-A student she'd probably been in school, she was already reaching into her bag for her notebook.

"You have to keep your head in the game. Always."

She pulled her empty hand out of the bag and rested it on the steering wheel. The expression in her eyes was a mixture of accusation and confusion. "What does that have to do with being sexy?"

"It has to do with staying alive. You can't for one minute forget what your purpose is when you're with Mitchell."

"I know my job."

"And I know mine. Dead women aren't sexy." He let that one sink in—for her, and for him—allowing an image of attending Grace's funeral to slip into his mind to keep his libido firmly in check. "Now, if we're going to do this job, we're going to do it right."

He leaned across the center console, arcing his arm around her to reach the seat belt. He was close enough to smell the damp heat gathering between her breasts. He forced her back in the seat as far as she could possibly go without him actually touching her, using a bit of subtle intimidation to remind her who was in charge on this assignment.

"And if you pull any more of that B-movie actress crap like you did on the firing range, I'll tell Carmody you failed the training. That you're mentally unfit for duty."

With a snap, he buckled her in and leaned back in his seat.

The word *fail* seemed to have a galvanizing effect on Grace. She sat up straighter, thrusting out those glorious breasts like fully loaded torpedoes. "You wouldn't dare."

"If I have to dress up in drag and seduce Harris Mitchell myself, I will. If I'm not convinced you can take care of yourself on this assignment, you won't go."

Didn't the damn idiot know when to back off from a challenge?

"Then train me as hard as you can." She stomped on the accelerator and drove the Mustang out of the parking lot. "Harris Mitchell is mine."

6

"WHAT'S THAT WIRE sticking out of your bra?"

Grace dropped her chin and looked straight down her cleavage. "What wire?"

"No!" Logan shoved his chair back from the conference table and stalked to the far end of the room and back before perching on the corner of the table and getting in her face for not thinking. "You have to come up with a cover line. If Mitchell or one of his henchwomen spots something like that, you have to tell them your underwire broke on your bra."

"Wouldn't they search me? They'll figure out that's a lie."

"That's the whole point! You have to come up with something so they don't even suspect you're lying. You can't let them get to the search part."

Logan had barred Grace inside this empty room at FBI headquarters, and together they'd pored over Mitchell's file, familiarizing themselves with all the pervert's quirks. Whether getting through a security screen or a one-on-one meeting with the man, Logan wanted her prepared for any contingency. She had to think on her feet. She might even have to think flat on her back, if Mitchell's reputation for the ladies played out.

But every time Grace showed a bit of promise, she made this kind of gaffe and backtracked through any progress they'd made. Logan swiped his palm across his jaw and noted the stubble of beard growing there. He needed a shave. He needed a stiff drink. Aw hell, he needed a vacation from this whole stupid idea. Grace Lockhart was bureaucrat material, not a field agent. How the hell did Carmody expect her to survive this assignment?

Grace set her steno pad, in which she'd logged every bluff line they'd brainstormed together, on the table and shoved it away. "Logan, we've been at this for seven hours. I'm tired and I'm hungry."

"Mitchell won't care how tired or hungry you are when he puts a bullet through your head. I said I was going to train you hard. Now are you up to it or not?"

Her shoulders lifted from their weary posture and she reached for the steno pad. She clicked her mechanical pencil twice and flipped to a clean page. "All right. Let's try another scenario."

If she had glared at him, he would have drilled her for another hour. If she had cried and tried to beg her way out of it, he would have taken her straight to Carmody and let her weeping prove she was unfit for this job.

But her big green eyes did him in. Wide and intelligent, they revealed a quiet determination that even his boorish commands couldn't diminish. She lifted her hand to adjust her glasses that weren't there and poked herself in the nose. He watched her smooth her fingertips across her brow, as if that had been her intention all along.

She was covering for her mistake.

It was a mistake she should never have made in the first place. But she was trying. Damn, but this woman didn't know when to quit trying.

"You're right," he relented, feeling something very like compassion stirring near his heart. He was smart enough to think of a compromise that would suit both the jaded agent in him, who didn't want her anywhere near this case, as well as the soft-hearted man who wanted her to succeed.

"I am?"

"You'll think better on a full stomach. Let's go eat." He grabbed his jacket from the back of his chair and shrugged into it. "I need to make a stop at my locker first. We're not done for the day."

ONE HELICOPTER and cab ride later, Logan and Grace were on to the next phase of her training. In the heart of Manhattan's posh business district, he would teach her a thing or two about old-monied living.

The tie around his neck had been a concession to the role he was playing. The Willingham Hotel restaurant had been a swanky place for lunch yesterday. But it was a country club buffet compared to Chez Dumond at dinner.

Logan adjusted the lapels of his charcoal flannel suit and touched his cuff links with the superior nonchalance of a man who wore Dolce & Gabbana every day of his life.

Grace's gray suit fit in just by the fact that she filled it out to magnificent proportions. All it took to dress it up was to undo the top button of her blouse, revealing a satiny expanse of skin, and add a pair of diamond drop earrings. The glistening prisms danced along her neck, reflecting the rosy hue of her skin and the strawberry highlights in her golden hair.

Simple. Classy. Gorgeous.

A perfect blend of brains and body. And though both traits were obvious, she wasn't flaunting either one.

As Logan studied her across the table, he couldn't help but notice the picture of understated elegance she made. And to know the secret of raw sensuality that simmered just beneath the surface of her conservative exterior made her an intriguing mix of lady and hussy that any healthy man would find hard to resist.

Just the way he liked his women.

Now if he could only get her to act the part she resembled so well. He gave his head an imperceptible shake as he scooped the sprig of mint from his soup. "Stop playing with your earrings."

"Why do you keep baubles like these in your locker?" she asked, referring to the jewelry box he'd given her on the helicopter.

"I'm not a Boy Scout, you know. In my experience, it pays to be prepared for anything."

"Like a pretty thank-you gift for your latest conquest?"

He ignored the damning reference to his checkered past and lifted his wineglass, saluting her as if he were sharing an intimate toast with a lover. "Like having the real thing on hand when I infiltrate a gang of jewel thieves."

She leaned over her plate. Accusation lit her eyes and guilt-by-association hushed her voice to a terse whisper. "These belong to the Bureau?"

He matched her position at the table, leaving little more than the centerpiece candle separating them. "Mitchell might give you a gift like that."

"For what purpose? I'll be his accountant."

"How do you think he inspires such loyalty from the women who work for him? They're paid well." He reached across the table and caressed one of the diamond fobs. "And sometimes they're given bonuses for a job well done."

Grace jerked away from his touch and sat back straight in her chair.

Logan retreated more slowly. "Enjoy them for tonight. They'll have to go back." He picked up his spoon. "Now eat your soup and convince me you're at home in a place like this."

"It's cold."

"It's chilled melon soup. It's supposed to be cold."

"I would have settled for a burger and fries to fill me up so we could get back to work. Not three different glasses for wines and doll-size servings of food I can't even pronounce."

Logan restrained the urge to shake his spoon at her. "What is it with you and fast food? You're not infiltrating a warehouse with a chop shop and a bunch of mechanics. You're going into Mitchell's multimillion-dollar estate and corporate headquarters. That's the champagne-and-chilled-soup crowd. If you don't fit in, he won't hire you."

Despite the defiant pout of her lips, she glided her spoon from the center to the back of the bowl and sipped the melon puree with well-mannered perfection. The spinach soufflé and veal medallions passed by in a similar sham of quiet etiquette.

He would have preferred their conversation include more than an evaluation of Chez Dumond's food and service, but at least she wasn't screwing up. She used the forks in proper order, spoke to the waiter with just the right hint of arrogance, and even stopped fidgeting with her earrings long enough to survey the restaurant with the bored indifference of a regular wealthy patron.

They had just taken their first bites of crème brûlée when the real Grace reemerged.

She snatched his wrist across the table, nearly knocking his spoon from his hand. "Oh, my God, Logan. Look."

He didn't need eyes in the back of his head to know he was in trouble. The adolescent animation in Grace's expression was warning enough.

He discreetly turned to glance over his shoulder at the restaurant's grand entrance. His chest expanded in a steadying sigh.

Harris Mitchell.

The man fit his profile to a T.

Six foot one. Trimly muscled, thanks to regular workouts. Chestnut hair cut and combed just so to mask the receding points of his hairline. Ice-blue eyes that revealed his Scandinavian heritage and emotional detachment from his conscience.

Mitchell was flanked by twin female bodyguards who served as both adornments and protectors. One woman looked like a Viking princess, the other a Nubian goddess. Though both wore revealing formal wear, there was no mistaking the bulge of handguns in their evening purses or the garters strapped to their thighs that undoubtedly anchored knives or smaller hardware beneath their short gowns.

While Harris chatted with the maître d' as though they were old friends, the *guards* surveyed the restaurant, not even acknowledging their boss when he escorted them both to a reserved table in the corner of the restaurant.

Grace's grip on Logan tightened and trembled in a blend of nerves and excitement. "He's more tanned in real life than he is in his pictures. But that's him. That's our man."

Logan switched his watchful gaze from Mitchell to Grace. Her neck had rotated ninety degrees to keep the mobster in her line of sight. "Quit staring at him. Your eyes are bulging like a rock star just walked by."

"This could be our first meeting. I should go over and introduce myself."

Logan turned his hand and grabbed her wrist, instantly reversing their positions. "As what?"

That one stumped her. "I—"

He stared hard into those big green eyes, trying to reach that stubborn brain of hers. "You're not ready. Backup's not set. You don't even have a fake résumé in place."

When she blinked and finally relaxed in her seat, Logan released her.

But she hadn't given up the idea. "This would be a chance to get that awkward first meeting out of the way. It'll make the job interview go that much more smoothly. I could pretend I've mistaken him for someone else."

"You can't afford an awkward meeting at any time. And, right now, you're exuding teenybopper instead of femme fatale. Mitchell won't give you the time of day." That last assessment of her acting skills finally washed the flush of excitement out of her cheeks. "Finish your dessert and let's get out of here. Better yet, let's just get out. The lesson's over for the night."

He signaled their waiter and asked for the bill.

"All right. Fine. Can't we at least observe him for a few minutes? Maybe we'll pick up something we can use."

Logan *did* prefer firsthand knowledge of a suspect before he went under on a case. The FBI profilers were thorough in putting together dossiers on criminals, but he preferred choosing the time and place to run surveillance instead of having it chosen for him.

He considered the idea for the time it took him to fold his napkin.

Grace was too new at this. Too eager.

Just like Roy.

Hey, Pierce. I'll take point on this meeting and you play backup. Roy had smiled with the smug arrogance of youth. *You're not the only smooth talker on the case.*

But smooth talk didn't stop bullets. And cocky young rookies eager to make their first undercover arrest didn't see the whole picture. They didn't notice the subtle signals from their suspect that they'd been made. They didn't heed their partner's warning to get out until it was too late.

"Logan?"

Grace's soft, husky voice reached deep into his thoughts and pulled him through time and space from that bloody dock back to the Chez Dumond.

"Are you all right?"

He looked down at the wrinkled linen napkin crushed inside his fist.

Then he looked up. Through the dusky light of candle glow he saw her sweet green eyes. They were a mite too large for her face, but that only added to their unique beauty. Like shiny emerald mirrors they reflected a curiosity that showed intelligence, a concern that showed her heart.

For a moment he found a haven in those eyes. He found a place where death and violence hadn't touched. He found a warm, welcoming place where his beat-up old soul longed to find a home.

And he knew that because those pretty, myopic eyes revealed so much, Grace wasn't ready for an encounter with Harris Mitchell.

Shoving aside the lingering memories and foolish fantasies, Logan rose from his chair, buttoned his suit coat and circled the table to her side. Conscious of the un-

answered questions in her eyes, he cupped his hand beneath her elbow and pulled her up to stand beside him.

"We need to leave."

He guided her toward the front doors. "What just happened? Where were you?"

She wasn't tough enough to understand the kind of hell
guilt could put a man through. "I was just thinking."

"About something awful, it looked like."

She wasn't nearly tough enough.

"C'mon. I have a long day planned for you tomorrow.
You'll need your sleep."

As they reached the maître d's station, Grace came to
a sudden stop. "I forgot my bag at the table," she said,
already retracing her steps.

"I'll get it," he offered.

But for a top-heavy woman wearing three-inch pumps,
she could move mighty fast. She was already leaning
over her chair, her butt curved out in the aisle at an enticing angle before he'd excused his way past the couple
behind them.

Logan saw it coming, but was helpless to stop it without creating a scene.

Harris Mitchell was crossing down the aisle behind the
African-American amazon cum bodyguard. Maybe to
take a private phone call, maybe to use the facilities. The
why didn't matter, only that Miss B-movie-queen Wan-
nabe was about to make a critical mistake.

"Innocent, my ass." Logan seethed, damning his own
fanciful notions as much as Grace's lying green eyes.

The bodyguard walked past. Grace straightened. She
slung her purse over her shoulder and stepped back...
right onto the instep of Harris Mitchell's Gucci loafers.

She gave a tiny yelp as her heel slipped and she stumbled. Mitchell caught her square in his arms and held her against his chest.

A waiter with an oversize tray on his shoulder blocked Logan's path. But the exchange of words was clear.

"Excuse me." That was Grace's breathy greeting.

"Not a problem." The deep, faintly accented voice was Mitchell's. "Don't I know you from somewhere?"

Of all the cheesy, cheap come-on lines. And Mitchell was supposed to be a player?

When the waiter moved, Logan could see this scene had gone from bad to worse.

Grace's cheeks were flushed with heat. Her fingers batted around her temple as if she were self-consciously searching for those nonexistent glasses. She held on to Mitchell's sleeve while he set her back on her feet.

And while her eyes were glued to the knot of Mitchell's tie, Harris's leering gaze was anchored a bit lower. Straight down the plunge of Grace's blouse.

"Um, I...don't think..." Grace was searching for words. "I mean, I would have remembered someone like you."

She couldn't see Mitchell's reaction, but Logan did.

Warning signals sounded inside his head. There was that little ticking sensation at the base of his skull that had clued him in to danger more than once in his career. And then there was another feeling, something territorial. Something personal.

She didn't need to become a femme fatale to snag this guy's attention. He was already interested. His hands lingered a little too long on Grace's arms, his eyes lingered way too long somewhere else.

Trouble was, Grace didn't understand what Mitchell thought she was offering. He needed to get her out of there. Now. Before the whole undercover plan blew up in their faces.

"Honey?" Logan called before closing his hand around her upper arm. He couldn't afford to startle her and give Mitchell another glimpse of that deer-in-the-headlights expression on her face.

Fortunately, she turned and gave Logan that startled glare. Carefully avoiding the use of her name, Logan smiled and pulled her to his side. Beyond Mitchell's reach. "We need to leave now if we want to make an appearance at the Guggenheim reception."

Play along. She tugged against his bruising grip, but he didn't ease up until the light of understanding relaxed the self-conscious tension from her face and body.

"Of course. The Guggenheim." Grace turned and batted those big greens at Mitchell. Her talents were getting ahead of her common sense again. Her voice was now smooth as molasses. "Sorry I stepped on your shoe."

"Lucky shoe." Harris smiled, finally lifting his gaze to Grace's eyes. "Enjoy the museum."

Logan quickly turned Grace away from Mitchell, hoping the crook hadn't gotten a clear look at her face. He would have followed her if it weren't for the poke of what felt like a ladies' beaded handbag in his back.

"Is there a problem, Mr. Mitchell?"

The bodyguard.

And no doubt her hand was on the gun inside her purse.

Logan forced himself not to react. He looked at Mitchell. Mitchell looked at him. Though Logan played the part of a dutiful escort and not an overprotective boyfriend, there was something more than a man-to-man exchange of casual greeting going on here. This was more like one man sensing a potential enemy and sizing him up.

Then dismissing him.

"I'm fine, Tanya."

The purse disappeared and Logan turned and quickly followed Grace out the door, not giving Mitchell a chance to change his mistaken first impression of him.

HARRIS MITCHELL.

Oh, my God, Harris Mitchell. She'd seen...she'd touched—talked—to Harris Mitchell.

No. Grace groaned with embarrassment and let her chin sink to her chest. She'd babbled to Harris Mitchell. Crushed his foot like a klutzy idiot. She couldn't even remember what color his eyes were because she'd been too addlepated worrying about what to say or think or to do that she'd never looked any higher than the pointy cleft of his chin.

No wonder Logan thought working with her was an impossible mission.

Seduce a man?

Hell. She couldn't even talk to one.

When Logan strolled out the door and chatted with the doorman, she wasn't fooled for a minute. He was pissed. His flinty eyes darkened like unbending steel and drilled holes into her.

He smiled as he slipped the doorman a tip to flag them a cab, but there was no smile for her. She was already backing up a step before he grabbed her by the arm and dragged her to the curb, beyond the earshot of the doorman.

"I know what you're going to say."

"Really."

She had a good defense for her actions, even if he

didn't want to hear it. "I was concerned about you. You looked so distant all of a sudden. I was trying to listen."

"So you attempted to put the moves on Mitchell because you were worried about me." His sarcasm rubbed salt into the wound of guilt and embarrassment that had already sapped her confidence.

"No. I mean, that's why I forgot my purse. There was no ulterior motive. I really did forget it." She shrugged helplessly, seeing her explanation was having no effect on his surly mood. Time to accept the blame for bungling her unexpected trial run at undercover work. "I'm sorry. I wasn't thinking."

He nodded sharply, hearing only the last three words. "No you weren't, were you?"

At last he released her arm. He snatched her bag instead. "All right, Gracie. Here's rule number eight to put in your book."

He fished out her steno pad and pencil and pushed them into her hands.

"Smart is sexy."

She dutifully wrote the words.

"You're book smart, Grace. But you need to get street smart. Fast."

He stopped her hand as she jotted it down. "Now quit being an idiot. You don't go anywhere near Mitchell until you're fully trained. Got that?"

He was her partner, damn it! Not her superior. He had no right to chew her out like this. "Was I really so terrible—?"

"You got that?" he repeated, leaving no room for discussion.

"Got it."

Until she could think of a way to fix the problem, she let Logan load her into the waiting cab, and said nothing more.

7

GRACE'S SALTBOX on the outskirts of Quantico had been the first item on her list of things to purchase once she was gainfully employed by the Bureau after college graduation. A permanent home. A comfy place to return to each night that she knew would always be there for her.

After a childhood of moving from trailer to apartment to her mother's current boyfriend's house and back to a trailer, she'd wanted roots. She wanted the security of knowing what address she was going home to. The satisfaction of knowing she could take care of herself.

She'd decorated the three-bedroom structure herself in country colors, muted reds and deep blues and pale greens. She'd spent countless weekends scouring auctions and estate sales to find antique furniture and knick-knacks. Her house had a sense of age and character that she'd always longed for.

But she found little comfort in the polished wood floors and china pitchers and handmade quilts tonight.

She was a failure. A hopeless failure as a field agent. A failure with men.

She leaned back into the checkered pillows that lined her denim couch and flipped through the pages of her steno pad. The answers had to be here somewhere.

She'd worked so hard to prove she was anything but a failure.

Her first encounter with Harris Mitchell had been a disaster. If he was looking to hire an accountant to provide comic relief at his business meetings, then she was his woman. But if he wanted another seductress to add to his collection, she didn't stand a chance of getting hired and infiltrating his syndicate.

The men she knew best in her life had been the users and well-intentioned losers who had paraded in and out of her mother's love life. She knew nothing about how to please a man sexually. Hell. At age twenty-six, she was just now beginning to learn about her own sexuality. And that was only because Logan had been forced to help her.

Logan.

She tucked her white fuzzy robe up to her neck and pushed her thick, black glasses up on the bridge of her nose. She couldn't shake the chill that had stayed with her, despite a hot shower, a cup of cocoa and her flannel pj's.

Logan Pierce was the real reason she was moping around the house after midnight. He was the real mystery she couldn't comprehend.

She'd spent the past forty-eight hours trying to learn the crafts that he knew so well. Forty-eight hours of seeing every side of that man. Arrogant. Angry. Frustrated. Disappointed. Amused. Turned on. Extremely turned on. Suspicious. Sad.

And while each and every mood presented something new to perplex her, she found herself obsessing about that last mood of his. She pulled off her glasses and nibbled on the earpiece. How could a man so in command of himself, a man so in command of the world around him, suddenly look so hurt? So far removed from the world that she wasn't sure he'd ever come back to her?

That night at dinner—and every time she mentioned Roy Silverton's name—Logan's remarkable gray eyes seemed to transform. The color dulled. The gleam of secret knowledge disappeared behind a veil of shadow.

She'd used his partner's unfortunate death as a last-ditch means to goad him into working with her. But Grace was beginning to wonder if training her was an uncomfortable reminder of Agent Silverton's first undercover mission. Did Logan think she was so incompetent that she'd end up the same way? Was he being so hard on her—and on himself—because he didn't want to deal with another partner's death?

Grace rubbed the fatigue from her eyes and put her glasses back on. When she'd been growing up and the chips had been stacked against her, she'd responded by getting tougher, working harder. She'd never complained because that hadn't done her any good. She'd never succumbed to worry because that drained the energy she needed to survive.

She wouldn't complain or worry now, either. She'd just add proving her abilities to Logan to her list of why she'd asked for this assignment in the first place.

She flipped to the page of cover lines they'd gone over today and settled in to do her homework.

Why do you carry a gun in your purse, Miss Lockhart? Grace practiced the responses out loud. "A woman alone isn't safe on the streets anymore. Smart women carry them for protection." She tried the next one with a sarcastic twist. "Once you've been mugged, you never leave home without it." But sarcastic wasn't exactly her style. "As an accountant, I'm sometimes required to carry a large amount of money—"

The telephone chirped on the end table beside her.

Startled, she waited for her heart rate to slow to an even beat and checked the time before answering. "Hello?"

Her cautious greeting was met with a loud, boisterous, "Gracie! It's Mother. I hope I'm not calling too late."

Grace's night went from worse to impossible. "It's almost twelve-thirty, Mother."

"I know it's late, but I just had to share my good news."

Oh, God. Grace squeezed her eyes shut and prayed. She'd heard that line too many times before. Somehow Mimsey's good news ended up being bad for them both. Just once, her mother deserved to have some good news without any strings attached.

Grace was used to the pattern by now. It was her turn to ask, "What is it?"

"I got the part. The part in Grant's play! I'm going to be in an off-Broadway show!"

Her mother's joyous enthusiasm was hard to resist. A cautious smile teased the corners of Grace's mouth. "That's wonderful. Is it the part you wanted? The aunt?"

"Yes! Isn't that wonderful news? It's like my career is starting all over again. The way I wanted it to all along."

Grace let her mouth ease into a full-blown smile. "You deserve it. When do rehearsals start?"

"Next Monday."

Monday? That was less than a week away. Grace's practical nature took some of the curve out of her smile. "Will you be able to find an apartment by then? You can't afford to stay in a hotel room indefinitely."

Her mother seemed amused by her concern. "You always did worry about little things like that."

"Do you need to borrow some money until your first paycheck comes in? Or did you sign a contract for money up front?'' Grace picked up the cordless phone and began to pace. ''I don't want you staying in some dive in a bad part of town. I could call the New York office and see—''

''Don't worry about that, sweetie. Grant's taken care of all that for me.''

An anvil of dread thunked down in the pit of Grace's stomach. ''He found you an apartment?'' She hoped.

''He invited me to stay with him at his penthouse. I'm calling from there right now. Oh, you should see it, sweetie, the view is so beautiful from up here, with all the city lights sparkling.''

''Mother—''

''And everything is decorated in ivory and gold. Except for Grant's bedroom, it has dark—''

''Mother!''

Mimsey sighed. Grace could envision her mother shaking her platinum head. ''Gracie, sweetheart. This is the new millennium. Men and women live together now. Grant has agreed to keep our relationship as platonic or personal as I want it to be.''

''Which is it—platonic or personal?''

Mimsey giggled. Oh, God. Grace thumped the phone against her forehead, wishing she could just as easily knock some sense into her mother's head. How many times had this scene played out in their lives? Mimsey putting her faith in one man, giving him her heart and trust, while the man wanted something considerably less noble.

How many times had Grace listened to Mimsey's tears when the man moved on to his next conquest? And she never would understand her mother's ability to forgive and move on to take yet another chance on love.

Voicing her concerns hadn't helped in the past, but she

had to try. "Would you think about getting your own place, Mother? At least until you're sure that Grant Stewart is the one for you."

"I know you worry about me, and I appreciate that." Mimsey's voice took on an uncharacteristically serious tone. "But Grant's different from the other men I've known." She'd heard that before, too. "Be happy for me, Gracie."

She'd surrender the battle. For now. But tomorrow she'd run Grant Stewart's name through the Bureau records. Just in case.

"I hope everything turns out the way you want."

"Me, too. Good night, dear."

"Good night, Mother."

Grace carried her steno pad and the phone upstairs to her bedroom and wondered if failure was an inherited trait in Lockhart women.

"Last call, Mr. Pierce."

Logan looked up from the bourbon he'd been nursing the past hour and nodded at the bartender. "I'm good, Danny."

So. He'd sunk to this. Closing down the local bar in an effort to drown out the emotions in his system. Four fingers of bourbon hadn't done the trick.

He could still see Harris Mitchell's eyes, glued to Grace's cleavage. While she fumbled to balance herself, he'd averted his icy-blue gaze ever so slightly to get a glimpse down the front of her blouse. Logan had wanted to ram his fist down Mitchell's throat for ogling Grace like that. For keeping his hands on her longer than what was politely necessary.

Grace was *his* to mold and train. He was teaching her *his* damn list of what was sexy, not Mitchell's. Well, she was taking his list and running with it. Oh, yeah. She was getting the sexy part down pat. Moving that body and making those sounds and...

Logan groaned at the pitiful picture he must make, sitting on a bar stool, half aroused, lusting after the most stubborn woman on the planet. He should be mad at her. He *was* mad at her.

But he still wanted her.

Every bit of frustration and impatience about training Grace Lockhart for this job seemed to be manifesting itself in his groin.

As he reached inside his pocket for Danny's tip, he caught the eye of the trim, leggy brunette sitting a couple of stools away. She and her cute redheaded friend smiled at him.

Maybe that was the answer. Pick up some willing chick—or two—and get the sexual frustration out of his system. He hadn't been with a woman since long before his last deep cover assignment. And that had lasted four months! That was it. Get laid. Then he could teach sex appeal without actually having sex and Grace on his brain 24/7.

Logan winked.

The two women practically jumped off their stools. He could have them both if he turned on the charm.

But the redhead giggled like a schoolgirl.

And the brunette really was too skinny for his tastes.

And neither one of them had big green eyes.

Logan slapped his money on the bar and picked up his tie. He'd better get home before he did something he might regret.

He toasted them with his glass and polished off the bourbon. "Good night, ladies."

The unusually warm autumn night didn't help cool a

thing as he walked the three blocks back to his condo. He tried to focus on the more unpleasant aspects of agent training. Weapons. Crime studies. Psychological torture.

But somehow, every time he tried to plug Grace into one of those scenarios, his brain went off on a sexual tangent. It was probably just that heavenly body of hers, he reasoned, that turned every training exercise into foreplay.

Logan jogged up the steps to his condo and went inside. He reset the alarm system and shrugged out of his jacket. He untucked and unbuttoned his shirt as he crossed into the kitchen and pulled a beer out of the fridge. The cold liquid chilled his throat and trickled downward, dampening the heat in his body, and giving Logan a usable idea.

Maybe denial was the wrong way to go about this. What if he could sleep with Grace—just once? That would get her out of his system. With her lack of experience, she probably wouldn't be any good in bed, anyway, and these hellish fantasies would finally go away in the light of reality.

Okay, so that theory didn't take into account how her natural instincts had nearly done him in at both the department store and the firing range.

Logan swore. No way was Grace Lockhart ready to take on Harris Mitchell. She wasn't comfortable with her body. She couldn't think on her feet. She analyzed everything to death—including his moods—which meant she lacked the spontaneity that was so critical to undercover work. And now they were down to three days of training!

Not nearly enough time to work a miracle, and way too long for his body to endure this tension.

Logan went up to the bedroom and kicked off his

shoes. He stripped off his belt and socks and sat on the bed, debating the benefits of a cold shower before going to sleep.

He drank a long swig of beer and set the bottle on his nightstand. Next to the phone.

A vengeful idea whispered in the back of his mind.

He'd call Grace. Right now: 1:00 a.m.

He could tell her to meet him at seven instead of eight tomorrow. He chuckled in his throat as the idea took form. As meticulous as Grace was, she'd probably snap at him for waking her so late. *That* would certainly put him out of the mood.

Before his less vindictive side could warn him that the liquor might be fueling his ideas, he'd dialed her number.

The phone rang two and a half times before she answered. He heard a click. Then a breathy sigh. The rustle of sheets.

"Hello?"

Big mistake.

"Hello?"

Logan's groin tightened as if she'd put her hands right on his crotch.

Just roused from sleep, her sinfully husky voice aroused thoughts of a telephone sex talk fantasy. The kind in which a man called and the woman said all sorts of nasty things to him. If Grace could talk dirty...

He grabbed the pillow beside him and set it in his lap. *Smooth move, Pierce.* He cursed himself silently. It seemed like every plan backfired when Grace was around.

"It's Logan." He used his gruffest voice, hoping to startle the sleepy seduction out of hers. "Did you get home okay?"

He heard some more of that shuffling sound. She was

sitting up in bed, adjusting the sheets and whatever she wore to bed. Oh God. What if she didn't wear anything to bed?

He squeezed his eyes shut and caught his breath, picturing Grace in a flannel nightgown buttoned all the way to her neck. A shapeless, sacky thing that hid her curves. He released one breath, but caught another as his chest tightened when his thumb settled against a button on his shirt. Next thing he knew he was unbuttoning that imaginary gown in his mind, pushing it up past her hips—

"Is something wrong? Obviously I got home fine. I'm here, aren't I?"

Oh, yeah. He wished he was, too.

Logan had never been one to butt his head against the inevitable. Unlike Grace, he could adjust to situations as they changed, make them suit his purpose. She owed him some cooperation. And his body was too tired to fight any longer.

"You alone?" he asked.

"Of course."

Logan adjusted the fit of the pillow in his lap. "Good. It's time for another lesson." God, he could be such a liar.

"Now?"

He'd caught her off guard. That should work to his advantage. "This is the kind of thing you need to practice when there's no one else around."

"Should I get my steno pad?" He could hear her scrambling around some more.

"No. This isn't something to write in your notes."

He had her full, waking attention now. "What do you mean?"

"Rule number nine, Grace." He paused for dramatic effect. "Talk dirty."

"What?" He smiled with relief. Okay, here was the telling-him-to-go-to-hell part. He'd get some sleep tonight, after all. "Are you serious?"

"A lot of men like that. And with Mitchell's kinky habits, I'm sure it's on his list, too. You can't laugh or blush with embarrassment while you're doing it, either, or he'll know you're a fraud."

"But I never—"

"I didn't think so." Logan tossed the pillow aside. He made his voice sound apologetic. "I didn't mean to shock you. I just wanted to prepare you for any contingency that might come up."

"Do you really think I need to learn how to talk dirty?"

An inkling of doubt marred his smug triumph over his obsession with Grace. Why wasn't she telling him off? He stood and tried to ignore his physical state. "We'll work around it. Tomorrow we'll get back to the physical training, bright and early. Talk to you then."

"Wait." Her expectant pause made him sit again. "I don't know what to say. Will you help me?"

Help her live out one of *his* fantasies?

She didn't wait for an answer. "I'm sorry about tonight at the restaurant. I really did forget my purse." Her breathy hesitation socked him somewhere north of his groin. "I don't want to screw this up. I need to get Mitchell."

"Why is this case so important to you? Why aren't you content to be a successful computer n—" He swallowed the last word, knowing the nickname didn't fit.

"Nerd? It's okay to say it. Up until two days ago, I looked the part. In a lot of ways I still am socially inept. That's what 'nerd' means, you know." Her breath puffed out on a self-deprecating laugh. "You probably didn't want to know that. See? I am a nerd when it comes to normal, human—especially male-female—interaction." Her voice faded away. "I'll shut up now."

Her matter-of-fact acceptance tugged at his conscience. "So you think the glamorous life of a field agent will cure your nerdiness? Take it from me, it's not all fun and glory."

"It's not the glamour. It's complicated to explain, but...I just need to succeed in the world on my own terms. I don't want to rely on anyone else to give me success or happiness. I want to earn it."

"You want to know that it's yours to keep?"

This soft, gentle talking, shared in the privacy of a late-night phone call, soothed his frayed temper and eased his conscience.

"Yeah."

"I want you to succeed. I do." This hushed conversation had suddenly grown very personal. "Undercover work is like that sometimes. Any humor you share or friends you make—it all gets taken away from you when the case is over. Sometimes it gets taken away from you before then."

"Like Roy Silverton?"

His soul turned inside out at the memory of his lost partner. "I don't know why you want to get into this line of work, Gracie. Sorry. I know you don't like to be called that."

"That's okay. I don't mind it so much when you say it." Her honey-soft voice poured like a healing caress over some very old wounds. "It sounds sort of... personal."

Personal. Logan leaned back against the pillows at the head of the bed. He was beginning to like getting *personal* with Grace. "It's hard when you come home from a case, too. It's like you've been living in a different world, and then suddenly everything is back to normal.''

''Did you ever want to quit undercover work?'' She sounded as if she were settling into bed, too.

''Once.'' After Roy had died he'd doubted he could ever work another undercover op. But he had. He'd overcome seemingly insurmountable obstacles and succeeded as an agent.

So would Grace. Come hell or high water, if he had anything to say about it—and he did—so would Grace.

A different kind of energy pulsed through his veins. Easier than the anger and lust that had tortured him before. This energy was sparked by a higher purpose. And it didn't necessarily have to do with Grace's training. ''So. What are you wearing?''

''My flannel pajamas. Why?''

''Even if you're wearing a burlap bag, you should tell a man you're in something sexy.''

''Is this the 'talk dirty' lesson?''

''Maybe. Let's just keep talking. So what are you wearing, Gracie?''

If she didn't want to play along, then fine, he could go to sleep with a lighter conscience. And if she did…well, he'd still go to sleep a happy man.

''Should I be naked?''

Whoa. Logan took a deep breath and offered some advice. ''Start with something else. Let the interest build to the good stuff.''

''Okay, then…''

He held his breath, wondering what she'd come up with.

''…I'm wearing that ivory silk bra-slip that you liked so much at the department store. You know, it was short and had the lace over the breasts.''

His breath seeped out. ''I really liked how I could see

through the lace. I could see the rosy circles around your nipples.''

She cleared her throat. ''What are you wearing?''

''Me?''

''Yeah.'' She laughed. ''And it better not be flannel pajamas.''

He shrugged out of his shirt, feeling the room temperature climb. ''Just my slacks from dinner tonight. I was on my way to bed.''

''No shirt?'' He shook his head as if she could see the movement. ''Is this when I'm supposed to talk dirty?''

His body was interested, but he wasn't ready yet. He doubted she was, either. ''Not yet. Let's start with what you see.''

''How do I know what I'm looking at?''

''Use your imagination. Close your eyes if you have to.''

She breathed in deeply. In his mind's eye, he could see those green eyes closing. A tiny dimple appeared on her forehead as she frowned in concentration. ''I see your chest. It's just got a sprinkling of hair, right?''

''And there's a line that goes—'' He traced the line of hair down to his waistband and stopped.

''That goes where?''

Logan reached for the pillow again. ''Down into my pants.''

''Oh. Yeah.''

Her shocked silence last long enough that he thought she'd stopped playing the game. Grace Lockhart's frustrating combination of lusty natural instincts and sexual inexperience was going to be the death of him yet.

But then again, this was the woman who refused to fail any challenge set in front of her.

''May I unzip your pants?''

Logan's chest shook with palpable relief. He pictured Grace's hands on him, opening his pants, freeing him. "Please. Tell me everything you're doing."

"I'm unzipping them. Slowly. I'm watching to see where the trail of hair winds up, but I can't find the end. I'm pushing your pants aside." He squeezed his eyes shut and savored the pressure building against the pillow. "Do I find boxers or briefs?"

"Which do you like?"

"Briefs."

"That's what I'm wearing."

Grace fell silent, dragging out a long breath of air. He imagined that soft breath blowing across his arousal. He reached beneath the pillow and unzipped his trousers, giving his straining member some room to swell.

"What kind of underwear do you have on?" he asked.

"I'm not wearing any."

The electric current that had simmered in his veins kicked up to a dangerous level. "Nothing?"

"Underneath my pajamas, no. Oh. I see." Instead of self-conscious embarrassment, she sounded disoriented. Lost. "I guess we're both naked. Underneath."

"Yeah?" For a long, silent moment he thought she'd quit the game and hung up. "Grace?"

"I'm sorry. You said I should..." Her voice caught on a breathy moan. "Could we keep talking? Oh, Logan, am I doing this right? Am I supposed to feel something, too?"

8

THAT NOT-SO-INNOCENT little vixen was getting turned on by this, too!

Was she supposed to feel anything? Only if she was doing this right. And, man, she was doing this oh, so right.

"Yeah, Gracie. Tell me what you feel."

"Hot. And heavy. Down there."

"It's called your clitoris. Put your hand down there. It's swelling up."

Oh, God. She'd done it. She'd touched herself. That deep, husky moan that was half a cry and half a breath left Logan openmouthed and gasping for air himself.

"Gracie?"

"I know what it's called. Is that what you want me to say? Should I talk like that?"

"Just keep talking." He squirmed on the bed, wondering if Grace was twisting herself up in her covers, too. "How does it feel?"

"It's…" She paused and he imagined she was testing herself. "I'm wet. It's slick. And sticky."

"I want you to touch me, too." It was half a plea and half an order. "Tell me how you're touching me."

"I rub my hands across your chest." Logan touched his fingertips to an aroused male nipple. "The crisp hair teases my palms." She caught a ragged breath. "Do men like to have their nipples touched?"

Logan nodded even though she couldn't see. "Put your mouth on it."

"Yes."

"Describe what you're doing to me, Grace."

"I lick it. I take it between my teeth and nibble."

"Oh God. Gracie."

The electric current zinged off the scale.

"Now I'm inside your pants and I touch your...your..."

Logan freed himself through the slit in his briefs. "My what, Grace?" Electricity targeted the spot like a lightning bolt. "Say it. My shaft? My penis?"

"Yes, I'm—"

"Say it."

"I touch your...penis. It's straining. And damp. Like me. I rub my hand up and down its length. I squeeze the end, just to lubricate my fingertips. And then I..."

Her seductive voice changed to innocent again. "Is that all right?"

"Yeah, baby. Just like that." Logan thrust himself against the pillow. "What else do you do with your hands?"

"Now I touch your..."

He imagined the blush staining her cheeks and helped her along. "My balls? Is that what you want to touch?"

"Yes. I just squeeze—"

"Go easy, baby."

Hell. Who'd have thought Grace would be so good at this?

"I run my fingertips lightly beneath them. I flick my fingernails just so." He groaned.

But Grace was starting to get into it. Her voice dropped an imperceptible level in pitch, aligning every husky

word to the frequency of desire racing through his veins.
"Do you like that?"

"Oh, yeah, sweetheart. You're making me crazy."

"I am?"

"Definitely." It was time to give his talented pupil a
taste of her own medicine. "You want to know what I'm
doing while you're stroking me?"

"I, um, I don't think—"

He pressed his lips together at her nervous hiss of
breath. "I'm kissing you. My tongue is in your mouth.
Pushing in and out, licking the outside rim. I'm doing
everything to your mouth that I'm soon going to be doing
somewhere else."

"Logan."

She was breathing hard now. Was she touching her
lips? Stroking her fingers around their lush contours and
then darting inside to suck on them? Or was her hand
still between her legs? Was she already doing those
things to herself down there?

"You like that? I'm kissing you again. Deeper this
time. So deep and hot and wet and wild that you don't
think it's ever going to stop."

"Don't stop."

Could her sexy voice sound any more turned on?
"Where do you want my hands?"

She hesitated. Was she going to give up the game?
Maybe he should. This had gotten way out of hand. He
could finish himself if this was too much for her.

But he'd forgotten about Grace's determination to see
a thing through to its end. "I want your hands on my
breasts. No, my butt."

Logan smiled and squeezed the pillow and the phone
in his fists. "I've got them both. I'm squeezing your butt
with my right hand. With my left hand I'm squeezing

your breast. God, baby, it's the most beautiful thing in the world to watch how it reacts to my touch. I've got the nipple between my thumb and forefinger, and I'm rolling it, squeezing it, pulling it."

"Logan." She squeezed his name out on a breathy moan.

"I want to rub my erection against you, baby. Is that okay?"

"Yes. Please."

"Can I put it in you?"

"No. Not yet. I...I want you to kiss my breast."

"I am. I'm kissing your breast. It's sweet and pebbly and hot inside my mouth. I'm sucking it hard."

Her husky moan vibrated through his straining arousal like a tiny electrical shock.

He wanted to feel it again. He wanted her to feel it, too.

"I'm putting my hand where yours is, Gracie. Right between your legs. Do you feel me?"

"Ye... Yes." Was she touching herself? Was she pressing her hand against her swollen, fragrant channel?

"I'm slipping my fingers inside you now. One." She moaned. "Two." He moaned. "Open for me, baby. I'm pulling you open."

"Logan...?" Her rapid, erratic breathing fueled his own. "I need... Damn it, how do I...?"

He was about to go over the edge, too. "Talk dirty, baby. Say it dirty."

"I want you in me. Now. All of it. Long and hard. Now!"

"It's in there baby. You're so slick and hot and perfect." He crushed the pillow in his lap. "I'm pushing in once."

"Now."

"I'm sliding out and pushing it in again."

"Logan—"

"This is it, baby." His hips bucked. "Gracie." They bucked again. "Sweetheart."

He heard a muffled scream, as if she'd pressed her fist to her mouth. Logan's hips rocked. He surged against the pillow.

Logan collapsed back on the bed. His mind numb. His body spent. His soul oddly longing for something more.

As the pounding in his ears receded, he could hear Grace's husky little whimpers calming into longer, steadying breaths.

"Did I do okay?" she finally murmured.

If she was any better at this, he'd be in the hospital. "You're a natural."

"Logan?"

"Yeah?" He didn't think he had the strength to talk any more right now.

"Will I have to talk this way to Harris Mitchell?"

If one thing could douse the euphoria of having perfect phone sex with Grace, that was it. For a few moments he'd lost himself in the fantasy of her beautiful body and lusty voice and carnal instincts. But it seemed reality was destined to intrude and spoil his time with her. "I don't know."

It was an honest answer—halfway between the false platitude of *No, the sex maniac wouldn't want anything like that* and his own, possessive gut reaction of *Hell, no! I'm the only man you do this with.*

Grace's answering silence made him wish they weren't separated by a phone line, that she was right here in bed with him. Even if she hadn't just given him mind-blowing sex, he wanted to hold her and to reassure her with one of those quiet little conversations that made a couple truly intimate—the way they'd been talking before this had all gotten out of hand. He needed to hold her. To reassure himself that she was okay, that he hadn't just made her life a whole lot tougher.

He should have told her something. But he had no reassurances for her.

In the end, it was Grace who spoke. "See you in the morning."

Logan listened to the silence after the click for half a minute before he found the strength to rouse himself.

He hung up the phone and sat up, his frustration simmering even worse than before. The stain in his lap brought him completely back to the futility of his growing need for Grace Lockhart.

He wanted her in his bed. The real woman, not just that voice.

And he sure as hell didn't want to share her with Harris Mitchell, or any other man.

Yet his job was to do just that—to make her sexy, to make her savvy, and then to send her into the arms of another man.

Logan stripped off his pants and briefs and walked into the bathroom to take the coldest shower he could stand.

So NOW she'd had two orgasms.

With just some touching and talking. Okay, so it was a lot of talking. Graphic, dirty talking. Logan said talking like that was a turn-on for men.

What a horrifying discovery to learn she liked it, too. So much for her misconceived ideas about sex.

Joel Vitek's idea of sex talk all those years ago had been a few grunts before crying out her mother's name.

She'd had no idea.

It boggled her imagination to think how she might react if Logan was actually doing half of those things he'd described over the phone last night. Words like conflagration popped into her mind. Explosion. Meltdown.

Maybe if he hadn't started with that quiet little conversation first. The one in which he'd tricked her into talking about herself. Snuck around her sleepy defenses with that deep, drugging voice of his.

That wasn't exactly fair, she conceded. He'd made her feel safe talking about her insecurities by talking about his own.

He'd made her feel safe and cozy. And sexy and strong and wild...

"Damn." He was her partner. Her *Bureau* partner. Whatever was going on between them—it was business.

Yet last night she'd been rolling around on the bed, touching herself at the seductive insistence of his voice.

That just wasn't her. First of all, Grace Lockhart took her job seriously. Grace Lockhart didn't have orgasms.

What was wrong with her?

She rolled the waistband of her sweatpants down around the waist of the mint-green leotard she wore and studied her reflection in the locker-room mirror.

She even looked different. The glasses that had once masked her face had been replaced by contact lenses, leaving her doubt-filled expression open for all the world to see. Her hair was a riot of strawberry-gold waves, bouncing around her ears and curling onto her cheeks. And the tight fit of the leotard clung to her top-heavy curves in a way her old T-shirts never had.

Where was the old Grace? The one who thought things through before she acted. The one who was in control of her environment and her future. The one who would never have talked sex with a man in the middle of the night. Much less enjoyed it.

The woman in the mirror looked nothing like the computer-whiz who put her job before her personal life and demanded that men pay attention to her brain instead of her body.

She didn't look like the Grace she knew anymore.

She looked like her mother.

Grace's jaw dropped open at the unsettling discovery. Twenty-two years ago Mimsey had achieved cult status in the sci-fi thriller, *Vampire Women of Asteroid X,* wearing an outfit much like this one. Change the black cotton terry to black leather and strap an Uzi around her waist, and she'd be a dead ringer for her mother's pre-"Buffy the Vampire Slayer" role.

Add the makeup artist who'd been Mimsey's lover for six months after the movie was wrapped, and it would be as if time had stood still.

Grace groaned and tore her gaze away from the image in the mirror. "I am *not* my mother."

Another female agent walked past on her way from the gym to the showers. "Don't I know it." She patted her hips and winked in some sort of secret agreement. "Every year it gets harder to stay in shape." By the time she'd moved on, Grace's cheeks burned a hot shade of pink.

She'd been reduced to talking to herself in a mirror. She'd lost her focus. She'd lost sight of what mattered here.

Infiltrating Harris Mitchell's syndicate and bringing him and his connections to justice was what mattered.

Her sexual curiosity and repressed fears would just have to wait until she got the job done.

She only had to play the part of a sexy woman. She didn't have to possess a wealth of intimate knowledge herself. She'd remind Logan of that fact the minute she saw him.

And keep reminding *herself,* too.

As she walked through the weight room to the exercise mats, though, her conviction got a little sidetracked.

Logan was already on the mats, moving through his Tae Kwon Do kata. He wore only a pair of black sweatpants that hung low on his hips, revealing a deliciously long serving of that T-bone-shaped back that fascinated her so. With each precise movement, the muscles along his shoulders and spine stretched and flexed. Droplets of sweat glistened at the small of his back. One tiny rivulet trickled down the length of supple skin and was lost beneath the waist of his pants.

The fluid exertion of strength and control left her mouth dry and her nipples tingling. The tips hardened as though she were chilled. Yet her temperature was definitely rising.

Too much man. Too sexy.

Too distracting for her to recall the speech she'd thrown together only moments ago about keeping everything between them strictly business.

Grace forced herself to look away and to take a deep breath. She crossed her arms over her chest, covering the telltale contours of her body's reaction to him in a mock suit of armor before speaking. "I still don't know what a morning workout has to do with my training for this assignment. We're trying to convince Mitchell I want to be in his bedroom, not his gym."

Logan completed a series of movements and bowed slightly to the east in traditional Asian fashion before turning to speak.

"Good morning to you, too." His sarcasm was tuned as finely as his body. "I want to see how sharp your self-defense skills are. Backup isn't always around when you work undercover. You need to be able to protect yourself.''

He slowly circled around her, scanning her from head to toe in a thorough evaluation. Whatever he was checking, by the time he faced her again, the questioning look in his eyes made her feel she didn't quite measure up. ''We'll review the basics. I'm one of the bad guys. I catch you rummaging through my desk. I'm going to charge you. Ready?'' He wanted to practice blocks and takedowns? ''Defend yourself.''

With no more warning than that, Logan bent his shoulder into hers and snatched her around the waist. She went down with an embarrassing whoosh and a thud, landing flat on her back with her hips pinned to the mat beneath his.

For a stunned moment he propped himself up on his elbows above her. ''You *did* pass the physical requirements for training, didn't you?''

''Of course, I did.'' She pushed at his chest, indignant to read the doubt flickering in his eyes. ''I just wasn't prepared. When you said workout, I thought we'd be lifting weights or running laps.''

''Let's try this again.'' With an easy grace belying his size, Logan rolled off her and pulled her up to her feet in one motion.

He backed off a few steps, assumed an attack stance, then relaxed. ''Don't stand like that.''

''Like what?''

''With your arms crossed.'' He pulled her hands from her shoulder and waist. ''You're hiding your figure again.''

Grace tugged her hands from his grip. ''This isn't what

I'm used to wearing for physical training. It's a little revealing."

He hesitated a moment before his expression hardened like granite. "You can't be self-conscious about showing your assets to Mitchell." The discussion had ended. He retreated into position and nodded. "Defend yourself."

This time she got her hands up to deflect his initial charge, but he overpowered her again and pinned her to the floor.

"My *assets* make me look like a dough brain. Mitchell won't hire me if he thinks I'm an empty-headed twit."

He helped her stand and indicated they try the move again. Grace put up her hands and glued her eyes to his as they circled each other. "Brains and a bod are not mutually exclusive."

"Try telling that to my mother."

"Defend yourself." This time Grace ducked and kicked out, catching him behind the knee and tossing him to the mat. The victory was short-lived, though. Almost as soon as she landed on top of him, he flipped her beneath him. With their legs still tangled together, his thigh insinuated itself between hers. "How did Mimsey get into the conversation?"

"I look like Colonel Cupcake."

"Come again?"

The heat from their workout seemed to intensify with the conversation. She burned from her crotch to her shoulders. The bare skin on his chest sizzled wherever they touched. She wedged her elbows between them, needing air to cool her body and clear her mind.

"I look like a sex-kitten mercenary Mother played in one of her movies."

Logan grinned. "That *is* the idea behind this training project, isn't it?"

Didn't he get it? "A helpless, brain-dead sex kitten."

"Sex-kitten *mercenary,*" he corrected, tapping the tip of her nose with his fingertip. "Which film was that? *Batamaran?*"

His amusement, and his familiarity with her mother's ridiculous movies, fueled her temper. Disgusted with the description of what she was evolving into, she shoved him off her, refusing his offer to help her stand.

"I'll come from behind now," he said, circling around her. "No man is ever going to mistake you for an air-head, Gracie. Your body says sex, but your eyes say smart."

His unexpected compliment caught her off guard, and he easily took her to the floor. With the wind startled out of her, she pressed her cheek to the mat and tried to catch her breath. She lay on her stomach, and Logan covered her. His hips cupped her buttocks, his shoulders cast a shadow over hers.

"But who bothers looking above my chest?" she asked between labored breaths.

Logan grasped her shoulder and rolled her over. "I do." He slid his fingers into her hair and brushed it off her face. "It's the whole package that makes you hot, Grace."

Hot. Fever crept into her cheeks and down between her legs.

She mentally forced herself to step back from her body's immediate, automatic response to Logan's slightest touch. Was the gentle reassurance just a plati-tude issued by a coach to his protegée? A pep talk to get her on her game for the sake of the assignment?

Or did Logan really see her as something more than a by-product of her mother's legacy? Was he offering her the notice—the respect—she'd fought so long and hard for?

The seconds that they lay there together, entwined like lovers, suddenly ticked into eons. She jumped from deep in her own thoughts to the here and now, conscious of other agents in the workout area turning curious glances their way.

Certain that their position looked more personal than professional, Grace kicked and lifted Logan with a twist of her hips. They rolled over, the strategic placement of her knee and his vitals giving her the upper hand. "If I'm so *hot*, then why do you keep fighting me over my qualifications to go after Harris Mitchell?"

She hadn't bested him at all. In a demonstration of his superior strength, he sat up, carrying her along with him on his chest. She slid down onto his lap and he held her there, her bent knees caught between the juncture of his hips and thighs.

"Tell me this," he whispered. "Did you like what we did last night on the phone?"

Her face grew hot with embarrassment. She immediately lifted her palms and hid her blush from public view.

"People are watching."

"Answer me. Honestly," he dared.

She understood the fundamentals of sex. She knew terminology to use and safety precautions to take. She'd seen movies and read books. She knew women who claimed to use sex as a means to control men, and she knew men who used women like her mother to fulfill their sexual fantasies. But she hadn't really *known* about sex.

Not until Logan Pierce.

She hadn't known she could actually like the way sex made her body feel.

She hadn't known.

"Did you enjoy it?" Logan's eyes darkened to intense shards of granite, demanding the truth.

Using psychological torture to reveal a state secret couldn't have been more painful for her. "Yes."

She shoved him back and climbed to her feet. The humiliating admission ended their workout session as far as she was concerned. With chin high, she avoided making eye contact with anyone else and headed for the locker room.

Before she reached the edge of the mat, though, Logan snatched her by the ankle. He tugged her off balance and Grace fell to her knees, her grand exit thwarted as he dragged her back beneath him. She twisted to free herself and pounded at his chest with her fists. But Logan was too strong, his wrestling skills too finely honed. In seconds, he had her shoulders and hips pinned to the mat.

"I enjoyed it, too." His hushed voice and half smile stopped her fists.

The fight drained right out of her. He enjoyed it? He enjoyed *her?* Grace's muscles quivered with an edgy, unchanneled energy. "Why did you call me last night?" she asked on a whisper for his ears alone.

"Because I couldn't stop thinking or worrying about you. I'm so damn obsessed with you that I can't concentrate on this case anymore. I need to focus if I'm going to prepare you properly. I need to be able to concentrate once we're inside Mitchell's estate if I'm going to keep you safe."

How could a man say such beautiful things and sound so upset?

He squeezed his eyes shut and turned his growing anger inward.

Seeing the struggle he was going through, if not necessarily understanding its cause, Grace reached up and rested her palm against his cheek. His skin felt as feverish as her own. "Lo—"

"Don't." He pulled her hand away, refusing her comfort as he opened his eyes and glared down at her. "I need to get you out of my system."

"I'm not quitting the case."

"I know."

"Do you have something else you want to suggest?"

Logan's mouth opened as if to speak, but then he snapped it shut, thinking better of whatever he'd been about to say. He stood and pulled Grace to her feet, but released her quickly.

Just like that, he ended the conversation. He ended the workout. He ended the frustrated tension building between them.

He ended all hope of Grace ever understanding how a man's mind worked.

A few minutes ago she'd been the one eager to leave. But now she followed him over to a bench where he picked up a towel, wiped off his face and hung it around his neck.

"C'mon, Logan. I've done everything you've asked of me so far. What is it?"

He combed his fingers through his damp hair, moving each strand into place, it seemed, before he turned and looked down at her. "Do you know you blush whenever I talk about sex or pay you a compliment or touch you?"

Grace shook her head. "Where are you going with this?"

"Rule number ten." He grabbed her by the wrist and held her in place when she automatically turned toward the locker room to retrieve her steno pad. "You can write this down later, see if it makes any better sense to you then than it does to me now.''

''What's rule number ten?''

His voice had dropped to such a low pitch that she had to lean in close to hear him. ''Appeal to all of a man's senses. Your breasts cover the visual part. Last night your voice had my blood boiling in my veins. But I wanted you to touch me. I wanted to smell you come. I wanted to taste your pleasure in my mouth.''

Grace blushed all over again. He brushed his fingertips across her cheek, proving that he'd made his point about her physical reaction to his sexual innuendoes.

''What's it gonna be, Gracie? Do you have the brains and the confidence to use that body as a tool to seduce Harris Mitchell? Or will you hang on to the mistaken idea that enjoying your body is a bad thing, and quit?''

She turned her cheek from his touch. A silent alarm speed the pulse inside her veins. ''I don't have to enjoy whatever games Mitchell tries to play with me.''

He shrugged. ''But you'll have to act like you do.''

''I know that.''

''Do you really?'' he challenged. Logan picked up another towel and tossed it to her. By reflex alone, she caught it. ''Monday morning you asked me to teach you how to seduce a man. I think we need to check into a hotel room tonight to see if you can.''

Grace blinked. Twice. Unsure that she'd heard him correctly. She clutched the towel tightly to her chest. ''That sounds like bad writing from one of Mother's movies.''

''Think of it this way.'' He dropped his knowing gaze to where she covered herself with the towel. ''If you're not comfortable with a man talking and touching and coming on to you, then how are you going to convince Mitchell you're a player in his league?''

Was he for real? Grace tried to drop the towel but couldn't. She didn't know whether to be offended or defensive or just plain mad. "You've planned a very thorough training, Agent Pierce."

"I don't want Mitchell's sexual overtures to surprise you and throw you off your mark. You can't afford to blow your cover once you're in, or you'll be dead."

Last night she'd felt so close to Logan. If he'd asked her then—on the phone—she might have said yes. But now?

"So you want to double-check that I can play my part without blushing. That I can anticipate what's coming at each stage of the game so I know when to make an excuse and get out of there. Otherwise my choices will be breaking my cover or having sex with Harris Mitchell."

"Basically. Yeah."

Logan's explanation made good sense. But his proposition sounded so impersonal, so clinical.

"Is that the only reason why you want to..." She couldn't even say what he was suggesting. "Meet tonight? To see if I pass your seduction test?"

"No." Logan traced a finger across her breast, just above the line of the towel. Her toes curled inside her shoes at the suggestive caress. But his hard gray gaze warred with the gentle persuasion of his touch.

"I want to find out if you're as good in the flesh as you are on the phone. Maybe then I'll be able to get you out of my system."

9

GRACE LIT THE LAST of the vanilla-scented candles and blew out the match. The clerk at the candle store had recommended several stronger, spicier, more exotic scents as the popular choices for a romantic evening. But Grace stuck with plain vanilla. She found its rich, delicate scent comforting. And she had a feeling she'd need whatever strength and comforts she could find to get through this evening.

She tossed the spent match into the trash and picked up her steno book and pencil from the bedside table. "Let's see, that's 'scent.'" She put a checkmark beside the word on the list she'd made. "'Touch.'" She'd handled that with the lotion she'd smoothed over her skin after her bath. "'Taste.'" That would be the tray of fresh fruit, cheese, crackers and dip she'd ordered from room service. "'Sight.'" She'd gone to a lingerie shop at the mall and splurged on a navy-blue lace bustier that was held up by a bit of boning and imagination, plus a matching thong. "'Sound.'"

She crossed to the desk and pushed the play button on her portable CD player. The melodic rhythms of a Celtic instrumental ballad filled the room. She adjusted the volume to a soft level and checked it off on her list.

Done. She'd followed all ten items on Logan's sexy how-to list in preparing for tonight's test.

She had to prove to Logan she had everything it took

to go undercover with a kinky crime lord, and she wanted to prove to herself that life under the covers wasn't always a game-playing fiasco.

She wanted to sleep with Logan. And, hopefully, to appease her newly awakened sex drive enough that she could get rid of the frustrated curiosity Logan said tormented him, as well.

Grace inhaled deeply and gave the room one last survey.

They had agreed on a neutral location at a hotel near the airport for this unofficial training session. The suite of rooms she'd selected was spacious but modest. No crystal chandeliers or mirrored ceilings, but there was a king-size bed and roomy bathtub.

Shuddering with nerves and excitement at the thought of actually going through with this, Grace tucked the collar of her white fuzzy robe up around her neck. She put her steno pad away in her bag in the sitting room and checked her watch. It was time.

"All set."

With the determination of an agent going after a most wanted criminal, she removed her watch and set it on the nightstand beside her cell phone. Then she marched back into the sitting room and perched on the edge of the chair facing the door. She was ready to do this.

She hoped.

Just as doubt began to rear its sabotaging head, there was a soft knock at the door.

She'd always admired punctuality in the men she worked with, appreciated the sense of security and predictability it gave her. But tonight's timely knock made her heart race with anticipation. She hoped the telltale blush on her cheeks blended with the makeup she'd carefully applied.

Grace stood and took a deep breath. She pushed an independent-minded curl off her forehead, walked to the door and breathed deeply again, slowing her pulse and hiding her nervousness beneath the cool, calm and collected facade of the old Grace Lockhart.

Finally, knowing that putting this off any longer could be interpreted as a concession of defeat, she opened the door.

"Hi."

"Hi." Logan stood in the hallway, dressed in his usual attire of jeans and a leather jacket. A smoke-blue Henley shirt peeked out at the collar. Judging by the bulge beneath his arm, she guessed he was wearing his gun and holster, as well.

"Expecting trouble?"

Logan grinned. "I like to be prepared for anything. And you, lady, are always full of surprises."

She smiled, feeling a few of those nerves dissipate at his teasing humor. "You can lock it in the closet safe with my sidearm, if you want."

"Right." His casual yet all-seeing gaze, looked beyond her into the softly lit room, then settled on her face. "You ready for me?"

"As ready as I'll ever be." She stepped back and opened the door wide. "Come on in."

While she locked and bolted the door, he removed his jacket. "I like what you've done with the place."

"Thanks." She came up behind him and took the jacket from his grasp. "I'll take that. Gun, too, please."

As he shrugged out of his holster, she admired the graceful ripples of muscle over bone across his broad shoulders. She could enjoy this evening, she reminded herself. If she gave herself permission to. As she put away his bulky jacket and gun, she couldn't help but think about the size and power of the man who wore them both. She inhaled the raw scents of leather and masculine musk and sighed at the delicious contrasts to her own delicate scent.

She gave herself permission to enjoy.

When she returned to the sitting room he was pouring them two glasses of the sparkling grape juice she'd ordered with the snack tray. "I went ahead and helped myself. I hope that's okay."

"Sure. Thanks." She accepted the glass he offered and looked straight up into his gray eyes. Rule number one. Eye contact. His were pale now, like fading storm clouds, his expression relaxed. She planned to change that. "I want you to feel at home here tonight. If there's anything that makes you uncomfortable, I want you to tell me."

"I should be saying that to you." Did he just shift nervously on his feet? Surely legendary ladies' man Logan Pierce wasn't having second thoughts about tonight. His hesitation gave her confidence an endearing boost. He reached into his pocket and pulled out a small box wrapped in plain brown paper and tied with a shiny gold bow. "Here. Open it."

"You didn't have to bring me anything." She set down her drink and quickly opened the package. And frowned. "A box of condoms?"

"I like playing games, but I don't like taking chances. For either of us."

A whole box of condoms. Yes, she was an apt pupil and, yes, she understood that sex was on the agenda for tonight. But a whole box?

Grace's breath stuttered and caught. Logan must be expecting big things of her.

Her first wave of panic kicked in and her mind went

blank. Plan? She had a plan for this evening, right? Oh, hell, what was it?

Stay in control.

Rule number two.

Thank God she'd worked so hard memorizing the rules he'd given her. Grace breathed easier. It was as simple as a computer program, really. Just stick to the formula and it would all work out. "Thank you for, uh, thinking of me."

"I was thinking of us." He handed her the glass of juice again. "Just so you know, I have a clean bill of health. I just didn't know whether you were on the Pill or not."

She hadn't even thought about protection. That Logan had been considerate enough to do so raised her confidence level another notch.

"For your information," she said, "no, I'm not on the Pill, but I have a clean bill of health, too. So we don't have to worry about anything like that."

"Good." He raised his glass in a toast. "To tonight."

She clinked her glass to his. "To tonight."

Grace watched him over the rim of her glass as he sipped his drink. His Adam's apple bobbed along the long column of his throat as he swallowed. She swallowed hard, her body tightening with a dramatic response to the purely masculine sight.

Rule number three had something to do with erogenous zones. She hoped that included finding out where his most sensitive spots might be. She hoped his throat was one of those spots. She really wanted to taste the tanned, taut skin along his neck.

"Grace?" She blinked at the sound of his deep-pitched voice. She'd been staring. She was supposed to seduce him. She had something to prove. Drooling over Logan wasn't part of the plan.

"Okay." D day had arrived. Agent Grace Lockhart would not fail her mission. "Where should we start?"

"You tell me."

"Right." She nodded, fortifying her courage. "*I* have to seduce *you*."

He nodded skeptically. "Right."

"Are you hungry?"

His eyes darkened to the color of gunmetal. He was hungry, all right. But judging by the feral gleam, he wasn't thinking about food.

"All right then…" She released a breathy sigh. So much for stalling. "I thought we'd start with a game of chess."

"Chess?"

Logan couldn't think of one single, sexy, seductive thing about chess. All this polite little small talk made him a tad nervous. He didn't want Grace to fail. She needed the confidence of knowing she could pull this off. And his libido, his concentration, his future as a field agent depended on her making tonight work. Once they'd done the deed, his hormones would be sated, his fascination with her appeased. He'd get Grace out of his system and go on with his life a happy, focused man.

He was curious how this would all play out. She was wearing a virginal-white fuzzy robe that reminded him of the comforter he'd cuddled up in on the couch when he'd had the flu. Grace covered in fluff from her neck to her ankles wasn't exactly part of the picture he'd envisioned of their fun, sexy night.

True, she'd made the stereotypic preparations of finger foods and candles and music. But she'd need something a little more innovative to catch Mitchell's attention.

Logan cursed at that thought, one that threatened to spoil the evening. With a desperate man's will, he pushed aside all thoughts of the case and concentrated on Grace's swaying butt as she led him to the two overstuffed chairs and coffee table where she'd actually set up a game of chess.

Now that was surprising. That was one of those rules on the list he'd given her. He didn't know where she was going with the old-fashioned game of strategy, but he was intrigued enough to play along.

She indicated he take a seat, then sat across from him, making sure that the robe was tucked and secured around her waist and neck. "At first I wasn't sure how to work in the smart thing, you know, rule number eight? But I think I came up with something—if you're willing to try."

Her eyes sparkled like clear-cut emeralds, dancing with anticipation. Logan's entire body smiled in response to her excitement. Maybe this was going to be okay, after all. "You're running the show tonight. Let's see what you got."

She set her drink on the table beside the game board and Logan followed suit. "You do know how to play chess, right?"

"Uh-huh."

"Well, we're going to play a regular game, trying to checkmate each other's king, but with an interesting twist." Her chest rose and fell with a steadying breath. "Whenever a player's piece gets captured, he or she has to do something for the other player."

"What do you mean, 'do something'?"

Her rose-painted smile dared him. "Play me and find out."

Play me? In that let's-have-sex voice of hers, her invitation became the ultimate come-on.

Intellectual strip poker.

Logan's body jumped at the chance to play.

It was only a matter of seconds before she'd captured his first pawn. Logan laughed. "So what do you want me to do?"

"Take off your shoes."

"My shoes?"

"I want you to be completely relaxed."

Obeying the lady's command, he reached down and tugged off his boots.

Two minutes later a second pawn was gone. Grace's lips pursed with amusement. "The belt."

"Huh?"

"Get comfy, remember?"

When his first knight disappeared at the hands of her bishop, Logan's competitive streak fired up. He saw pure calculation behind the laughter in her eyes. "Take off your shirt."

She was beating the pants off him. And while that wasn't an entirely disagreeable idea, he wanted to have some fun, too. If he wanted to see something interesting, he'd better step up to the plate. A little underhanded distraction should help his cause.

Keeping his eyes fixed on hers, Logan stood. He untucked the tails of his shirt and unbuttoned it at the neck. He watched her gaze dart to follow each movement of his hands. With her full attention, he pulled the shirt up his torso, and watched her gaze slide over his stomach. He hitched the shirt over his chest and shoulders, losing her eyes as he pulled it over his head, but noting the tip of her tongue darting out to moisten her bottom lip once he was naked from the waist up.

Good. His body hummed a little tune of its own, knowing a beautiful woman was looking at him and liking what she saw.

He sat and resumed the game.

Finally. He had one of her pawns. Where to begin?

"Well?" Her breathy tone betrayed a hint of nerves. For her sake, he'd take this slow.

"Give me a glimpse of what you've got on under that robe."

"Just a glimpse?"

"Yeah."

He watched with unblinking fascination as she loosened the sash and slowly peeled the fuzzy white material off one shoulder. He followed the path of her hand as it slid across bare skin. Lots of pale, rose-tinted skin. Oh God, was she...?

Her hand stopped as soon as it uncovered a whisper of dark blue lace rising above the curve of her breast. Ladylike. Mysterious. Pure temptation. His own knight strained to attention. He knew what he was asking for next time. He was playing to win.

But Grace was no dough brain, as she had claimed that morning. Three moves later, Logan was sitting in his black briefs, his arousal jutting up beneath the cotton knit, aching to become part of the game.

He studied the pieces on the board, glanced up at Grace's watchful eyes, then moved his queen and knocked her bishop to the floor.

"The robe goes."

Inclining her head in a deferential nod, Grace shrugged her shoulders. The fuzzy, white, cozy, homey, virginal robe slipped off her arms and pooled at her waist.

Logan's breath hissed between his teeth. That wasn't warm and fuzzy he was feeling right now. And there was nothing virginal about the stark contrast of fair skin and dark lace. He looked straight through the paisley-patterned holes and saw her rose-colored areolae and taut nipples tipping her full, firm breasts like strawberries on cream.

"All of it."

He was a greedy bastard, all right, but when Logan played, he played to win.

And, oh, what a prize there was to be won.

Grace stood and wiggled her hips. His straining shaft wiggled in response as the robe fell to the floor. A small triangle of navy lace played peek-a-boo with the thatch of golden curls that crowned her thighs.

The bustier ended above the indention of her belly button, and several inches of bare skin passed before his gaze reached the ribbon-thin straps that held the thong in place.

"Are you liking this game?" she asked.

Logan nodded. "It's a wonder more people don't play."

When she sat, her breasts jiggled, and twin half moons of rosy pink peeked out above the top line of dark blue lace.

Thus distracted, Grace made her move.

"Check."

He blinked and brought his gaze down to the board. Her rook was in a straight line with his king. "You're not playing fair, Gracie."

"I'm playing smart." Oh, yeah. Smart women were sexy. Logan could hardly wait to fulfill her next demand. "Kiss me."

Game, set and match! Logan reached across the board for Grace's hand. When he stood, he pulled her up and away from the table. Standing barefoot in front of him, with that shy downturned face and those sweet green eyes looking up to anticipate his every move, he remembered how vulnerable and inexperienced she was.

He ran his fingertips, across the delicate bones of her wrists, across the fit strength of her upper arms, across the satiny smooth skin of her naked shoulders. His fingers left a trail of goose bumps in their wake and Logan smiled.

"You're a beautiful woman, Grace." He cupped his hands on either side of her face and let his fingers catch in the silky curls of her hair. He gently tilted her head, bending closer, zeroing in on her parted lips. "Absolutely beautiful."

It was a gentle kiss. He pressed his lips against hers and savored their soft texture and shape. He angled his mouth the opposite way, catching sight of those big green eyes looking deeply into his own. He nipped at the corner this time, slid his tongue along the sensitive rim. He kissed her again. Harder. And her lips moved in a quiet response.

Logan tunneled his fingers into her hair and pulled her up onto her toes, demanding more from her kiss. His breathing jerked as her warm hands touched his waist.

Inexperienced, yes, but not without imagination.

With a husky moan deep in her throat, Grace leaned into him, slipping her hands around his waist and flattening those bounteous breasts against his chest. Her mouth opened wide and her tongue slipped into his mouth to mate with his.

The hair on his chest caught in the lace of her bustier as he ran his hands up and down her back, pulling her closer while he buried himself in their kiss. He stroked the soft skin inside her lip, playing a daring game of tag with their tongues. He caught hers and sucked on it, tasting the sweet bite of the grape juice.

Logan's palms skidded across the rough, fine texture of lace that enclosed her and kept her most precious treasures from him. He struggled with the top hooks at the back of the bustier and cursed the man who had invented the thing. Conceding an impatient defeat for the moment, he slipped his hands lower, finding her bare bottom, exposed by the thong. The smooth, firm curves fit perfectly in the grip of his palms and fingers. He cupped and squeezed her, then lifted her up to his aching loins.

He wanted to carry her to the bed. He wanted to lay her down on the floor. Take her up against the wall. He wanted her. Period.

"Gracie." He licked and nibbled his way along her jaw. "Sweetheart."

She ran her tongue along the arch of his neck, using her wicked mouth to follow the sound in his throat. Logan pressed his nose into her hair, inhaling the rich scent of vanilla. The game was forgotten and he was consumed by Grace, her taste, her feel, her scent, her sounds, her beauty.

But she hadn't forgotten the game.

In a feat of self-control that left him panting for breath, Grace unwound her arms and pushed away. Once her feet touched the floor, she stepped back.

He nipped at the consoling fingers she stroked across his lips. The smile on her kiss-swollen lips was pure vamp. "You haven't won yet, Logan." She sat back down in her chair.

Resuming his own seat, he prayed he had the strength to see this game into overtime.

Determined to make the winning move, Logan bent to the game board, captured her last knight and cornered her king. "Check. Now I think that deserves something special." He leaned back in his chair, adjusted the straining bulge in his briefs in a blatant display of his ultimate intention and gave his command. "Strip."

Her hand slipped up to her shoulder in that familiar, self-conscious habit she had of hiding her bounty from the world. But Logan wouldn't allow her to give up on this perfect seduction now. "This is your game, Grace. It's too late to change the rules."

"There's no music. I need to change the CD."

"I'm not interested in the music."

Just as she had taken his dare and run with it last night on the phone, she accepted this challenge.

With his hand resting lightly at the base of his shaft, he watched his best fantasy become reality.

She reached behind her and unfastened the remaining hooks of the bustier. His hand jerked with each little pop as the navy lace crept forward, revealing millimeter by tantalizing millimeter of smooth, pale skin as each hook was released. Finally, as the back sprang free, she cupped her hands over her breasts. He watched her thumbs and forefingers press together, squeezing her distended nipples through the lace. Her eyes drifted shut and her lips parted on a breathy sigh.

She was pleasing herself. Logan's thumb and forefinger mimicked the act on his distended penis. She pleased herself again. Pleasing him.

Then she opened her eyes and dropped her top.

Pink and pert. Big and beautiful.

If the Olympics ever offered a medal for sheer perfection of feminine pulchritude, Grace would earn gold.

The thong went next. Slipping her index fingers beneath the straps, she slid them around to her back. Turning around, she slid her fingers along the strap that curled into the seam of her buttocks. Logan's gaze traced the path of her fingers and lingered. When she stepped out of the thong and tossed it into his lap, he barely noticed.

She was naked. Completely, gloriously naked.

Logan's eyes narrowed in a passion-drugged stupor.

"A perfect ten." That hoarse whisper of desire didn't sound like his own voice. "Now get back here and finish the game."

His queen was the last defensive piece to go. Grace handed him a condom from the box. "Sheathe yourself."

"I'll have to take off my pants to do that."

"If you insist."

She braced her elbows on the table, propped her chin in her hand and leaned forward to watch him. Her right nipple nearly touched her king. Man, he had to capture that piece! He had to win.

When they both sat naked, except for one strategic piece of latex, Grace made her move. She slid her queen across the board.

"Check."

Logan didn't wait for her command.

He circled the table and picked her up bodily from her chair. With one hand at her back and the other beneath her thigh, he carried her to the bed. She wound her legs around his hips and gripped him tight. Logan ravaged her lips, her earlobe, her neck—anything he could reach with his mouth.

When his knees hit the edge of the bed, he tumbled forward, splitting her legs wide apart as he fell on top of her.

This was a race to the finish now, a head-to-head competition that required more speed than style.

Logan guided one glorious breast to his mouth, licking and sucking. He rolled the nipple with a rasp of his tongue and nipped a gentle bite on the rosy pucker of skin surrounding the beaded tip. At her urgent moan, he opened wide, taking her into his mouth and pulling hard.

Her fingertips stroked through his hair and clutched at his scalp, guiding him to the other breast, demanding his attention there.

While his mouth feasted on her rosy globes, he moved his hands lower, to the juncture of her splayed legs. She was slick and hot as he stroked his thumb along her feminine crevice. He ran both thumbs along the slit, bending his knuckles and pressing them against that willful nub of passion. She twisted and buckled beneath his tender assault, alternately pushing into and pulling away from his kneading hands.

"Logan—" Her voice alone left him quivering with explosive need.

He slipped his thumbs inside her and pulled her open.

"Mmm—" Her incoherent plea matched his own.

The scent of potent female honey teased his nose and turned his brain to one blinding purpose. To consume her. To possess her. To claim Grace Lockhart as his rightful prize.

He left a damp trail along her thighs as he pushed her legs apart and plunged inside her.

He abandoned her breasts only to capture her mouth beneath his. He thrust his tongue in and out, copying the same hammering action of his rocking hips. She tried to close her legs around him, but he forced her knees apart, plunging deeper, faster.

When the spasms of her own release erupted around him, Logan buried himself to the hilt, grinding into her, swallowing her keening cries of rapture deep in his throat.

After Grace was spent, he followed her over in the most amazing finish of his life.

The game done, he crawled farther up onto the bed, pulling Grace with him. Once under the covers, he cradled her in his arms and nuzzled his nose in the vanilla scent of her hair. He kissed her gently on the cheek. And then beside her ear, he whispered, "Checkmate."

10

GRACE HAD SEDUCED HIM on her own terms.

A game of chess. Who'd have suspected?

Logan chuckled to himself, his body supremely satisfied and his mind at peace. Savoring the good feeling, he slowly opened his eyes to the dim glow of candlelight that still flickered in the darkness of the wee hours.

He'd never be able to flip past the International Chess Federation Tournament on the public broadcasting station again.

He was going to have to alter his list of things he found sexy and add "playing board games." Or maybe it all depended on who he was playing with.

That's when he realized that the bed beside him was empty, that his playmate had abandoned him. Moving beyond the unexpected twinge of disappointment, Logan listened for the sound of running water. Maybe Grace had slipped into the shower. He sat up in bed, suddenly fully awake after his short nap. He'd love to join her there, see if her chess-playing skills could be adapted to water sports.

But there was no running water. Logan frowned at the surrounding silence and his nagging sense of unease returned. Where was Grace? Had she abandoned him? Technically, they had agreed to a one-time seduction. They'd done the deed. But now he wanted more.

Did she?

He rarely had trouble reading women's desires, but Agent Lockhart was an exceptional case who confounded the hell out of him.

Maybe she'd met his challenge, was satisfied with her success and was ready to move on. Or maybe he'd scared the hell out of her and she wanted nothing more to do with him.

A little frisson of fear quaked inside his body. Had he been too rough? He'd been wild with his need for her. Desire had overwhelmed consideration. Logan heaved a massive sigh. Great. More guilt. He had to know how she was feeling. He had to know the truth.

Logan threw back the covers and swung his feet to the floor. He wouldn't find any answers just sitting on his duff.

Training his eyes and ears to his surroundings, Logan waited for something to seem out of place. There. He angled his ear toward the source of the sound. The crackle of paper. A page being turned. Was Grace reading a book?

He smoothed his fingers through his short, spiky hair and stood. Given that his clothes were strewn about the sofa in the sitting room, Logan walked out of the bedroom stark naked.

The first thing he noticed was that the chess board had been neatly put away. Next, he spotted his discarded clothes, folded and stacked in a pile on the chair he'd occupied during that memorable game. Sitting like a crown at the top of the pile was the box of condoms. Her lacy temptation outfit was nowhere to be seen.

So Grace had tidied up. Cleaned up any visual reminders of what they had shared. Her easy dismissal of something he would never forget ate up a little more of his good humor.

He followed the narrow beam of light coming through the crack between the bathroom door and its frame. Was she all right? Logan hurried his pace a step and knocked on the bathroom door. "Grace? Sweetheart, are you okay?"

Since the door was already ajar, it swung open at the force of his knock. Inside he found Grace sitting on the toilet lid, wrapped from neck to toe in that fuzzy robe again, her black glasses hiding half her face.

As the door moved, so did she, scrambling to her feet, slamming shut her notebook and pushing her glasses up onto the bridge of her nose. "Logan!"

Her mechanical pencil clattered onto the tiled floor and skidded beneath the sink. Logan stooped to pick it up for her, but she was already there. She snatched up the pencil, stuffed it into her robe pocket and straightened. He stood more slowly, but not before seeing her catch sight of the notebook in her hands and quickly stuff it behind her back.

To say she wasn't expecting to see him just then would be an understatement.

Logan didn't know whether to be amused by her rumpled, frazzled appearance or irritated by her efforts to hide something from him.

"What are you doing? Is something wrong?"

"You're naked." Her gaze slid down to his privates, her cheeks stained with color, and then she looked up at him again, forcing a smile. He didn't buy it.

"And you're not in bed. I'll ask again, is something wrong?"

"No. No, I, uh..." She slipped past him, sucking in her breath to avoid touching him, and hurried into the cooler, less confining dimensions of the sitting room. "I was just jotting down some notes."

"About tonight?"

Should he be shocked or flattered or just weirded out by her continuing efforts to jot everything about life into that damned notebook of hers? He followed her and discovered her stuffing little bite-size cubes of cheese into her mouth.

"Yes," she answered between nibbles. "I wanted to see how I measured up to what I've learned this week. Hungry?" She offered him a piece of sliced apple, blithely unaware of the symbolic temptation.

He decided to be irritated. He took the apple, set it back on the tray and reached for the steno pad. Since she seemed tardily determined to hold the front of her robe together, he easily overpowered her struggles and commandeered the notebook.

"Give that back." She sounded genuinely worried. "Logan."

He turned his back on her and flipped through the pages to her last entries. The nearest lamp was beside the couch, so he turned on the switch and sat to read.

Show a little skin.

Lacy lingerie.

Strip.

"Strip?"

"Logan, please." She grabbed for the steno pad but he snagged her by the wrist and held her at arm's length. "Don't read any more."

Which was just what he intended to do.

He found the list of ten rules he'd given her, all with little notes in the margin beside them. He found a list of the five senses, all checked off. He found her critique of tonight's seduction.

Remember condoms.

Loved the kiss!

Black underwear +++!

Don't hide body. Don't cover body. Don't stress about body.

Body okay.

Then, a little angry face drawn beside the words *Mimsey flaunts it—why can't you?*

Logan's irritation softened into something sad. Something more protective, more curiously afraid. A hundred different questions of concern floated through his head. The agent in him wanted answers. The man in him wasn't sure he'd like what he'd hear.

Third orgasm! It can be done. Joel Vitek be damned. "Who's Joel Vitek?" he asked, skimming her notes about preparation time and future shopping trips. He looked up and saw Grace hugging herself in that self-conscious way that minimized the glorious shape of her body. "Grace?"

"Give me the damn thing, Logan."

He reached up and removed her glasses, verifying the sparkle he'd seen behind her lenses. "Shit." He wiped away the tear that had spilled onto her cheek with the pad of his thumb. An uncomfortable lump of guilt turned over inside his stomach. "I'm sorry, sweetheart. I didn't mean to..."

To what? Be a jerk? Make you cry?

Obviously her notes were more than just scribbles about her work. It was a journal of sorts. A diary. With a reverence that came too late, he closed it.

"Baby, I'm sorry."

She snatched the steno pad and her glasses and dashed across the room to her bag. The steno pad quickly disappeared.

"Joel was my first...my only...lover before you."

She pulled out a tissue and dabbed at her eyes beneath

her glasses. He needed to tread lightly here. Undo the damage he'd inadvertently caused.

Logan stood, but held his ground, thinking better of crossing the room and putting his hands around her quaking shoulders. "And he didn't appreciate your talents?"

"Talents?" She laughed, but it was a self-deprecating sound that held no humor. "He didn't even know it was me."

"How could he not know who he was going to bed with?"

"He thought I was my mother. He wanted to be with Mimsey Lockhart." She turned to face him, one hand clutching her robe together at her neck, the other crossed at her waist. "At least you used the right name."

Some jerk had used her. Some selfish bastard had taken advantage of her innocent trust and hurt her. No wonder she'd denied the sexual side of herself for so long. "Gracie—"

"Look, it's no surprise that I'm self-conscious about my body. I've been this way since junior high."

There was more? "Gracie—"

"I mean, I didn't just develop ahead of my peers, I developed *big* ahead of my peers."

He tried to follow the path of her confession. "Kids can be hard on each other. But we're adults." He took a step closer, but she backed away and over to the desk when he would have touched her. He spread his arms wide, standing there naked and completely exposed. Surely she had to trust his honesty when he made himself this vulnerable to her. "I love the size and shape of your body."

Maybe she didn't hear him. "Can you imagine what it was like as a teenager to have grown men hitting on me like I was Mimsey's twin sister instead of her daughter?''

"What?" Fierce emotions, territorial and unexpected, churned through Logan's blood. His supplicant hands tightened into fists. "How old were you?"

"Not old enough. When Mimsey found out, she gave them the boot."

"Good for her, but she should have called the cops."

Grace's tears had subsided to a flush of anger across her cheeks. She paced back and forth in front of the desk. "You see why I'm not any good at this? I have to learn these skills from you and write them down because I wasn't blessed with Mimsey's acting abilities. The Bureau has given me the opportunity of a lifetime, and my success or failure all comes down to the one thing I know nothing about." She stopped at the corner of the desk closest to him, and lifted her fiery emerald gaze to his. "So did I pass the seduction test or not? Will I be able to fool Harris Mitchell?"

"Enough!" He grabbed her by the shoulders and shook her. "Do you hear yourself? Do you think tonight was just about a test?"

She released the death grip on her robe and shoved at his chest. "I made you play chess, for gosh sakes. How pathetic was that?"

He crushed the soft, fuzzy material in his hands, trying to reach out to the softer woman underneath. "Do you think I was just doing my job coming here?"

"Yes. Isn't that why—"

Logan hauled her up by the collar and kissed her. He claimed her mouth and silenced her protests and tried to say with his body the message she refused to believe from words alone. He lapped up the salt of tears that had dried on her skin, tried to ease her pain with his lips and his tongue. Her fists opened and she flattened her palms against his shoulders as the need to strike out began to fade. Her mouth opened, as well, and Logan seized the advantage and swirled his tongue inside. With just his mouth, he tried to show her what the Joel Viteks of this world were missing out on.

"I wanted you. *You*," he whispered against her mouth. "Grace Lockhart. Every sexy, desirable, lovable inch of you. I still do." He kissed her again and slipped his hands inside the gaping front of her robe. He found smooth, hot skin and luscious curves, and not a stitch of clothing to get in his way. As always, his own body responded to the alluring call of hers. He slid his hands down to her bottom and pulled her closer. And though she was no longer pushing him away, he willed her to put her arms around him and eliminate the distance between them entirely. But he didn't push. Not yet.

He nudged aside her fuzzy collar and licked and nipped and kissed the bundle of nerves at the juncture of her neck and shoulder. He knew he had the right spot when her fingertips clenched and dug into his shoulders. "Did you seduce me tonight only because of this case assignment? Wasn't it really just the excuse we needed to get naked together?"

"I—" She caught her breath as he flicked his thumbs across her exposed nipples.

Okay, so he wasn't eloquent. But he was honest. "I wouldn't have agreed to this if I didn't think there was already something between us."

That thing between them was already growing. He blazed a trail to her sternum with his lips and began working his way down toward heaven. For now he was just kissing and touching, but already he wanted more. How could she believe she wasn't a wild, sexy woman?

Just as his lips reached the swell of her breasts, she grasped his head and pulled him away. When she tilted his face up to hers he could see she was thinking. He could see the wheels of consideration spinning in her eyes. "So you'd do it with me again? Just because?"

"Just because I want you," he corrected her. "Now, Gracie." He took her hand and guided it down to his straining shaft. Her big green eyes widened with surprise, but he kept her hand there, rubbing himself inside her grip. "This is what you do to me."

Logan rested his forehead against hers and struggled for an even breath as she repeated the same rubbing action on her own.

"I do this to you?"

"Oh, yeah."

She was wavering. She wanted to believe. But she didn't. Not yet. She removed her hand and pulled off her glasses, tucking them into her pocket. Then she reached up to frame his jaw between her fingertips. She stood so close he could see each tiny fleck of blue that haunted her emerald eyes. She was searching, he could tell, searching for some verification of the truth.

Logan had never considered patience to be one of his virtues, but with Grace, tonight, he would wait however long it took for her to believe she was an impossibly sexy woman. Moving his hands to the more neutral location of her waist, he tried to intellectualize his arguments the way she would to make her point.

"Did you like it when those other men—and I use the term only in reference to their gender, not because bastards who go after underaged girls have earned the title— did you like it when they touched you?"

His little flare of temper earned him an indulgent smile before she answered. "No. Not really."

"What about this Joel guy?"

The smile disappeared. "I thought he liked me. It was okay until..." Her voice trailed away. He could only imagine what it must feel like to be loved as a substitute for someone else. Joel the Jerk better never show his face around Logan, or he'd learn what was like to be the substitute for a punching bag.

But Logan kept his vindictive feelings to himself. "Just okay?"

She nodded.

His chest expanded in a steadying breath as he braced himself for the unexpected importance of her next answer. "Do you like it when *I* touch you?"

She stroked her thumb across his bottom lip as if she was petting him. Calming him because he might not like her answer. "Yes. But I'm not supposed to—"

He pressed his finger over her mouth, shushing her denial.

"Do you like it?"

She pulled her thumb away, but her gaze stayed true. "Yes."

Logan smiled, never questioning the relief that lightened the gloom and anger he'd been carrying since this conversation started. "I like it, too. The way you touch me. The way I touch you."

"But we're partners—"

"We're lovers now. In every good sense of the word." He wet his finger on the tip of her tongue and traced the decadent curve of her bottom lip. He felt her shudder, felt her eager response shudder through him. "I wasn't thinking about the case tonight, and whether you were sexy enough for Harris Mitchell. All I was thinking about was us. And how you're just the right kind of sexy for me."

"Logan?" She kissed his lucky finger. She made him an even luckier man when she took his hand and placed it against her left breast. She breathed in deeply, pushing herself into his palm. Logan closed his eyes and squeezed, savoring the delight. With her other hand she reached down and took him, caressing him in her hand just as he'd shown her earlier. "Can we do it again? Just to see that the first time wasn't a fluke?"

"A fluke? Haven't I proved my point yet?" Logan played with her breasts the same way she was playing with him. She was one tough cookie to convince, but worth every effort.

"Please?"

"You don't have to beg." He seized her mouth in a wet, openmouthed kiss, plunging his tongue deep inside. He gently pried her hand from his straining shaft and twined her arms up around his neck. "Hold on, sweetheart," he coaxed her. He pulled her tight, closing his arms around her beneath the robe, flattening the luscious pinpoints of her breasts against his aching chest. "I want to be inside you right now, baby. Is that okay with you?"

"Yes." He slid his fingers down her spine, traced the seam of her buttocks, reached beneath her thighs and lifted her, split her. Guided the tip of his shaft toward her heat. "Wait. A condom."

Logan nearly collapsed as she struggled out of his grasp. This woman drove him nuts! A good kind of nuts, though. After a raw, lingering kiss, he grabbed the condom box and ripped it open. He pulled out one foil packet and let the box and its contents fall to the floor.

Where was the confounding slit to rip the damn package open? Grace's laugh pulled him from his savage need to defeat the foil wrapper. "Here. Let me."

After a cautious rip, the acrid smell of latex stung his

nose. She wanted to put it on him. He gripped the back of the nearest chair and tried to focus on anything but the fumbling caress of her fingers as she smoothed the rubber over the tip and began unrolling and stroking her way down his shaft. But she was new at this and his patience was failing. He palmed the back of her head and bent to give her a fierce kiss. Then he put his hands over hers and speeded up the process. ''I can't wait, baby.''

He picked her up, wrapped her legs around his hips, and plunged right into her slick, hot folds. With his hands beneath her thighs, her fingers clawing to grip at his shoulders and then losing themselves in his hair, he backed her up against the wall and pinned her there, ramming himself home.

She screamed out his name as they plunged over the edge together in one endless, driving plunge.

Once the fevered heat had passed, Grace collapsed against him. Logan nuzzled her exposed neck and idly wondered if this driving desire for Grace Lockhart would ever really leave him.

Setting her down only long enough to lose the robe and find the condoms, he carried her into the shower where they washed each other with soap and warm water and he loved her all over again.

He'd proved his point. Grace was one sexy, irresistible woman. And he was damn lucky to have her.

Even if it was only for one night.

BY THE TIME dawn crept in through the window's sheer curtains, Logan had proved his point time and again. Grace knew all about what it meant to get laid now. They'd set up the chess board again and he'd taken her there, on the sofa and on the floor beside the bed when their passion for each other ran faster than their time to get between the sheets. He'd licked sweet cream dip from her breasts and drank sparkling juice from her navel.

He was exhausted, content, and falling in love with the vulnerable sleeping beauty he held in his arms.

The burgeoning idea didn't bother him nearly as much as he'd expected it would. He didn't have to worry about lengthy commitments or if he was the best man for her or whether or not he could change his bachelor living habits. Because he knew their time together would be short. Dangerous. Decadent. But short.

And then he'd move on to his next case. He'd go out into the field on his next assignment and risk his life, and Grace would go back to her safe cubicle.

He didn't worry about developing feelings for her because he knew he wouldn't be around for the long term. It was a trend in the Pierce family. People you loved went away. So you loved them for a little while. Then you got over it and moved on.

His mother had been taken from him, his father had abandoned him, and women had come in and out of his life with no strings attached.

When this case was done, Grace would move on, too. He'd enjoy her for now, for as long as she was willing, and then he'd let her go.

11

AN ANNOYING BEAM of bright sunlight hit Grace in the eye, stirring her from her contented slumber.

Though this September weather had blessed them with an Indian summer, she knew the toasty warmth that surrounded her had nothing to do with the temperature outside. She smiled and eased back against Logan's large frame. They'd fallen asleep beneath the covers, spooned together, his leg thrown over both of hers, his hand resting possessively on her breast.

She'd bared her body to him time and time again. But more than that, she'd bared her soul. She'd shared all her doubts and damning self-image. And Logan wanted to be with her, anyway.

She felt beautiful in his arms and in his eyes. *Sexy.*

Maybe she'd been wrong to hold on to all those self-conscious hang-ups about boobs and brains and heartless men.

Logan seemed to think she could have it all. Brains *and* beauty. Respect *and* sex. Lots of sex. Lots of lusty, fun, tender sex.

How could she thank him for that? How could she take all that she had learned out of this room and apply it to the rest of her life?

Pushing aside the weight of his arm and leg, Grace rolled over to face him. Her body still ached in a few places at even that simplest of exertion, but she felt alive in those same spots. Needed and wanted and blissfully alive for the first time in her life.

And she had Logan Pierce—renegade loner, ace superagent, legendary lover—to thank for that.

Grace smiled and reached up to brush a stray spike of that teak-brown hair off his forehead. Asleep like this, he didn't look so tough. She traced her fingertip down the straight, sharp angle of his nose, skipped over those imminently wonderful lips, and touched the point of his chin. A shadow of beard had sprouted during the night, and the soft stubble of it teased her finger. Relaxed in sleep, the deep lines on his face—evidence of life and sunlight and laughter—softened and made him look younger. More vulnerable.

Grace frowned as her secret observations took an inward course. What made Logan Pierce vulnerable? What fears and insecurities did he have that needed to be protected? That needed to be treated with the same loving care he'd shown her throughout the night?

Maybe Logan didn't have vulnerabilities. He certainly seemed strong and fit and knowledgeable about things in this world she was only just beginning to discover for herself.

Of course, there was Roy Silverton. His partner's death had turned Logan into the reputed lone wolf of Quantico's finest. Did guilt over a death he couldn't have prevented still plague him? Did it make him question every decision he made? Did it color every task he undertook?

Grace could understand if that was the case. She'd grown up in her mother's shadow. And though she'd never doubted Mimsey's love, she'd often doubted her mother's wisdom when it came to taking care of her child or herself. Her childhood and her skewed relationship with Mimsey colored Grace's life. But Logan was teaching her that it didn't have to.

Could she teach him that his anguish over Roy's death could be a part of the past, as well?

Like a ferocious beast, gentled by loving and tamed with sleep, Logan lay beside her, breathing softly on his pillow. His broad chest and long body bespoke his strength and even a battle scar or two. He was generous with his kisses and potent with his lovemaking. Not ever in her wildest dreams had she pictured herself sleeping beside a man like him.

Grace grimaced, sliding deep into thought. Her wildest dreams had never included a man, period. She'd resigned herself to a lifetime of loveless duty. That's why she'd been forced to find a man to teach her about sex. To teach her to like sex. To teach her that she wouldn't die or explode or be sentenced to hell for liking sex.

To teach her that a man would like having sex with her. With *her!*

But like that fable of old, Grace feared that this magic she'd discovered with Logan would fade with the rising of the sun. The intimacy they'd shared would disappear beyond the other side of that door.

While her thoughts were taking a downward spiral, she traced matching circles across the plane of his chest, tightening the circumference of each circle until she closed in on a flat, male nipple.

"You'd better watch that."

She tipped her face up to the sound of that deep, drowsy voice. Sleepy gray eyes blinked open and she smiled. The magic hadn't faded yet.

"Good morning." She pressed her lips to the aroused nipple she'd been teasing, licking and nipping and suckling the way she'd learned he liked last night.

"Mmm." His appreciation vibrated through his chest. His hands came up and settled on her shoulders as she began the same gentle assault on the other nipple. "Good morning to you, too."

When she felt his interest begin to butt itself against her thigh, she stretched up beside him and planted her lips against his throat. Her tongue rasped against the prickle of his beard, drawn to the warm beat of his pulse beneath the salty tang of his skin.

"Last night wasn't a dream, was it?" she asked, stretching farther to nip at his chin, dragging the tips of her breasts across the curling, coarse hair on his chest. She repeated the motion, and the pert, rosy peaks strained to attention. A thousand little pinpricks of sensation awoke throughout her languid body, from her tender nipples down to the aching juncture between her thighs.

Logan slid his hands down to her waist, his calloused palms waking each bundle of nerves they touched. He angled his mouth to hers. "If it was, I'm not ready to wake up yet."

Grace lifted her mouth to his, as eager to possess as she was to be possessed. The stubble of beard abraded her lips, but he soothed her tender skin with the warm lap of his tongue. She feasted and supped and gave and surrendered.

A warm serenity lit deep in her belly and close to her heart. Logan's lazy, thorough kiss blew life across the embers of her desire, stoking the fire more slowly this time, unlike the spontaneous combustion of their earlier joinings.

She was beginning to understand the choices on Logan's list. The thrill of surprise. The secret power of erogenous knowledge. The pleasure that came with confidence.

But she would add one more item to his list, she thought as her head fell back to give him access to that erotic spot at the base of her neck. With each tortured breath, her body brushed against his, arousing his need, arousing her own.

Love.

Grace needed love to make her seduction complete.

She needed to give Logan her love before she could truly appreciate the wonder of last night's gift.

She wasn't ready to admit it, and she doubted Logan was ready to hear it. He might never want anything more from her than her body.

But he would have it, whether he knew it or not. This dangerous, powerful, gentle man would have her love. In the only way she knew how to give it.

"Thank you for last night," she whispered, sliding her palms to the center of his chest.

"My pleasure," he answered, nibbling at the point of her shoulder.

"But that was last night." She gave him a shove, rolling him onto his back. Throwing the covers back, she rose up and straddled him. "And this is this morning."

Logan's eyes darkened with anticipated pleasure. His hands rested lightly on her knees. "What did you have in mind?"

She felt wicked and powerful and full of love. "You worked so hard last night, I wanted you to relax this morning."

He wiggled his hips, sliding the jut of his arousal along the seam of her buttocks. "It's a little late for that."

"We'll see." She leaned forward and flicked her thumbs across his nipples.

Logan smiled. "Nice."

With her eyes pinned to his, she brought her hands up

to her breasts and cupped them in her palms. Then she flicked her thumbs over the rosy tips, playing with her nipples just as she had played with his.

Something almost like a growl rumbled deep in his throat and Grace smiled. "That is really nice."

She reached down and flattened her hands over his nipples, then she rubbed them up and down—long, slow strokes down to his waist and up to his shoulders and down again. She reveled in the tickle of crisp hair on her sensitive palms, the warmth of smooth skin at her fingertips.

She covered her own breasts and gave herself the same sensuous massage. Up over her breasts, down to the crease of her thighs. She created a delicious friction as she stretched and preened and rubbed herself. Logan's observant gaze missed nothing, darting to capture every detail. The beading of her nipples, the flush of color on her breasts, the whisper of heated breath blown between her lips. His warmth became her warmth. His pleasure became hers.

Taking care to avoid his rigid shaft, she moved down to sit on his thighs. Then she reached for him.

She stroked him gently, lubricating her fingers with the drop of moisture at the tip. Each stroke taking her further, closer, until her fingers nestled in the thatch of dark hair surrounding him. She reached beneath, found that ultrasensitive ridge of skin. She cupped his testicles, then traced her fingernails lightly across their length.

"Gracie." His chest rose and fell in a deep, erratic sigh. He clutched handfuls of the sheet in tight, shaking fists.

She gave him a moment to recover. Only a moment. And then she touched herself.

She rose up on her knees above him, stroked herself

just as she had stroked him. She opened her mouth to catch her breath as she rubbed her fingers against her sensitive nub. Then she dipped her fingers inside, feeling her own feverish core blossom with heat. Slick moisture coated her fingers. She braced one hand against his thigh and let her eyes drift shut, feeling her body begin to pulse, feeling herself drip onto her hand.

But this was for Logan. So she tore her mind from the precipice of rapture and pulled her fingers free. She touched his penis, coated the engorged shaft with the liquid proof of her desire.

"Gracie. Sweetheart." He clutched at her thighs. His hips twisted beneath her.

Muscles clenched between her legs. Her buttocks pressed together. Her toes stretched. Her breasts tingled with her taut need for release. She dipped her fingers inside herself and squeezed the nub.

As the orgasm took her, Logan grabbed her hand and thrust her wet fingers into his mouth. He suckled them, holding her captive with just his mouth while he freed his hands to open a condom and sheathe himself. Before she could reach to help, he shifted his body and pulled her down over his hot, throbbing shaft.

She loved the stretching, filling, consuming sensation of taking Logan inside her. His hands anchored her thighs beside his hips and he began to move, thrusting himself impossibly deeper. He moved his thumbs to her aching nub and began pushing, rubbing, pressing her together from the inside and out.

It was too much. Too much. She was coming again!

"Logan—"

"Touch yourself, baby." His hoarse command echoed her own trembling need. He guided her hands back to where they were joined together. "Come for me."

He grabbed her breasts and squeezed them roughly, pinching the tips while he bucked beneath her.

Riding her lover like the thoroughbred he was, Grace arched her back. She cried out as the exquisite torment seized her for a second time. Logan hammered into her with one final, mighty thrust.

After he had pulsed inside her, she collapsed onto his chest. He gathered her into his arms and kissed her roughly, quickly, as short on breath and energy as she.

She tasted herself on his mouth. Tasted the wonder of sexual rapture, the sated flavor of love fulfilled.

Then she nestled beneath his chin, riding the rise and fall of his chest as he regained his equilibrium. He pulled the covers up to her waist and held her loosely in his arms, stroking his fingertips up and down her spine.

"How about that?" He smiled at the crown of her hair. "We finally made love in the bed."

Grace giggled, too exhausted to laugh. "There's a first time for everything."

Logan's loving hands were relaxing her muscles and putting her to sleep. "I think there's been a lot of firsts for you in this suite."

She snuggled closer. She hoped the discoveries she'd made wouldn't also be her last.

SOMETIME LATER, after dozing on and off atop Logan's chest, Grace was roused by a shrill chirp. She cuddled against his warmth and tried to stay asleep, but the chirp sounded again.

The sudden stiffness in Logan's chest was what finally woke her. At the fourth chirp, she pushed her hair out of her eyes and lifted her head. "What...?"

Logan's gunmetal gaze had locked onto her eyes. A hint of sadness darkened them that Grace didn't immediately comprehend. She reached up and laid her hand along the rugged angle of his cheek, intending to soothe him.

A fifth chirp intruded.

And then she understood. The outside world. Reality had found its way into their blissful fantasy world. Her training was over.

"You want me to get it?" asked Logan. Though he held her in his arms with the same tender care as before, his tone sounded flat and impersonal.

Hearing his withdrawal made it a bit easier for her to push herself away from him. She shook her head. "It's my phone."

A crushing inevitability flooded through her, making her movements awkward and unsure as she crawled to the far side of the king-size bed. She reached for her glasses first, then picked up her phone from the bedside table.

"Hello?"

"Grace? Sam Carmody." She didn't need the name to identify the clipped authority of her commander's voice.

She pulled up the sheet to cover herself primly as she sat on the edge of the bed and planted her feet on the floor. "Yes, sir."

Logan swung his feet off the opposite side. With the fatigued slump of his shoulders and the width of the bed between them, he seemed miles away. Though he didn't look her way, she got the impression he was waiting to listen to her half of the phone conversation.

"The call went out," Carmody informed her. "Mitchell just contacted the Sheers & Fine Accounting office." Grace knew the FBI had been monitoring all the local accounting firms who hired out freelance employees. Her cover as one of those freelancers had already been set in place. "You have an interview scheduled over cocktails tonight at six at Chez Dumond."

"Six o'clock?"

"Do you have your program ready to go?"

"Yes." Her undivided attention finally kicked in when he mentioned numbers. She opened the drawer in the bedside table and fished out one of the hotel's ink pens, but a scrap of paper was not to be found. "I've copied it onto a disk. All I have to do is locate Mitchell's master computer terminal and download the program onto his system. I can copy anything that looks incriminating at the same time."

Grace twisted around on the bed. There must be a notepad in the nightstand on the other side.

"And if his system is password protected, you'll still be able to get in?"

She nodded, then realized he wouldn't be able to hear her answer. "With all my research, I've got a pretty good idea how his mind works. And I've been able to crack other protected systems."

"Good." She knew Commander Carmody wouldn't have given her this assignment if he had any real doubts about her computer skills. It was her survival skills that he'd found lacking. After a few intense days—and nights—with Logan, she hoped she was prepared in every area. "We've tailored your résumé to meet Mitchell's specific requirements. Remember, tonight, six o'clock, Chez Dumond."

She started to write the information on the sheet beside her. But suddenly her steno pad materialized in front of her. Delivered by one splendidly naked messenger. Logan had retrieved it from her overnight bag and held it out to her, unopened. She looked up into his eyes, wondering if he remembered the secrets she'd written inside. Of course. Logan knew all her secrets now.

All but one.

Grace took the pad, opened it to an empty page and jotted down the time and location of her meeting.

"And, Lockhart?" Her boss's crisp demand for attention kept her from exploring the cause of her suddenly somber mood.

"Yes, sir?"

Carmody paused for dramatic emphasis. "Get the job."

After she hung up, she stared down at the information in her hand. Her first field mission started tonight at six. For a moment she couldn't remember why she'd been so determined to get this assignment in the first place.

Oh, right. Respect.

She was Grace Lockhart, FBI agent. Her own woman. A mind to be reckoned with. Mimsey Lockhart's avenging angel. Not her shadow or twin.

Logan glanced down at the information she had written. "I'm gonna hit the shower. We've got a lot to do before you go in tonight. You go ahead and pack what you need to take with you. I'll help carry it all out when we're ready."

Grace nodded as he turned and walked away.

She made no effort to follow. Despite his nudity, Logan's demeanor had been all business. All superagent. She wasn't sure a lover would be welcomed.

A night of seduction probably wasn't the best way to earn a man's respect. She suspected that proving herself on the case would be the only way Logan would ever think of her as anything more than a one-night stand. At least she was certain of two important things. He knew he'd taken *her* to bed. And he'd enjoyed his time with her.

But she had a terrible feeling that one night was all they'd ever have together.

If Harris Mitchell didn't tear their lives apart, the reality of their different lives in the outside world probably would.

12

FOR HER INTERVIEW with Harris Mitchell, Grace had selected a dark rose suit with a short skirt and zip jacket, which she'd unzipped to the shadow of her cleavage.

Logan's words had been appreciative—professional, yet with an understated invitation to sex. But his eyes had reflected stone-cold granite while his impersonal hands had secured a computer-chip-size microphone and wire beneath her mauve silk camisole. Though he'd be posing as her assistant later, for this initial meeting he'd remain out of sight in a surveillance van where he, Commander Carmody, and a team of agents and technical support would be eavesdropping on her every move.

It was to be all about business between them from now on, she supposed, and her heart mourned the loss of that special connection that had bound them together as lovers the night before.

He'd given her a pep talk of sorts, "Remember, Job One is to gain Mitchell's trust. Once you've secured that, we'll need the schematic of his computer network. That'll help us pinpoint our search of his estate for the master terminal. Then the reprogramming will be up to you. Be smart. Be sexy. Keep your head in the game."

Grace had only nodded, feeling too overwhelmed by the enormity of the task she was facing to allow herself the luxury of deducing the cause for Logan's mood swing into cool, calm and calculating.

They rode together in silence in the elevator from her room at the Willingham Hotel down to the parking garage. With all the detached wariness of a personal bodyguard, he stepped through the doors ahead of her and surveyed the garage before taking her by the elbow and escorting her to her red Mustang.

"Keep the top up," he advised her, scouting the cars parked around her while she unlocked the door. "You'll be driving at night."

When she opened the door, Grace assumed there'd be no goodbyes. But for one brief instant, the Logan from last night reappeared. He slammed the door shut and turned her into his arms, backing her against the shiny red frame of the car and covering her mouth in a raw, passionate, earth-shaking kiss.

Just as quickly as it had happened, he released her. He stroked the back of his knuckles beneath her chin, apologizing for his harsh possession while she clung to the front of his leather jacket and tried to make the brief connection last.

His dark, hooded eyes probed her face, as if memorizing each curve and line for the last time. "Give 'em hell. And watch your back."

And then his eyes blinked to granite gray and the moment was gone. He pried her fists from his jacket and opened the car door for her.

After she started the engine, he moved to the entrance and watched over her departure. She could still see him standing there in the rearview mirror when she turned the corner a block away.

"MISS LOCKHART."

Harris Mitchell rose from his table and took Grace's proffered hand. He sandwiched her hand between both of his own when she would have pulled away. She noted his fingers were long and smooth, a testament to time spent at the spa in lieu of regular physical labor. They were hands that lacked character. Grace immediately decided she liked the calloused imperfections of Logan's hands better. Those were hands that had seen the worst the world had to offer. Those were hands she trusted.

"Thank you for seeing me." She lifted her gaze directly to his and earned a bright white smile.

"My pleasure." With Grace's hand still clutched in his, he turned to his two dinner companions, the Amazonian African-American and the statuesque blonde. "These are my associates, Tanya and Ilsa."

The bodyguards. "Nice to meet you." Grace smiled, but received no response in return.

"Ladies, if you'll excuse us." Harris dismissed them. He pulled out one of their vacated chairs and invited Grace to sit beside him.

She had passed the initial test. Mitchell was interested enough to want to spend time alone with her. The small success buoyed her confidence. She just had to think of this as any other job interview. Be polite and knowledgeable. Know the business.

And be just a little bit friendlier than a professional relationship called for.

As Mitchell pushed in her chair, she thought he bent a little too close. He surely wouldn't put the moves on her here in a posh public restaurant! But then she heard a hiss of breath. He was sniffing her!

Hopefully, he liked the Oriental musk she'd chosen to wear. The scent was a lot more powerful than her preferred vanilla body splash, but the salesclerk had guaranteed this new fragrance was as good as an aphrodisiac.

Apparently Harris Mitchell thought so, too. "Eastern Fire, isn't it?"

"Excuse me?"

"The perfume you're wearing." When he sat down, he let his arm rest along the back of her chair. "I like it."

He turned sideways in his seat, effectively trapping her in the back corner of the restaurant. Grace kept her hands in her lap, forcing back the instant flare of panic. He was hitting on her already. That was a good thing, right?

Never explain away a man's compliment.

Grace remembered her training well.

"Thank you," she answered simply.

"What'll you have?" Harris turned and signaled to the waiter.

"Soda with a twist of lime, please."

He butted her elbow with his and offered a cajoling smile. "C'mon. I invited you for cocktails. My treat."

Stay in control.

"I understand. But I never drink when I'm on the job." She let her eyelids drop to half-mast and sent him a sultry woman-who-knows-what-she-wants look. "I like to keep a clear head when I'm conducting business."

Her expression wasn't lost on Mitchell. He gave her the slightest of nods, then turned and placed their order with the waiter. With his attention momentarily diverted, Grace took a deep breath to steady her nerves.

Harris Mitchell really was a handsome man, she decided. If one liked the pretty-boy type. His chiseled features were perfectly balanced. His skin was evenly tanned, emphasizing the doctored white of his smile. His dark hair with occasional auburn highlights was a striking foil to his ice-blue eyes. He exuded wealth and power and cultured charm.

But he wasn't Logan.

How was she ever going to pretend...?

She snapped the hooded look and Mona Lisa smile back on her face the moment Mitchell turned around.

"Grace. May I call you Grace?" He continued on without waiting for permission. "I can't shake the idea that I know you from somewhere." His gaze slid down to the demure glimpse of cleavage she afforded him. She closed her hand into a fist to keep from reaching up to cover herself. "Something about you seems familiar."

She offered him an embarrassed laugh. "Well, I *am* the lady who tripped over your foot the other night. I had no idea I'd be interviewing for the personal accountant's position with you, or I would have tried to make a better first impression."

"Your first impression's just fine."

His eyes stayed glued to the top of her zipper. He was talking to her boobs! Good God, the man was literally talking to her boobs. She resisted the urge to shout, *Up here, buddy!* Instead she gave him a little show, dropping her napkin, then twisting in her seat to retrieve it. So much for chivalry. He made no move to retrieve it for her, but he probably got a crick in his neck, contorting himself to watch the dip and sway of her twin peaks.

The drinks arrived and Harris shooed the waiter away impatiently. He was still pondering their previous acquaintance.

Maybe if he studied her face, looked into her eyes and learned her personalities instead of guesstimating whether her cup size was a D or DD, he'd have a better memory.

Grace asked about the type of services he expected from his personal accountant. She tried not to let her nervousness or her affronted anger get to her. When her pulse quickened, she breathed harder. And each time her chest expanded, Harris's smile seemed to brighten another notch.

"I'm sure we've slept together. I remember those breasts."

And she remembered how to take a man to the floor and render him incapable of fathering children for the next two weeks.

She'd had enough. She reached out and placed two fingers beneath his chin and lifted his face until he looked her in the eye. "The job particulars?" she insisted.

Oh, Lord, what had she done?

Harris's cheeks flushed with a ruddy rise in body temperature. His blue eyes sparkled and he smiled. He liked that she'd touched him. He liked that she'd taken control of the interview.

"Yes, ma'am."

Knowing, of course, that Harris Mitchell had to have developed some business skills to establish a syndicate and make millions in illegal dollars, she was nevertheless surprised when he spent the next twenty minutes outlining the prescribed duties of his personal accountant with the clear, no-nonsense demeanor of any legitimate big businessman. Keep the books, oversee payout for personal employees, manage Harris's private investment account.

"I understand you're thinking of expanding your business." The FBI had proof of phone calls and meetings to establish such an expansion to the West Coast, but Grace didn't want to appear too well-informed. "How would my role change if you go bicoastal—if I should get the position?"

Harris folded his hand around hers where it rested on top of the table. "I like you, Grace."

Warning bells flashed on and off inside her head. This sounded like the beginning of a brush-off.

"I like you, too, Mr. Mitchell."

"I tell my employees what they need to know as they need to know it." He tutted his tongue against his teeth. "You're asking some mighty curious questions, and you're not even an employee."

Carmody said her résumé was foolproof! She fit the profile of what Mitchell had been looking for. She had to get this job! If she didn't, the case was finished before it ever got started. Goodbye respect. Goodbye making a place of her own in a man's world. Goodbye any chance of being promoted to field agent permanently.

Think, Grace. Think!

"What kind of businesswoman would I be if I didn't research the job I was applying for?"

Harris squeezed her hand, deliberately reminding her that *he* held the power at this corner table at Chez Dumond. "Just curious about your research, is all. Why do you want to work for me?"

Because I want to take down a murdering, cheating, kinky crime lord? Somehow honesty didn't seem like the best policy right now. She quickly played through the list of scenarios that she and Logan had gone through down at Quantico. She could answer this one several ways. But, ultimately, she chose the answer she was least comfortable with.

Taking a deep breath to steady her nerves—and that had the added benefit of distracting Mitchell's focus for the moment—she turned her hand in his, transforming his barely professional touch into a definitely personal one. She dropped her voice a notch in pitch and actually batted her eyes.

"You're going places, Mr. Mitchell. I want to go there

with you. You're a powerful man in the investment world." She moistened her lips and tried not to gag on the part she was playing. "I like powerful men."

He watched her for a moment. Watched her mouth. Watched her eyes. And, oh, yes, he watched her breasts as she slowly breathed in and out, waiting for his response.

"What I meant to say was, you're not my employee—yet." He lifted her hand and pressed a kiss to the warm pulse point on her wrist.

Shocked by the brazen intimacy of his cold lips against her skin, Grace automatically tugged, trying to free her hand.

Mitchell's fingers tightened in a painful grip. Grace flinched as his bright white smile vanished and his fingers dug into skin and muscle. His pale blue eyes transformed to nearly colorless chips of ice. "What's wrong, Grace? You're not one of those women who blows hot and cold, are you? I'm not a man to be toyed with."

He released her only to move his hand beneath the table and slide it along her thigh, right up to the hem of her skirt. She clenched her knees together in reflexive defense. And though he moved his hand no farther, he didn't remove it, either.

So this was what Logan had been talking about. This was the heinous part about undercover work. She had to let this man ogle her, touch her. And she had to like it. On the surface. She couldn't blush with embarrassment or curse his name or kick him in the groin. She had to let him pinch her wrist and put his cold mouth on her and feel her up, and find a way to deal with it all.

The blush was too late to stymie. She bit back the curse on her tongue. And the kick in the groin? Well. His time would come. She'd see to that.

She'd handled men like this before. Countless times. Of course, she'd been the ice queen, not the B-movie actress who'd never learned to say no to a man who touched her heart in any way.

Caught in the snare of Mitchell's hands, she had no recourse other than her haughty tone. "This is hardly professional behavior, Mr. Mitchell. I could sue you for harassment."

"You'd sue *me?*" He almost laughed.

She didn't. "In a heartbeat."

He removed the hand from her thigh and reached up to trace the groove that became a dimple beside her mouth. *Stay in control!* She didn't flinch. She glared.

"Anger makes you frown, Grace."

"Then don't make me angry, Mr. Mitchell. Do I get the job or not?"

"Harris, please." He released her completely and sat back in his chair. "Sometimes, I'm a naughty boy. Can you deal with that? For say, two hundred thousand a year? With optional bonus payments for…special projects."

Special projects? Did he mean personal? Or illegal? Or both?

Without his smooth, clammy hands on her, she could think more clearly. She reviled this man. But she could play her part.

"Just how naughty do you get, Mr.—" She stopped herself with a husky sigh that seemed to please him. "Harris."

"Well, now that all depends on the company. I have a feeling you'd try to keep me in line."

"I would."

His smile returned. Had she said something funny? Harris seemed to think so. He was laughing out loud by the time he picked up his martini glass and saluted her. "You're good with numbers, aren't you, Grace?"

"Of course."

"I'm glad. It'd be a shame to hire an accountant who wasn't."

TWENTY MINUTES MORE of arranging the place and time for their meeting tomorrow at Mitchell's estate, and Grace could finally escape. He hadn't liked the idea of her bringing a male personal assistant to the team, but without Logan on the ticket, Carmody wouldn't let her in on this assignment. So she'd been insistent. Mitchell had finally agreed to her male associate as long as he maintained a background role at his estate. She would be assigned permanent quarters in the main house, but *this Logan fellow* would have to stay at the guest bungalow.

"I don't like seeing men about, you know." She supposed he felt threatened by any competition. How else could he account for his penchant for female employees? But Mitchell's explanation was more aesthetic. "They spoil the scenery."

She'd endured enough passing touches on her back, her knee, her butt and her thigh to know she wanted Logan there to run interference for her. To protect her from Mitchell's groping hands when possible. To protect Mitchell from her growing fury at his base treatment of her.

She'd gotten the job. Big deal. She should be celebrating her first victory. She was in. But by the time she'd gotten outside into the fresh air, she wanted nothing more than to peel off her clothes and stand in the shower until she could erase the dirty feeling that coated her skin.

Grace handed her valet stub to the parking attendant and zipped up her jacket against the unexpected chill in the air. Maybe autumn was finally on its way. Or maybe she just didn't have the nerves of steel necessary to pull off working undercover, after all.

Grace crossed her arms and let her hand slide up to her shoulder, ostensibly to get warm. But that subconscious need to protect herself from gawking eyes and long-held insecurities was trying to reassert itself. Her brain knew there was no going back to the old Grace who hid herself away from the world while, at the same time, demanding its notice and respect. But the new Grace was having doubts. A few second thoughts. The new Grace...heard the snarling sound of a well-tuned Harley-Davidson motorcycle turning the corner and pulling up in front of Chez Dumond.

Like a modern knight on shining armor, Logan idled the engine and rolled to a stop at the end of the red carpet leading to the curb. Even before he raised his visor, she recognized him by the length of leg, the breadth and bulk of black leather jacket, and the snug—not tight—fit of his jeans.

"Need a ride?" The timbre of his dark voice made her think of the ride she'd taken with him just that morning. "You're blushing, Grace."

She lifted her palm to her cheek, betrayed by the heat Logan could generate in her. She quickly pulled down her hand and moved closer so they wouldn't be overheard. "Do you think you should be here? Mitchell or his bodyguards might be watching."

"We're partners. They'll see us together soon enough." His matter-of-fact tone practically dared Harris Mitchell to question his right to be a part of this.

"Harris won't like you. He's expecting my assistant to be some quiet, effeminate man who's rarely seen and never heard." She swept her gaze across the power and polish of the machine hugged between Logan's legs. "That role should be quite a stretch for your talents."

"It won't be a problem."

"But he saw you the other night. Won't he suspect—"

"He never got a good look at me. He'll buy what I tell him." For once impatient with the importance of playing an undercover part convincingly, Logan abruptly switched topics. "We need to talk."

"About what?"

"About what just happened in there."

Why the sour face? Why the low-pitched anger in his voice? "What's wrong? I got the job." Logan should be celebrating that his training was paying off. "It wasn't always easy to stay in character. But I used some of the things you told me. I tried to handle the situation the way I thought you would."

"Since your hand's not rammed down Mitchell's throat right now, I doubt it."

"Logan." He sounded downright predatory. The way he had when he thought she was unsuited for this kind of work. He was using the same impatient, derogatory tone he'd used when he'd gone to Carmody to try to get her taken off the case. Grace's defensive hackles shot up. He hadn't gone behind her back, had he? While she was on the front lines, putting up with Mitchell's busy hands, had he been pleading to Carmody to have her reassigned? "Maybe I didn't handle everything with the smoothest style, but I got the job, right? That's what counts. I think he even likes me a little because I stood up to him."

"Don't defend him."

"I'm not!"

"Keep your voice down."

She pointed to her chest, indicating the microphone

and wire taped to her skin. "Am I still wired for sound?" She spoke down to her chest. "Commander, can you hear what he's saying to me?"

"You're off the air, Gracie. I unplugged you when I left the van." He glanced behind her at the curious interest of the couple walking into the restaurant. "We're on our own until you report to Mitchell's tomorrow."

She threw up her hands in surrender. Leaving the case now was nonnegotiable. "Fine. You go your way. I'll go mine. See you in the morning. I don't want to be late."

"Ma'am?" The parking attendant walked back around the corner instead of driving her Mustang. His apologetic slouch didn't bode well. "Apparently, your car's missing."

"What?"

"I'll call the police right away."

"Save it, son." Logan pressed a twenty-dollar bill into the young man's hand. "I arranged to have it picked up. My girl wasn't expecting me back in town this evening. I thought I'd surprise her and take her home myself." He lied with a glittering smile on his face that had the young man accepting Logan's story as the truth.

"Enjoy your evening, sir." He pocketed the twenty and left to help the next customer, abandoning Grace to her fate with Logan or the first cab she could flag down.

She planted her hands on her hips and shook her head. "I don't know who's more full of himself, you or Harris Mitchell. Did you honestly think I couldn't handle myself for one hour with him? Without you coaching me every step of the way? You're the one who trained me. Or did you leave out something important?"

The quietness of his response put her on alert. "I think you can do anything you put your mind to. That's what scares me." He reached behind him in the storage compartment for his second helmet and held it out to her. "C'mon, Grace. We'd better get out of here before Mitchell decides he's not staying for dinner."

She took the helmet and put it on, reluctantly agreeing to let him chauffeur her back to the hotel. "Where's my car?"

"Agent McCallister is enjoying it this evening. With his luck, I'm sure he'll put it to good use and find some action."

"In *my* car?"

"It's the Bureau's car, Gracie. Now get on the bike. *It* belongs to me." Was there some double meaning in his words about who was really running the show here?

He held out his hand and she used it to balance herself as she swung her leg over the back of the motorcycle and climbed aboard. Her short skirt hitched up almost all the way to the crease of her thighs as she spread her legs wide to straddle the seat. Thank God she'd worn panty hose.

When Logan reached back to tug down the hem of her skirt to a more decent level, and then let his hand rest atop her thigh, she wondered again about the possessive tone of his words.

Just what did Logan own in his life? A barely lived-in condo? A rugged leather jacket? His bike?

Who belonged to Logan? She knew from his records that he had no surviving family. Except for those few tragic months with Roy Silverton, and this week with her, he'd never had a partner. There'd been no signs of a feminine influence at his condo. There hadn't even been any pets.

Was *she* what he claimed as his own? What he worried about? What he wanted to protect?

Was he still so haunted by his first partner's death that

he could never absolve himself of responsibility for her?
That he would never trust her to be safe without him
watching her back?

She slipped her arms around his waist and hugged him
tight. For the sake of the ride. And for something more.

"I'm okay, Logan," she whispered against his back.

At first she thought her words were lost beneath the
monstrous growl of the Harley as he revved the engine.
But then his hand closed over hers where it rested on his
belt buckle. He gave her fingers a reassuring squeeze. He
made no comment. He simply returned his hand to the
clutch and rode the bike into traffic.

HE WAS SUCH a jerk.

He was such an overbearing, territorial jerk.

Too many years of looking over his shoulder kept Logan's eyes watchful as he downshifted the Harley and
rode it into the parking garage beneath the Willingham
Hotel. But his thoughts were on the woman behind him.

Grace had handled herself perfectly during her drinks
with Harris Mitchell. Yeah, there'd been a couple of close
calls when the prim and righteous parts of Grace's personality had threatened to overshadow her savvy, sensual
veneer. But she'd talked her way out of trouble each time.
She'd even charmed Mitchell in the process with her
tough talk.

But he wasn't ready to let her fly solo yet when it came
to undercover work. Without a visual, the silences in her
conversation with Mitchell had terrified him. What was
he doing to her? Was she safe?

The rational side of Logan's mind knew that Grace
could take care of herself. She'd found a way to survive
the ugly taunts of her adolescence, and deal with a
mother who needed mothering herself.

But the emotional side—the side of the man who'd watched his first partner die in his arms, the side of the man who couldn't get this crazy need for her out of his system despite an exhausting night of seduction—wanted to take care of her. Wanted to shelter her from men like Mitchell who chewed up and spat out people's savings and feelings and lives for entertainment and profit.

He wanted her back in that hotel room where the most dangerous enemy to contend with was the shortage of time together.

It had been a stupid, male thing to do—asking Travis McCallister to pick up her car and then bringing her here himself. But he needed to see her. Needed to touch her. Needed to keep her safe.

Screw the assignment. Screw Harris Mitchell. Screw the FBI.

Grace Lockhart needed to stay safe.

He parked the bike in a shadowy corner of the garage near the elevator. They removed their helmets and he offered her his arm for balance so she could climb off. When he stood to follow, she stayed him with a hand on his shoulder.

"Don't come up." Her gentle rejection of his company was absorbed by the concrete walls and deep in his heart. "We have work to do tonight. *I* have work to do. And if you come up—"

"I know." He sat back down on the bike, hearing the wisdom of her words. "We won't get anything else done but have wild, wonderful sex. And you need your sleep."

Her cheeks flushed a pretty shade of rose at his honest words. He pulled off his left glove and reached out to brush his fingertips across the telltale heat beneath her skin.

"I just wanted to be sure you were okay." He pulled

his hand away. "I didn't keep a close enough eye on Roy."

Her sweet green eyes lit with a smile. She meant it as a reassurance, he knew, and he tried to believe in it. "Tonight wasn't easy for me, either. But I learned from the best. Thanks." She stretched up on tiptoe and kissed him. A light, friendly, go-home kiss. "Good night."

There was no good-night for him.

When she turned to go, Logan grabbed her and pulled her up onto the seat in front of him. He covered her mouth with a kiss that poured out his jealous anger, his fears, his frustration. She sat an awkward sidesaddle in his lap, but he wound her arms around his shoulders, giving her an anchor to cling to. Then he tunneled his fingers into her hair, holding her still beneath his passionate assault.

He unzipped her jacket and squeezed her silk-sheathed breast. He slipped his hands beneath her butt and lifted her high onto his chest. He spread her legs when he set her back down, pushing them apart so that she straddled his lap atop the bike.

Logan couldn't help himself. He wanted her closer. He needed her to be a part of him. He reached up beneath her skirt, right between her legs, and grabbed her crotch. He damned the man who had invented panty hose, and damned himself for his own insatiable need. He rubbed his thumb along her hot, swelling nub, and squeezed her from below, feeling her first beads of moisture sticking to the nylon.

"I'm sorry, baby," he breathed the apology beside her ear a moment before he reached beneath her skirt with both hands, found the seam of her nylons and ripped it apart. Her body shook at his savage compulsion. "I need you."

In record time, he unzipped his jeans and freed himself, quickly rolling on a condom from his pocket. There was no finesse to this mating. No sweet words. No delicate sighs.

He leaned back on the bike and lifted her higher. He guided himself through the tear in her panty hose and brought her down on top of him, encasing himself in her damp womanly heat. He pumped into her once, an instinctive jerk. Then he hammered into her again and again. With nothing to cling to but his shoulders and neck, she bobbed helplessly above him.

Her breasts jiggled near his face. He buried his nose between them, lapping at skin and silk and the spicy, overpowering perfume that filled his nose and fevered his brain. That minutia skirt she wore bunched up around her thighs. She was so open to him like this. Open and vulnerable in a way that fired up his need to protect and possess her all over again. He thrust up into her one last time, long and hard, pulling down on her thighs as he strained and pushed and finally erupted deep inside her.

With their bodies still linked, he gathered her into his arms. He kissed her and kissed her and kissed her until all he knew was the sweet, distilled taste of Grace returning his kiss. Until her pure essence was in his mouth, her brave, giving spirit providing the only healing antidote for his lonely, ravaged soul.

When he knew himself again, he gentled the kiss. He slipped free of her body as he lowered her back to the Harley's leather seat.

"I'm sorry, baby." He stole another gentle kiss. "I'm sorry I didn't make it good for you."

"Shh." She pressed her fingers against his lips, refusing his apology. "Are you kidding? What a rush it was to know you needed me like that. So quick. So out of control.''

"Next time it'll be all for you, I promise."

Suddenly aware of their daring position in the semi-public location, Logan eased her into a more comfortable position, fastening his pants and sitting her sidesaddle on the Harley again. Though she could now close her legs, he regretted to see that he'd ruined her hose and had wrinkled her skirt so that she could no longer pull it down to its intended length.

Logan took off his jacket and laid it in her lap like a peace offering. "I'll, uh, pay for those."

She looked up at him and smiled. He'd even done damage there, seeing the raw marks of his beard on her rosy fair skin.

"No you won't. The Bureau footed the bill for my clothes, remember?"

Her wry attempt at humor should have made him laugh. It almost did.

Instead, he saw another mark on her body. Five marks, to be precise, encircling her left wrist. Five small bruises too dark with color for him to have just put there.

He lifted her arm, gently cradling it by her fingers and elbow, to inspect the bruises. Though the size and spread of the marks weren't as large as his own dimensions, they definitely fit the scope of a man's rough grip.

A different kind of fire lit in his veins.

"Did he put his hands on you?"

Grace's big eyes blanched to the color of fading grass. "Yes." She pulled her arm away and tucked it beneath his jacket on her lap. "We knew that he would."

"Not like that. Where else?" He lifted her chin, ran his fingers along her neck, pushed aside her hair at her forehead and temples, searching for signs of further abuse. "Where did he touch you?"

"Logan, don't do this." She stopped his hands, folding them within hers like a supplicant prayer. "It's part of the job. That was the goal, remember? To make me sexy. To get Harris Mitchell interested in me. We knew this was going to happen if we did our job right."

"Knowing it and seeing it are two different things." He brushed his fingers across her cheek, wishing more than anything that he'd been there to stop her from being hurt. "I heard your voice over the microphone. I picked up the panic. I heard your temper start to go. I don't want to hear what happens when he picks up on it, too."

She leaned her cheek into his palm, accepting his touch for the good it would do her. "If you heard all that, then you also heard how I kept it all together. I didn't let my emotions rule my reactions. I kept my head in the game. That's rule number seven in your book, I believe."

"You're not a set of numbers, Grace."

"And you're not my keeper. You're my partner. Every now and again, you're my lover." She climbed off the bike and walked beyond his reach before turning to face him. "Work with me, Logan. Help me the way you have all week long by teaching me to help myself. Make me a better agent. Don't make me a prisoner of your guilt."

13

IF THEIR CIRCUMSTANCES hadn't been so dangerous, Grace would have laughed at Logan's new look when he showed up, without his Harley, to ride with her to Harris Mitchell's estate that morning.

It was a transformation in reverse. The tall, broad, buff man at home in jeans and leather that she'd gotten to know so well had become, well, a male version of the old Grace.

His tough-guy fashion style had been replaced by a brown, droopy-cut suit pieced together in such a way that the bulk of his shoulders and the trim narrowness of his waist and hips disappeared behind one straight, shapeless line of gabardine. A bow tie and horn-rimmed glasses completed the disguise.

But it was the slicked-back hair and slouched shoulders that reminded her so much of who she used to be. Someone who followed the rules. Someone who hid her talents and her heart's desires behind a guarded wall of anonymity.

Logan had taught her to shine. To stand tall and find confidence in her strengths, to trust her instincts. To think with her heart as much as her head. To take chances.

But as they climbed up to the pillared front porch of Harris Mitchell's estate in the old-money, horse-racing district outside New York City, she wondered if she had taken too big a chance.

Did she still have enough of that old Grace in her to see her through this? To drive her to become something more?

Having a tall, dark and nerdy assistant at her side seemed like little deterrent to the unpredictable danger awaiting her on the other side of that door.

But the big hand Logan squeezed around her shoulder still bespoke a man of strength and ruthless calm. "You ready for this?"

"As ready as I'm gonna get." She fixed her gaze on the doorknob and tried to steady her breathing as they waited.

"Remember, I'll be listening in on everything that happens. If I'm not actually in the room with you watching your back, don't worry, I'm just a signal away."

"Don't be ridiculous." She tried to sound just as professional and detached. "Your job is to search every room to find his hidden mainframe computer access terminal, while I keep Harris occupied. It's only if I download my program into the server that we'll be able to expose his network of contacts. Worry about that, not me."

He pulled his hand away and adjusted his glasses. A listening device installed in the earpiece picked up the transmission from the chip-size microphone hidden in her bra. "Right. Just remember to keep talking so I can track your whereabouts if there's an emergency."

He'd completely ignored her words. Grace's breath whooshed out on an impatient sigh. "Damn it, Logan, you can't compromise the mission because you're worried about Mitchell's groping hands."

"I don't intend to compromise anything." He reached out and pushed the doorbell, then settled his grip around the handle of his briefcase. "You do your job, Gracie, and I'll do mine."

Ever since their heated exchange on his Harley last night, his words and actions had been like this—strictly business. The bruises Mitchell had given her had awakened every protective, predatory instinct he possessed—which, in a man with Logan's talents, was considerable. And frightening.

But she'd stood up for herself and pushed him away with the guilt trip, turning him into a cold, distant man who worked the only way he knew how.

The man standing at her side with the briefcase and pocket protector might look the part of an introverted accounting assistant, but she knew better. This was Logan Pierce in pure agent mode. Not even the sardonic, dismissive Logan she'd first tried to woo into helping her less than a week ago. Certainly not the Logan who'd made her believe she was sexy, the one who made her believe a hot hunk of a man could find her sexy, too. There was no warmth here, no passion, no fire.

This Logan was completely attuned to his surroundings, the one whose unblinking gray eyes missed nothing. There was no humor, no challenge, not even an inkling of the sexually charged energy that had linked them so irrevocably throughout her training.

He was her partner. Her ally. Her backup.

Nothing more.

Five days ago she'd wanted only to prove herself at a man's job in a man's world. Right now she knew a desperately female need to see one of Logan's lopsided smiles.

But then, when had Grace Lockhart gotten what she really wanted out of life without a fight? If she wanted Logan to give up his agent persona and show her a genuine smile again, she had to complete this mission. And she had to do it right.

"It's time, Gracie." At the sound of footsteps in the foyer, Logan leaned down and whispered into her ear. "Let's go get him."

A tall, blond woman in a figure-hugging catsuit opened the door. "Good morning. I'm Ilsa." The faint lilt of a Scandinavian accent welcomed them, though the sidearm strapped to her hip indicated she was something more than the housekeeper. "Renee will take your bags up to your room, Miss Lockhart. Mr. Pierce's will be delivered to the bungalow. I'll show you those rooms later, but right now, Mr. Mitchell is waiting for you in his office. This way, please."

Atop her two-inch, spike-heeled boots, Ilsa stood nearly eye-to-eye with Logan. Grace couldn't help but notice the way Logan's gaze followed the lean, balanced curves revealed by their escort's formfitting outfit. The woman's blatant sensuality could be used as a weapon, Grace realized, noting the apparent distraction in Logan's focus. Though she exuded strength and power, she also was unmistakably female. Maybe a man would have trouble reacting to the threat she presented. Even if he wasn't drooling over her, he might still hesitate to strike out against a woman.

Grace was finally beginning to see the intelligence behind Mitchell's penchant for hiring beautiful, sexy women. While they beautified the scenery, as he'd said last night, they also provided a psychological as well as physical defense grid against his enemies.

They also made her feel woefully inadequate. Unwittingly, her arm crept up around her waist. Grace had always been shorter and bigger and out of proportion than the beautiful women of Hollywood and most of her classmates. Surely, there was some joke behind Harris Mitchell choosing to add her to his menagerie of women.

Oh, God, why hadn't she stayed in her cubicle?

Suddenly she felt the light brush of Logan's hand at the small of her back. He leaned over and whispered two words into her ear. "Rule four."

Sex appeal is all about attitude.

Just like that, a secret code of sorts was established between them. Grace dropped her hand to her side and stood a little taller. She could do this, she reminded herself. She was smart, she was stacked, and she had a plan. She'd left her cubicle because she knew she could do something more. Be someone more.

She'd come so far this past week, she wasn't about to blow it now. Besides, Miss Sweden with the sidearm up ahead probably hadn't aced her college calculus class. Grace smiled wickedly, psyching herself up. Miss Sweden probably couldn't even spell *calculus.*

"If you'll wait here, please." Ilsa stopped and nodded to the African-American woman standing outside a pair of white, brass-accented doors.

"I'm Tanya. It's good to see you again, Miss Lockhart." She stepped away from the door, and held out a black-and-silver wand that Grace recognized as a metal-detection device. "This is just a formality."

Tanya ran the metal detector up and down and around Logan's and Grace's bodies. Grace held her breath, praying FBI technology was more advanced than Mitchell's security system. Thank God for the plastic components on their surveillance equipment, plus the lead lining in the secret compartment of their briefcases where she and Logan had hidden their guns.

By the time Tanya had finished patting them down, Ilsa had reappeared in the open doorway. "He's ready."

Tanya nodded. "They're clean."

Ilsa smiled and ushered them inside the plush appointments of Harris Mitchell's office. Grace couldn't help but gawk a moment at the lavish use of blood-red velvet and gilded paint. Shelves filled with books and priceless-looking knickknacks of brass and silver and marble lined three walls, while the fourth sported floor-to-ceiling walnut paneling. A large portrait of Mitchell hung on the paneled wall. The room bespoke wealth, flamboyance and self-indulgence.

A perfect match for the polished man buttoning his suit coat and circling the corner of his ornate rococo-style desk.

"Grace!" He took hold of her outstretched hand and pulled her closer, pressing a kiss to her cheek instead of shaking hands. "Welcome to my humble abode."

This was it.

Grace fixed a professional smile on her face that was tempered with a bit of a haughty pout. "It's lovely. Thank you for having me." She turned to introduce Logan. "Harris, this is my assistant, Logan Pierce. He tracks files and, uh, carries heavy equipment for me—" she winked "—if you know what I mean."

"Yes." Harris's conspiratorial smile vanished when he turned to greet Logan. "Ilsa will show you to your room in the bungalow. If Miss Lockhart needs you, we'll send for you."

Grace opened her mouth to protest, but a sharp, warning glance from Logan kept her silent. "Yes, sir." He lifted his stooped gaze to hers. "I'll get started on that accounting template for you."

She hoped that meant he would get started on their search for Mitchell's hidden computer. Grace nodded, playing along. "Thank you, Mr. Pierce. I'll talk to you soon."

"Yes, ma'am."

Summarily dismissed, Logan turned and followed Ilsa out the door. Meanwhile, Harris turned to the freckle-faced redhead who'd been sitting beside his desk, apparently taking dictation and showing him a length of leg, judging by the steno pad she carried and the micro-mini skirt she wore. "Heather, you may go, as well. Get started on those letters. I'll sign them after lunch."

"Yes, sir."

After the room had cleared, Tanya took up guard again outside the door and closed it.

Harris took Grace's briefcase and set it on the corner of his desk. Her Undercover .38 was no longer within arm's reach. She breathed deeply, trying to subdue the sudden jump in her pulse rate before she betrayed her nerves in a blush on her cheeks.

He came back to face her, cupped her elbows and ran his hands up and down her arms. "I'm so glad you've chosen to join me, Grace. I think we'll make a fine team."

She was glad she'd chosen the heavier weight blazer of mint-green wool for her first day on the job. Though it wasn't body armor, it did provide some measure of protection from the stroke of his familiar hands. Other than the soft color and smooth fit, the suit itself wasn't sexy. But the fact that she wore a stretchy lace camisole instead of a blouse beneath it hadn't escaped Mitchell's notice. With his gaze fixed on the rise and fall of her chest, he was grinning like a child with a new toy.

"There's so much I want to show you." He lifted his gaze to hers finally, checking her reaction.

Grace arched one skeptical eyebrow. "Really."

Harris chuckled, then revealed his perfect, bright white teeth in a full-blown smile. "Maybe we can do *that* later. Right now I want to show you my books, give you a good feel for the scope of what I'm asking you to take on."

Books were good. Books were evidence. Books she could handle.

Grace relaxed enough to let her smile match his. "Sounds fascinating. Let's get to work."

He released her and crossed to the shelves at the far end of the room. He pulled out a leather-bound book then reached into the empty slot and pushed a button recessed in the side of the bookcase. To her surprise, one of the walnut panels behind the desk popped open. Harris quickly replaced the book and swung the panel open like a door.

"What's back there?"

Over his shoulder she could make out what looked like a row of metal filing cabinets set against a stark white wall. "A vault. Plus, it's a fireproof room where I can store my records."

A perfect place to stash a hidden computer, thought Grace.

"Here." He set a cache of computer disks on his desk. "Did you know I'm a self-made millionaire almost a hundred times over?"

"Impressive."

Harris made several more trips, carrying out stacks of records books and piling them beside her briefcase on the desk. Meanwhile, she circled the room slowly, touching a book or chair here and there, hiding the fact she was actually pinpointing the location of the switch he'd used to enter the hidden room.

There. Grace's eyes widened as she read the book spine.

Kama Sutra. Fitting, she supposed, given the man who'd designed the secret vault system.

"There. All set. Do you prefer to work on paper or the computer?"

Grace didn't answer. At that moment, she focused in on one of the small statues sitting on the shelf in front of her.

Silhouettes in copper and steel wire of a woman on her hands and knees with a man kneeling and entering her from behind. She looked up at the shelf beside her. A piece of carved teak in the image of an African goddess, with enough mammary mounds to feed an entire tribe. Sitting on the lamp table beside one of the wing-backed chairs was an oblong chunk of sculpted ivory with the smooth, defined shape and detailing of a man's erect penis.

In fact, she now realized, the only piece of art in the room that had no lewd overtones was the portrait of Mitchell himself. Or maybe the fact that it was included in the decor meant he thought he himself was a work of art worthy of such a collection.

Grace bit down on the inside of her mouth, stifling the urge to laugh. The man's ego was astronomical.

Without having heard him come up behind her, Grace jumped when Harris slipped his hand around her waist.

She stopped laughing inside.

His displeasure at being ignored was evident in the clipped tone of his voice. "Come, Grace. You can admire the collection later. We have work to do."

She stopped laughing and started thinking about survival.

"WHAT DID YOU FIND OUT?" Logan nearly pounced on Grace when she entered the bungalow almost five hours later. He'd checked to make sure the place wasn't bugged, then stripped off his jacket and tie to do some snooping, but had left on his fake glasses to keep track of his partner on the inside.

"That the man's a pervert." She kicked off her high heels and sank onto the floral-brocade couch in the sitting room. He noted that she pulled her jacket together and hugged one of the throw pillows in front of her before continuing. "There's a hidden room in his office I'd like to check out. Beyond that, the only room I had access to was the main bathroom, and there's no computer hookup in there."

Logan perched on one of the overstuffed chairs across from her, giving her the space she'd demanded last night, giving him the space he needed to keep his hands to himself and his mind on the game. "What about his office computer?"

Grace shook her head. "I was on it all morning. I played around while he took a call. It's freestanding. The main server that he uses to access his illegal files and contacts is somewhere else."

"The bungalow's clean. I discovered that his chauffeur, Raisa, and I share a mutual admiration for well-tuned engines. I got into the garage and checked the office there. Nothing. It's got to be in the main house."

"Right." He felt her weary sigh through his bones. "So how are we going to get in? Ilsa and Tanya patrol the halls twenty-four/seven."

"Not exactly." Logan was formulating a plan now. "I watched the staff today, tried to pinpoint their schedules. One of the two bodyguards is with Mitchell at all times while the other patrols. The rest have set duties, but seem to be limited to certain areas of the estate. They're easier to avoid than Ilsa or Tanya.''

Grace's energy level picked up a notch as she caught on. "If I keep Mitchell busy, that would account for at least one of his bodyguards.''

"And I can stay a step ahead of the other.'' He stood and began to pace. "I'll start with the west wing, back in the kitchen and servants' rooms. I doubt he'd place the mainframe there, but there might be someone he trusts enough to guard it. It'll help us narrow the search.''

"I can check the guest rooms upstairs tonight.''

"No.'' He shook his head and scratched at the stubble of beard that was just starting to poke through his skin. "I'll handle the search. You just keep Mitchell and his bodyguard busy.''

"So now I'm reduced to bait?''

He should have tuned in to the temper edging its way into her voice. "That was the plan. You got us in, you created the flush-out program. Now it's my turn to do what *I* do.''

He intended for them to find and corrupt Mitchell's computer network fast and methodically then get them the hell out of Mitchell's grasp.

But he wasn't going anywhere yet.

When he spun around, he found Grace blocking his path. Her fists sat on those voluptuous hips, her chest heaved in a deep breath, and her eyes were spitting nothing but emerald fire. His body lurched in automatic response at the delicate scent of her standing so close. But he fisted his hands at his sides and glared down at her upturned face, refusing to acknowledge the desire that forked through him.

He wanted to kiss that damn smirk off her face and bundle her up in his arms and take her home all at the same time. But he did neither. She wanted her space and some respect, not necessarily in that order. And, damn it, if that was all he could give her, he would.

"Let me get this straight." Her temper had reenergized her body. Never knowing for sure what was going on in that brain of hers, Logan wisely retreated a step. "You're going to search an entire twenty-five-room mansion all by yourself while you're dodging Amazons who wear guns and a man with a penchant for castrating the competition. And all the while, you're going to listen in on your earpiece to be ready to rush to my rescue should Mitchell get his hands out of place."

Logan didn't balk. "That sounds about right."

Her expression suddenly softened, throwing him off guard. "Who's watching *your* back while you're doing all this?"

He hadn't expected that one. Her concern sucker punched him right in the gut and he visibly flinched. But he was stronger than this. He was stronger than emotions; he was stronger than desire. He had to be. He'd barely survived losing one partner on a botched undercover assignment.

He didn't intend to lose another.

"I've always watched my own," he told her, moving across the room to pour himself a glass of ice water at the bar sink. He drank a long swallow. "You don't need to worry about me. Just focus on what you're doing."

"I see." When he turned to face her, she'd hugged herself up in that self-conscious embrace that made him want to rail at the world that had somehow made her think she wasn't good enough or pretty enough or sexy enough. He wanted to swallow her up in his own arms and show her time and again that she, Grace Lockhart, was a sexual force to be reckoned with. A beautiful woman in her own right who didn't need to live in her mother's bombshell shadow. "You can be afraid for me, but I can't be afraid for you?"

Ah, hell. Afraid for *him?* Logan shook his head, stemming the rising swell of warmth inside him.

"That's right." He set his glass down on the counter. He didn't want to like that she cared about him. For the moment, he pretended he didn't need anyone to care. "I know all the tricks, Gracie. I can work more quickly and efficiently on my own without having to worry about you wandering away from Mitchell. The minute I locate that computer, I'll contact you. You can download your magic and we can get the hell out of here before he's any wiser."

"You don't think I can do this, do you?" she accused. Her hug wound tighter around her middle. "Then what the hell was all that training about? I changed my looks, I fired weapons, I wrestled you to the floor, I…we…had sex."

No. They'd made love. Despite the best intentions of his randy libido, there'd been emotions involved. Connections had been made. Expectations had been kindled.

But he couldn't tell her that. He couldn't quite get a handle on those feelings himself. The only thing he'd allow himself right now was the driving need to protect something good and wonderful and innocent. He hadn't protected Roy. But, by damn, he would protect Grace.

Even if it meant never fully understanding the new and painful emotion gripping his heart.

"We were good together, Gracie, I won't deny that." *Good* didn't even begin to describe what they'd shared. *Good* was doing her a disservice. "But you're on the front line now. Harris Mitchell's the only man I want you to worry about."

"I can't promise you that."

"You—?" Logan sputtered on his frustrated anger. He marched across the room. Right up to her. Close enough to smell her. Close enough to see the blue flecks in her eyes. Close enough to touch. But he didn't. "You can't—? Do you think this is easy for me? This is the reason I work alone. Because you can't trust a partner not to go off and do some stupid, foolhardy thing that's gonna get him killed."

"Him?" she challenged, forcing him to relive every life-altering moment of Roy Silverton's death. "Take a good look at me, Logan. I'm not Roy. History isn't destined to repeat itself."

Heat radiated between them. Fiery, combustible heat.

"I'm smart and I'm a survivor," she went on. "And I had the best coach in the business."

He breathed hard. Grace dropped her arms to her sides, his temper touching off her own. She breathed hard. Their chests expanded in deep, erratic gasps, until their mutual frustrations synchronized themselves. With their gazes locked in stubborn combat, Logan breathed in. Grace inhaled. Her firm, high breasts reached out and touched his chest.

Logan jumped back as if he'd been zapped by an electrical shock. His groin tightened and his heart expanded.

But instead of reaching out to her, he turned and walked away. "Rule seven, Gracie." She knew that damn list he'd given her better than he knew it himself. But he needed to remind her—and himself—to concentrate on where they were and what they were doing. He slipped on his brown suit coat and pulled the tie out of his pocket. "You'd better get back to the house. Mitchell's expecting you for dinner."

"Fine." From the corner of his eye, he saw her slip into her shoes and comb her fingers through her hair. "I'm checking out the guest rooms and the hidden room in Mitchell's office," she announced with a prim, perfunctory lack of emotion. She picked up her briefcase and headed for the door. "What you do with your own time is up to you."

"Damn it, Grace." He reached beyond her shoulder and braced the door shut. He kept moving forward, trapping her against the door. He pushed aside her collar and kissed her neck. He wrapped his arms around her, filling his hands with her breasts and squeezing them tight. He wedged his knee at the seam of her buttocks and lifted her onto his thigh. "My job is to keep you safe. My job is to get you home in one piece. I don't want to lose you. I don't want to lose anybody else."

"No." She pushed aside his hands, pushed herself back from the door. She turned around and flattened her hand against his chest, pushing him away. She was fighting, fighting something hard inside her. Her hand trembled for a moment against his chest. But then the fingers became a fist and she was pushing him back another step. "Your *job* is to help me bring down Harris Mitchell."

Her big, expressive eyes had darkened to a nearly turquoise-blue. "You keep telling me to stay focused, to pay attention to the job at hand. I need you to do that, too, Logan. It's natural to worry about your partner, and I appreciate that, I do."

"But?" Logan moved away on his own, severing contact with her entirely. He knew she was right. He knew he could never completely trust her on her own because of what had happened to Roy. He knew that he wasn't letting her do her job.

"But I'm not proving anything if I let you call all the shots. If I make a mistake, I'll deal with it—"

"It only takes one mistake, Grace."

She paused long enough to let the import of what he was saying sink in. But she didn't change her mind.

"Then I won't make one."

With that he let her leave.

14

"SHOW ME YOUR BREASTS, Grace."

Logan stopped dead in his tracks, hearing Harris Mitchell's hushed request over the tiny monitor in the earpiece of his glasses. While Grace had worked late in Mitchell's office, guarded at the door by Tanya, Logan had worked his way through the west wing of the house. No computers.

His eavesdropping on Grace had become a harmless buzz of background noise in his ear. The conversation between Grace and Mitchell had involved numbers and expansions and investments. There had been a few brief detours into shared interests, such as fine art and gourmet food. But each time, Grace carefully steered him back to subject of business holdings and whether or not particular investments had paid out.

As the time crept toward midnight, this particular request had come out of the blue. Logan slipped silently into a closet to listen to how Grace handled this latest blatant flirtation.

It had caught Grace off guard, too, judging by the breathy catch in her voice. "Excuse me?"

Stay cool, sweetheart, he encouraged her telepathically. *Don't let this guy push your buttons.*

"We've worked long hours today. It's late. This Indian summer night is warm. You haven't even taken off your jacket."

"I'm fine with the temperature, thanks."

There was a beat of silence. Then the crackling sound of paper being crumpled into a fist. Mitchell's? Grace's? "Now you know I'm not really talking about the weather."

Logan's pulse rate kicked up a notch. God, he hated listening to this.

"We're almost done with your portfolio. One thing you'll learn about me is that I hate to leave a job unfinished." She was trying to steer him back to an impersonal topic just as she had numerous times before.

But this time Mitchell wasn't buying it. The paper crumpled again. "I'm the same way. Now take off your jacket."

Logan held his breath, his search temporarily forgotten.

There was a shuffle of paper, the creak of a leather chair. Was she obeying his command? Shit. She didn't have anything on under that jacket except that lacy little tank top and the bra with the microphone chip. And she was taking it off for him?

He heard the double click of Grace's mechanical pencil and remembered to breathe. "Shall we get back to work?" she asked in that husky phone-sex voice of hers.

No, no, no! He'll get the wrong idea, Logan warned her with a useless thought.

"You go ahead." Mitchell seemed to have gotten the very idea Logan hadn't wanted him to. "I like watching you."

A few moments later Grace moaned. Logan inched his way toward the closet door. "What's that for?" she asked.

"I'm helping you relax."

"Mmm. That feels nice."

He was touching her. Logan's blood boiled in his veins and pounded in his ears.

Teach me how to seduce a man.

She couldn't. She wouldn't.

He heard a wet, gloppy sound and a short hiss of breath. The leather chair creaked and skidded across the floor as either Grace or Mitchell moved it too quickly.

"What are you doing?" Panic had raised Grace's pitch a notch.

"You've been driving me crazy all night." Harris's voice remained eerily calm. "Acting like you don't care. Wearing those come-screw-me pumps and practically daring me to break your cool facade."

"Um—"

No, baby. Logan was out the door at the familiar stutter of nerves in Grace's voice. *Rule two. Stay in control.*

His hand strayed to the gun he now wore strapped to the back of his belt. After passing Tanya's initial inspection, he didn't intend to be without it again. He slipped through the empty wing of rooms and made his way down the back stairs.

The scene he was forced to listen to continued to unfold.

"I know I've seen those breasts before." Harris was trying that lame line again. Logan could envision Grace standing there, folding her arms around herself, hiding her generous bounty and blowing her cover. "Where was it? A centerfold?"

"No, I never posed—stop that!"

Logan heard a slap and froze. His lungs seemed to press against his ribs as he fought to keep a slough of expletives inside him.

"So you like it rough, do you?"

"What?" She was scared. Logan ran. "No!"

Shit. He might as well be a hundred miles away. How was he supposed to get to Grace without breaking her cover? How was he supposed to help her without putting her in even greater danger? He suspected Mitchell's wrath would be a far more ominous threat than his lust.

He heard the crash of pottery breaking. "Get worked up for me, Grace," Mitchell ordered. "Let me see what you've got."

"No." That was Grace. Logan recognized the sounds of struggle. Bodies slamming into things. Little grunts of sound.

Cover be damned. Grace was out of there. Now.

He wheeled around the corner into the servants' hallway and slid to a stop. He backpedaled a step and ducked behind a wooden settee as two women strolled past, dressed in workout clothes and headed for the gym.

One was the cook, Gertrude, a big, beefy foreign woman with a lusty laugh and biceps nearly as big as Logan's. She'd be a pain to take down if she spotted him. The other was the raven-haired chauffeur, Raisa. She packed a gun like the two bodyguards.

Damn the man and his eccentricities!

"You want to throw me down again, Grace?" Mitchell's voice sounded winded and excited at the same time.

"No, I don't." Logan took heart. He recognized that prim, go-to-hell tone in Grace's voice. Had she bested the bastard in a fight?

"Sure, you do." There was a squeal from Grace and a muffled oof as one of them hit a piece of furniture.

Gertrude and Raisa exited into the kitchen, and Logan was off again.

"Stop it." More struggle.

"You know you like it."

"Stop!"

Dead silence filled his ears as he hurried into the east wing. His feet made no sound on the marble-tiled floor. He had the double doors of Mitchell's office in sight. Damn. Ilsa was on watch.

Logan faded into the shadows and silently cursed the woman. How could she sit there, reading a magazine, while there were sounds of a struggle on the other side of that door? As long as Mitchell wasn't the one in trouble, she'd probably sit through rape and murder.

Thankfully, the sounds of heavy, erratic breathing filled his ears once more. Grace was all right. She'd been through a fight, but she was all right.

For now.

He heard Mitchell's deep breaths, too, playing like low-pitched static in his ear. "I thought you understood what I meant about *special projects*."

"I did," argued Grace. "I do."

"You don't want me to kiss you gently. You don't want me to kiss you rough."

"I don't want you to kiss me at all." *No, no, Grace,* Logan thought. *You're going too far.* He heard her catch her breath. "It's a little eccentricity I have."

Logan dared half a smile. Good girl. She was thinking on her feet. Tell a lie and make him believe it.

Her voice slipped back down to that irresistibly husky pitch. "I don't like to be touched on my mouth."

"Where do you like to be touched? How?" They'd gone back to the hated silence. "Like this?"

"Sure."

"How about this?"

"Uh, okay."

Logan sensed her panic. *Damn it, sweetheart, play along.* Should he announce himself to Ilsa? Tell her he needed to speak with his boss? Would his untimely arrival be enough to end the groping session? Or would his black-on-black outfit raise too many suspicions and jeopardize Grace's safety?

There was that wet, sloppy sound again, almost echoing in Logan's ears. That meant the sound was closer to the microphone. Closer to Grace's breasts. Too close.

"Harris, wait." Logan's thoughts halted at the precise command in Grace's voice. He hoped Mitchell's did, too. "You're right. We've been working all day. If this is how we're going to cap things off, then I'd like to freshen up."

"Wash me off your lips?"

Logan ran his tongue around his own mouth, remembering the sweet, soft taste of Grace there. It made him sick to think of Mitchell defiling that sweetness. Sick to think of Mitchell having anything at all to do with Grace.

"Yes. We each have our own little fetishes, don't we," she lied.

But, oh, thank God, Mitchell was buying this. "Of course. And if I've offended your sensibilities, you'll have to punish me somehow."

Logan shifted his attention from the voices in his earpiece to the sound of the doorknob turning beside Ilsa. "When I get back. I'll think of something appropriate for you when I get back."

Ilsa stood as the door opened. Grace was framed in the doorway. Her skirt was wrinkled, her hair bounced about her head in a scattered disarray, and she'd stripped down to that stretch of lace material that clung to each curve like a second skin.

Mitchell had had his hands on her! On *his* woman!

"I'll be back in a few minutes, Harris," she cooed.

"I'll be waiting."

GRACE STUMBLED blindly down the hallway, searching for the first empty room she could find. When a bathroom appeared on her right, she went inside and closed the door behind her. With her steps guided by a night-light beside the vanity, she went to the sink and ran cool water to splash on her heated face and neck.

Then she took a drink. She rinsed out her mouth and spit. And rinsed and spit again. Now if she could only wipe the man's touch from her breasts.

Grace shivered with revulsion at the scene that had just played out. Harris massaging her shoulders. Kissing her neck. Grabbing her breasts and kissing her mouth. She'd slapped him then.

And when his hand moved up between her thighs, she'd lost it. She'd simply reacted, smashing his instep and taking him down to the floor.

But he'd liked that.

She rinsed her mouth again, almost choking as she stood and watched the reflection in the mirror. The bathroom door opened. She jumped. A black wraith slipped inside with her and the door closed.

"Gracie?"

At the sound of that low-pitched voice, a wave of relief so profound that she could no longer stand swept through her. On weak knees, she threw herself into Logan's arms, linking her hands behind his waist and snatching up handfuls of his black sweater in an effort to get closer to his warmth and security.

"Oh, Logan." She buried his nose in his chest, inhaling his leathery, male scent on a silent sob. "You were right. I can't do this."

Logan bundled Grace up in his arms and cradled her head against his chest. He shushed her gently and rocked her back and forth, trying to absorb each hurt and insult and insecurity.

"I'm sorry, sweetheart," he whispered against her ear. "I heard everything. I'm so sorry you had to go through that."

"I can't go back there. He thinks…" Her body shook against his in a silent sob and Logan held her even more tightly. "He thinks I like what he's doing to me. He thinks I'm getting turned on."

Logan wouldn't torture himself any further by asking for details, and she didn't offer any.

"Are you okay?" He had to ask. "Did he hurt you?"

Grace shook her head against his chest. "Not like you mean. I might have a couple of bruises on my legs from when he threw me on the sofa." She shivered in his arms. "He actually wanted to fight with me."

Logan swore, softly and viciously, in her ear.

Here was the perfect opportunity to take Grace home. To sneak her past the guarded iron gates and whisk her safely away from Mitchell's grasp. Grace was finally surrendering to the horrible demands of this assignment.

"Take me home, Logan. Please, just take me home."

Logan backed toward the door, pulling Grace with him. He had every intention of granting her request. All he had to do was slip past Ilsa. Climb over the gates without tripping the alarm.

He could do it. He could get them out of there. He knew he could do it.

This wasn't just about possessive jealousy, about sharing the body of the woman he craved with another man. This was about some deeper emotion, one that twisted around his heart and made him think about Grace and home all in the same thought. She shouldn't have to do this. She was shy and self-conscious, damn it! Except with him. She hadn't transformed and come out of her shell for anyone else but him. It was his right to guard that gift. His need to keep her and her insecurities safe from slimy predators like Harris Mitchell.

"Someone else can take care of that damn program of mine," she murmured into his sweater. "Someone else can do it."

That program of mine. Mine.

And that's when Logan knew that he couldn't take her away.

He backed against the wall and let her lean against him, taking strength in her need for him. Offering his own strength to revive her unquenchable spirit. He saw her disappearing goals through his jaded eyes and knew he couldn't live with himself if he allowed her to give up. Not Grace. Tougher than a pitbull and sexier than his wildest dreams, yet fragile as a butterfly, she needed this victory. She needed to complete this mission.

And as much as he wanted her out of here, he wanted to see her happy and proud and so full of confidence that he knew she'd still be okay when it was finally over between them and he had to leave.

This was going to be one of the hardest things he'd ever had to do.

"I have to send you back to Mitchell, sweetheart. I can't let you quit."

Logan loosened his hold as she backed away. With his eyes having adjusted to the dim light of the room, he could see her own emerald gaze, dark with emotion and wide with shock. "What do you mean? Isn't that what you wanted all along?"

He framed her face in his hands, holding her still when she tried to get away from him. She had to understand. He had to make her understand. "You know it is. But this isn't about the case. This isn't about me. This is about you. About proving yourself to the world. That's what you've wanted all along.'' He brushed a strawberry-gold curl off her cheek and willed her to understand. ''What kind of partner would I be if I let you work this hard for this long, and then suddenly let you quit?''

''You'd be the partner I want right now.'' She pushed away from his touch, hugging herself up in that protective stance of hers. ''How can I go back in there? He thinks we're going to end up in bed together. How can I act sexy? How can I look like I'm enjoying it when everything he does makes me want to either laugh or puke.''

''I'll give you the look.''

''What?''

The idea was crazy. The idea was wild. But the idea might just work.

''Take off your skirt and hose.''

''Why?''

He turned her around, searching for a zipper to start undressing her himself.

But Grace's hands batted at his. She was fighting him. She didn't understand.

''Grace, let me.''

''Why are you doing this?''

''Because you're not a quitter. Not the Grace I know.'' She ceased to struggle for a moment, trying to make sense of what he was telling her. In that moment, he found the zipper and slid it down. ''The Grace I know is sexy and confident and full of attitude. And she's at her best when she's making love with me.''

He pulled the skirt and panty hose and shoes off her in one sweeping move. Then he picked her up beneath her bare bottom and set her on the vanity ledge beside the broad porcelain sink. He kissed her once, briefly, deeply, scattering her confusion beneath the instant haze of passion that flared between them.

"You and I always seem to end up in tight spots. Tonight I'm going to do something about that."

She slipped her hands up to frame his face. "You're crazy. Even if I stay, I said I'd only be gone a few minutes. We don't have time." She scraped her palm across his cheek. "Besides, Harris would be suspicious if I showed up with beard burn on my face."

"Relax." Logan smiled gently, then wickedly. "I can make you come without kissing you. Without entering you."

Her pupils dilated at the erotic arrogance of his statement. "How?"

"You're cheeks are already pink with that flushed, turned-on look just talking about it." Her hands flew to her face to test the temperature change for herself and Logan seized the opportunity to move in between her legs. "Just close your eyes and let me do my magic. Close your eyes and listen to my voice. Feel my touch." He flattened his hands against her breasts, doing nothing more than squeezing the nipples in his palms. The tips tightened and shot out in instantaneous reaction. "That's it, baby. Just feel."

Just feel? Grace's breath squeezed out of her chest as a bolt of instant heat shot from her nipples straight down to the juncture of her thighs. It was always like this with Logan. Instant and hot and sudden. But how? There wasn't any time. Harris was waiting for her.

Logan tugged at her nipples now, rolling them between his fingers, pulling on that invisible string that jerked a dampening reaction between her legs. The porcelain was cold beneath her bottom. Cold and hard and impersonal. But she could feel the heat building inside her, coming out of her, making at least one strip of that porcelain very, very hot.

She knew he was right. That she couldn't leave. That she'd never be able to hold her head up again if she quit this case. And Logan believed in her. For whatever reason he'd done this about-face, he believed in her.

"Ah!" She cried out loud when the nip of his teeth replaced his hands.

Quickly, his hand covered her mouth. "No, baby." He reached for the hand towel behind her. "Someone might hear us."

"It's taking too long," she whispered, just before he stuffed the rolled-up towel into her mouth. Logan grazed his lips across that sensitive bundle of nerves at the base of her neck and she bit into the towel.

He'd said this would be fast. He'd said there'd be no kissing, no intercourse. Without this slow build of sensual heat, could she ever possibly come before Mitchell or his guard became suspicious of her extended absence?

Logan's chest expanded in and out beneath her hands. He'd come so quickly on his Harley the night before. Fueled by lust and need and simmering frustration, he'd pumped into her before she was ready. It had been a glorious meeting of the heart, though. He hadn't been able to help himself. His need had been so intense, he hadn't been able to resist her. And though her body had been left unsatisfied, her heart and her mind were content.

Was that what this was about? Did he mean he would bring out that caring, nurturing contentment again? Or could he truly give her an orgasm? The clock was ticking.

She pulled the towel from her mouth. "Logan, the time—"

He pushed the towel back in and whispered roughly against her ear. "Touch yourself, Gracie." He moved her hands from his hard, solid chest to the softer, straining contours of her own. The pattern of the lace was a rough caress against her palms. He moved his hands over hers, silently instructing her on just the right way to pluck and squeeze and rub and excite herself. "Stay busy up here, baby. I'm going south."

She moaned into the towel as he touched her intimately. He pushed her thighs apart and squeezed them in his palms, rubbing the pad of his thumbs against the sensitive nub between her feminine folds. "Keep touching yourself, baby." He continued to rub. "I get all crazy when I watch you like this."

She made *him* crazy?

"I'm going inside, Gracie," he warned her a split second before he dipped a finger inside her. Then two. Her thighs automatically clenched against the electrically charged zap of pleasure and pain.

But she couldn't close herself. Logan was there. His hips penned her knees apart. She could only squirm and push against his hand to try to ease the torment.

The time. Oh, God, this was too slow. She wouldn't finish. She couldn't finish.

With his fingers massaging her inside and out, she felt herself swell. She felt his fingers get slick with her need. The scent of her own honey-sweet aroma filled the tiny space of air in the bathroom. But it wasn't enough. She wasn't coming!

She reached up to remove the towel but Logan moved his hands beneath her thighs and lifted her, pulling her right to the edge of the vanity. Thrown off balance, she had to lean back and brace herself with both hands.

She was so open like this. Open and wet and vulnerable. Logan's fingers plunged into her again and her thighs convulsed. She had to close. She needed to close to savor the tension, to ease the driving heat.

But Logan had other plans. "Spread your legs," he ordered on a husky command. "Spread your legs. I want to suck you."

His hands pushed against her and her thighs fell open. Then he was kneeling in front of her, his dark hair an enticing contrast against her pale skin. In a contest of strength and subconscious will, he held her open. His tongue lapped at her crevice and she bucked in reaction. With his lips protecting her, he nipped at her swollen clitoris. His scratchy beard stubble rasped against her most delicate skin.

Grace contracted. Logan pushed. He plunged his tongue inside her and he began to suck in earnest.

Grace's breathing picked up the same frantic rate. He drank her honey and pulled on her some more.

It was too much. His inner strokes were more than she could bear. She squeezed her thighs and buttocks, demanding her release.

But against Logan's hands, she couldn't close herself. She could only move herself closer, drive herself against the marauding assault of his hands and mouth.

Sensing her breaking point, Logan slipped his fingers beneath her bottom and lifted her right onto his mouth. With his superior strength he lifted her off the counter and bit down with one final plunge deep inside her.

Grace screamed into the towel. Everything inside her clenched, then flowered and flowed with her release.

He'd done it! They'd done it!

Before she came down from the pinnacle, Logan set her on the counter and gathered her into his arms. "God, you're so beautiful," he praised her. "So absolutely beautiful."

Weak and spent she could only cling to him to try to catch her breath.

The obvious bulge in his pants against her thigh brought her back to the reality of the moment. She reached for him, intending to return the favor. But Logan caught her wrist and moved her hand away. "That was for you, sweetheart. I'm okay."

He pulled the towel from her mouth and placed it between her legs to clean her. But even that rough texture on her sensitized skin threatened to arouse her again!

Logan smiled and stepped away, giving her space to close herself around the towel. He punched a button on his watch and the iridescent dial lit up. "Five minutes," he said. "We've been in here five minutes."

"Is that all?" She was both surprised and disappointed. "Well. Do I have that look?"

He turned her face toward the soft glow of the nightlight and smiled. "Oh, yeah. Feeling more confident?"

Grace felt herself blush clear down to her toes. "Oh, yeah."

He helped her climb down and while she washed herself and dried, he turned her panty hose right side out. She was dressed in a matter of minutes, though she and Logan kept bumping into each other in the small room, stirring her desire for him all over again.

When at last she was ready, Logan took her gently by the shoulders and backed her up against the sink. Grace tipped her head back as he leaned over her. Her lips parted as he moved in close enough for a kiss. But he paused, mere millimeters away. Their breaths mingled, their gazes locked, and the tension in the room stretched itself almost to the point of snapping.

But then he pulled away, leaving her breathless and hot. Her body still reeled with the aftershocks of his most intimate kiss. If they could stay locked together in this tiny room, she'd want to do it again. And again and again.

"You're a man of your word, Logan. Thank you." She plucked at the knit of his sweater, then smoothed it flat against his chest.

"I told you I could do it without kissing."

She smiled at his boyishly male arrogance. Then she threw her arms around his neck and pulled herself up on tiptoe, hugging him tight in her arms and thanking him.

"I meant thank you for not letting me quit." She kissed him beside his ear and unwound herself so she could look him in the eye. "I know this is hard for you. It's hard for both of us. Thank you for being strong when I couldn't be."

He smoothed the hair away from her face in a gentle caress. In the room's dim light, she couldn't tell if she saw regret or something more caring darken his eyes. "You're the strongest woman I've ever known, Gracie." He turned her out of his arms and urged her toward the door with a swat on her rump. "Now go give Mitchell a kiss and tell him he's the one who gives you that hot blush. I'll keep searching the house for that computer terminal."

Logan hung back in the shadows and watched Grace return to Mitchell's office. There was a confident wiggle in her tush as she sauntered down the hall. She exchanged pleasantries with Ilsa and disappeared from sight.

Automatically, he closed his eyes and tuned in to the sounds through his earpiece monitor.

"Well." Grace's nervous laugh put him instantly on guard. "Isn't this a surprise."

What?

It sounded like Harris Mitchell needed to die a very

painful death. "I thought I'd take off some of my clothes so you'd be more comfortable taking off yours."

Was the bastard naked?

Grace shouldn't have to do this. Although she needed to be a field agent. Though she was damn good at undercover, she shouldn't have to do this.

This kind of work was meant for men like him. Men who'd lived in hell. Men who'd rubbed elbows with the scum of the earth and learned the gift of street-wise survival. He was the kind of man who dealt with perverts like Mitchell so that innocents like his mother and Roy Silverton and Grace Lockhart never had to.

"I'm not really into cross-dressing, Harris." Was that pointed observation intended for Logan's ears? He pulled himself out of his spiraling depression to listen to Grace. "I don't know if I like a man who wears a camisole just like mine."

"I have other selections," offered Mitchell. "We don't have to dress alike."

Logan almost grinned at the notion of the notorious ladies' man wearing ladies' underwear. Almost.

He did his best to tune out the painful sound of some kind of embrace.

"I'm exhausted, Harris. Tell you what, let me get a good night's rest, and tomorrow night I promise to make it all worth the wait."

"We have dinner with an associate of mine tomorrow."

She was probably touching him somehow. Touching him in a way that would turn Mitchell's will to her own. Just as her touches had turned Logan's will to mush. "Dinner won't last all night, will it?"

Harris laughed. It was a low, secretive sound not meant for anyone's ears but Grace's. Logan heard it, anyway.

He heard it and hated the sound. "Anthony Benzetti is a boring old fart. We'll take care of business and end the evening early so that *we* can get down to business."

"Sounds perfect," said Grace.

To Logan, it sounded like a nightmare.

15

"QUIT TUGGING at your dress."

Grace's hands stilled at the low-cut neckline of her simple black dress. With all its boning, the knee-length silk sheath fit her like a second skin.

She'd make a good impression, she knew, judging by the appreciative interest in Logan's eyes, which somehow always seemed to be watching her, no matter what he was inspecting around her bedroom.

"It's just that it shows so much," she explained, aligning the spaghetti straps that were there for decoration rather than support. "This is supposed to be a business dinner."

"It's supposed to be an opportunity to clear out the house so I can search the last two rooms." He pulled the tiny microphone chip from his pocket and walked over to stand in front of her. His hands hovered above the horizontal line of black silk and the pale swells of her breasts that mounded above the top edge. "Are you sure there's space in here for the microphone?"

"Now who's worried about revealing too much?" she teased. She took the chip from him and tucked it down inside her strapless bra. "I'll be out of range at the restaurant, but as soon as we get within the one-mile radius of the estate, I'll start talking about tonight's...festivities...with Harris."

She could talk about it now, discuss how she would

seduce another man besides Logan. But only because it was part of the job. Only because Logan needed her to keep Harris Mitchell distracted long enough to find the main computer terminal. Only because that seduction talk would warn Logan that Mitchell and his bodyguards were returning to the estate grounds.

No matter how hard she tried to apply Logan's ten rules of sexy living to her relationship with Mitchell, they just didn't work. Sure, Mitchell was attracted to her, challenged by her. But she felt nothing for him but pure revulsion. The achy excitement of having a man find her irresistibly sexy only seemed to work when that man was Logan Pierce.

Logan clasped her by the shoulders. His thumbs stroked across her breasts, straying toward the plunging neckline, making Grace's skin prickle with an arousing heat.

But then he seemed to think better of giving in to the seductive connection that coursed between them. He pulled his hands away and pushed at the air in mock surrender. He walked back to his briefcase, pulled out his gun and checked the clip and firing pin before tucking it behind him in the waistband of his black jeans. It was almost as if he needed to keep his hands busy to keep them from touching her.

"I'm still really curious about what you plan to do tonight to entertain Mitchell. After meeting with Benzetti, he's expecting a big show."

She wasn't fooled by the businesslike tone in Logan's voice. She knew he wasn't comfortable with her role in this assignment. But he trusted her to be able to fulfill her part. That trust alone deserved a reassurance. "Well, hopefully, by the time we get back, you will have found the hidden computer, downloaded the program, and we won't have to stick around to find out.''

Logan nodded. ''There's just the hidden room behind his office, and his bedroom.''

Grace went over to the mirror above the dresser and touched up her ruby-tinted lipstick. ''Remember, the switch is hidden behind the *Kama Sutra*. It's the last book on the third shelf on the north wall.''

''How could I forget?'' Logan came up behind her. He cupped her bare shoulders in his hands and pulled her back against his chest. Grace lifted her gaze to meet his in the mirror. ''I wish I could kiss you.''

The low-pitched rumble of his voice vibrated along her nerve endings. ''I wish you could, too.''

They stood there like that for an endless moment, gazes locked, absorbing each other's sheltering heat.

Finally, Logan smiled. It was a wry expression that revealed frustrated regret rather than humor. ''Don't let Mitchell try any of that *Kama Sutra* stuff on you.''

''I'll be fine.'' She turned to face him, sharing her own concern. ''Don't get caught. Tanya and Ilsa are going with us, but there still will be other staff members on the estate.''

Logan brushed a loose curl off her forehead. ''You don't think I can charm my way out of trouble?''

She gave him back a little of the possessive streak he was giving her. ''I don't want you charming anybody but me.''

''Whatever you say, boss.'' He touched her hair again, not quite able to let her go. ''You remember everything I taught you, okay? Keep your head in the game, stay in control—''

''I know. I was trained by the best.'' Grace moved before her heart refused to let her walk away. She picked up a matching silk stole and pulled it around her shoulders. "Remember, you'll have about two hours. Find that computer.

"I shouldn't keep Harris Mitchell waiting."

DINNER AT CHEZ DUMOND was an elegant affair. The food was delicious, the service impeccable. The only thing marring the evening was the possessive squeeze of Harris Mitchell's hand on her knee beneath the table the entire evening.

Well, not the entire evening. Occasionally he moved his arm to the back of her chair and let his fingertips graze the bare skin of her back. Sometimes, he broke up the monotony by leaning over and nuzzling a wet lick against her ear.

The only thing that kept her from gagging on her salmon steak was the relatively normal, straightforward conversation of her other dining companion, Anthony Benzetti. Even though Benzetti was a known suspect with several alleged connections to organized crime, he proved to be pleasant enough company. Refusing to discuss business until after dessert, he chatted of his home in Sicily, his grandchildren, and the boat he wanted to buy to sail the eastern seaboard.

But even with that to distract her, she could only take so much of Mitchell's fixed stare down at the shadow of her cleavage. An old-world gentleman, Benzetti stood as she rose to excuse herself to the rest room, while Mitchell ordered a mixed drink, looking put out by her sudden abandonment.

As she scooted past Harris's chair, his hand snaked out and latched on to her wrist. "Don't be gone long," he warned, his voice barely loud enough for her to hear. He pulled her arm so that she had to bend forward and give him a gaping view of her breasts. ''Or I'll send Ilsa after you.''

The two bodyguards watched with detached interest from a nearby table. Benzetti pretended not to notice Mitchell's bruising grip. Grace squelched her panic and pushed herself upright, quietly pulling free.

''I'll be just a few minutes.'' She managed to hold the answering smile on her face until she pushed her way through the door to the ladies' rest room lounge area. ''Oh, God.''

She had just enough time to breathe a sigh of relief, adjust her gown and curse the day she'd ever been born with busty genes, before the door swung open again. She should have recognized the sudden burst of energy that filled the room before even hearing that shrill, maternal voice.

''Gracie! What on earth are you doing here with that man?''

''Mother?'' She turned in surprise, bracing herself for Mimsey's ebullient hug. But it never came. Instead, Mimsey took Grace's arm and led her through a second door into the rest room area. With a furtive glance over her shoulder that had Grace checking behind them, too, she pulled open the door to the double-wide space of the handicapped stall and pushed her inside.

''Mother.'' Grace avoided tripping over the toilet and whirled around. ''We can't stay in here.''

Mimsey planted her strappy silver sandals on the tile floor and refused to budge from the locked stall door. ''I saw you with him.''

''What are you talking about?'' This was so Mimsey. This was too weird.

''Honey, he's no good.''

''Who?''

"Harris Mitchell."

Grace froze at the announcement. Then she urged her mother to hush her voice to a whisper. "You know Harris Mitchell?"

Mimsey nodded. She patted her platinum hair and then wrung her hands. "He doesn't look much older than when I dated him in the early eighties. He must color his hair. And those teeth—"

"*You* dated Harris Mitchell?"

"Yes. And it was one of the biggest mistakes of my life." She wrapped her hands around Grace's where she clutched her evening bag. She'd never seen her mother like this. Not without the cameras rolling. "Think about it, Gracie. Think of all the mistakes I've made. *He* was one of the worst. All that talk of marriage and financing a real, grade-A movie for me. I fell for his line. We needed the money so badly. I was losing our apartment in Burbank. And he took care of us. He took such good care—"

"Mother." She switched the position of the hands, holding on to Mimsey now. *I've seen those breasts before.* Maybe Mitchell's come-on line wasn't as sick as it could be. She and her mother did share a body type, if little more. "Are you telling me you and Mitchell had an affair?"

"Yes. Isn't that what I've been saying?"

Grace's pursuit of Harris Mitchell suddenly took a very personal turn down memory lane. He wasn't just *like* the men who had hurt her mother. He *was* one of those men.

"He's a criminal."

She had no idea.

Mimsey clasped her hands at the cleavage of her red-sequined dress. "He's worse than that. Oh, sweetie. He has a temper on him. I dated him for a couple of months before I found out the truth. I was late meeting him one afternoon after an audition and he showed his true colors. He had a whip, Gracie.''

"Mother." Oh, God. She went back to classifying Mitchell as sick.

"He didn't use it on me. He wanted me to use it on him."

"What?"

"He said I owed him for standing him up. But I wouldn't do it. I couldn't." Mimsey stuck one of her red-lacquered nails in her mouth and started nibbling. "He got so mad. He slapped me a couple of times, and threw me to the floor. I think he was trying to get me angry enough to hit him." She stopped at the toilet and faced her. "Remember that day I came home with the black eye and said I'd fallen on the bus?"

Grace remembered it well. She'd only been five years old, but that was the day she got her first lesson in ice packs and first aid. It was the first of many times she'd played mother to her mom.

"He did that to you?"

Mimsey nodded. "I wanted to break it off right then. But he followed me. I was filming *Batamaran* that summer, and he'd come onto the set. He said he liked it when I wore my bat costume. He wanted me to bite him. Oh, honey, he's just no good." Grace already knew that first-hand. "That handsome agent friend you were with the last time I saw you—I'm sure he's a much better man."

Logan? He was the man she loved. Though he didn't seem to believe in such things as happily ever after, she loved him. When this case was over, he'd walk out of her life just like so many men had walked out of her mother's. But she loved him anyway. "He is, Mother. He's a very good man."

Mimsey looked visibly relieved to hear the admission. In contrast, Grace's own heart felt a bit heavier. Logan had no reason to stick around when this was all over. Great sex might be the stuff dreams were made of, but it would hardly be enough to sustain a long-term relationship.

Mimsey's hand on hers brought Grace's thoughts back to the bathroom stall with her mother. "Look. Would you take a bit of advice?" That would be a first. But Grace nodded. "Until I could get away from Harris—until he moved on to his next interest—I found I could distract him with dress-up games."

"What do you mean?"

"You know. He wanted to 'act' with me. Lion tamer and the naughty lion, principal and the naughty schoolboy, lady bat and the—"

"I get the picture, Mother."

Hadn't Harris asked to be punished for being too forward last night?

Oh, God. Logan better have found that computer.

In a way, she appreciated Mimsey's concern. Though it came a little late in her life, it was the first time Mimsey had offered Grace advice. The first time—other than where their next meal ticket was coming from—that she'd showed concern for Grace's welfare.

Acting on a long overdue impulse, Grace reached out and hugged her mom—and was tightly held in return.

After nearly a minute had passed, Grace thought of her surroundings and Harris's order to return before the guards came to find her. She pulled away and both women straightened their tight dresses.

"By the way, Mother. Why are you here?"

"Oh." Mimsey beamed, suddenly remembering something besides her daughter. "Grant and I are celebrating.'' She held up her left hand and flashed an embarrassingly extravagant diamond on her third finger. ''He asked me to marry him. After all these years, Gracie, I finally found someone who loves me. Just me. Not my name or my boobs or my theatrical reputation. He really loves me.''

Maybe it was too much to expect for Logan to love her in the same way. But that didn't diminish her hope for her mother. ''I'm happy for you. You deserve it.''

''Thank you, sweetie.'' Mimsey unlatched the door, but halted before leaving. ''I mean it, Gracie. Harris isn't a good man to stay with.''

''I won't be with him long, Mother. I promise.''

''Call me soon. Let me know you're safe.''

Though Mimsey's motherly concern had kicked in twenty-six years too late, it was a start. In the gold-appointed bathroom of New York's Chez Dumond, a tenuous relationship between mother and daughter had finally blossomed, with each assuming their traditional roles.

Grace gave Mimsey's hand a reassuring squeeze and smiled. ''I will, Mother. I will.''

IN THE SECRET ROOM behind the office? No. Like an old-fashioned game of Clue, through process of elimination Logan had finally determined where Mitchell's secret computer was kept.

His bedroom.

Though there was enough evidence in these file cabinets to charge Mitchell with money laundering and extortion, there was no computer terminal. No list of names, no link to Mitchell's network of buyers and their money transfers. If he wanted to take down all of Mitchell's network—and he did—he'd still have to download Grace's flush-out program.

Logan pushed the light button on his watch and checked the time. Almost nine. Grace and Mitchell's entourage should be arriving within the hour. He intended to be in and out and back at the bungalow calling in Carmody and the backup team before Mitchell ever set foot inside the front door.

But while the panel behind the *Kama Sutra* had let him into the secret room, Logan spotted no such panel inside. How did he get out without forcing the door?

He moved the beam of his flashlight around the walls of the vault. Besides the gray metal filing cabinets with records of Mitchell's illegal dealings, there were piles of cash, a stack of bonds, a jewelry case with several authentic-looking pieces of diamond jewelry.

"Are those for you, big boy?" Logan imagined Harris Mitchell wearing them, remembering Grace's description of the women's underwear he'd worn. Was Mitchell's cross-dressing wardrobe as extensive as his collection of pornographic art?

Logan swept the beam past a stack of lewd paintings and settled on the lifelike bust of a...bust. Though carved out of gray marble, the piece represented the figure of an aroused, well-endowed woman, complete with distended nipples and puckered areolae in a pale rose-tinted marble.

He wondered if Mitchell got off on all the suggestive works of art or if they were just for shock value to put potential victims of his lust off their guard. Then he had a more businesslike thought. "Oh, no. You wouldn't be that predictable, would you?"

Logan examined the bust more closely. The base of it sat flush against the wall on top of a cabinet next to the light switch. He reached up and palmed the figure's left breast. Cold. Hard. Lifeless. He preferred the real thing. He preferred the warmth and give and pulsing life of Grace's breast. The inevitable tightening of his crotch made Logan laugh. He definitely preferred Grace.

But it would be just Mitchell's style to...he moved his hand to the other marble breast and squeezed. "Gotcha."

The whole breast twisted a quarter turn to the right and the panel door popped open.

Checking first to make sure the office was still dark and empty, Logan hurried out and found the switch behind the bookcase to close the hidden panel. Then he snuck through the quiet house and up the stairs.

A nagging sixth sense alerted him to the idea that the house was too quiet. He'd left Gertrude and Renee playing cards in the kitchen. Heather had gone home for the night, and Raisa and the two bodyguards were with Mitchell and Grace.

So there shouldn't be anyone sneaking around except for him, right?

Logan shook aside his paranoia and slipped his lock pick into the door. After the lock tumbled open, he peeked over his shoulder into the dark hallway. He was still alone. Pushing open the door, he slipped inside and closed it behind him.

He flipped on his flashlight and swore. The room's kinky decor was both laughable and dangerous. A variety of whips and riding crops lined one wall. A construction-size spool of chain sat in one corner, with a bucket of combination and key locks sitting on top. There was a mirror on the ceiling and a heart-shaped bathtub set off in the adjoining sunporch.

On the shelves he found every scent of lotion and oil he'd ever seen, plus a few he hadn't. In a basket beside the shelves he found sex toys—everything from vibrators to penis rings to clips and dildos that looked as if they would cause more pain than pleasure.

The massive four-poster in the center of the room was draped in heavy red velvet. A series of heavy metal O hooks had been drilled into each post as well as the headboard. A pair of handcuffs hung from each post.

Mitchell's bedroom was a high altar for dirty, decadent sex.

"No way in hell are you ever setting foot in here, Grace."

He felt the cold steel at the back of his skull an instant before he heard the woman's thick German accent. "Dat's not for you to decide, now is it?"

Logan slowly raised his hands in surrender, offering no struggle as Gertrude pulled the gun from his belt and took the flashlight from his grip. At the command of her Browning automatic, he slowly turned around and faced both Gertrude and tiny Renee. The petite gymnast of a woman who'd hauled their bags to their rooms now held an Ithaca Stakeout 12-gauge shotgun with comfortable ease.

"Whaddya wanna do with him?" asked Renee, her twangy Southern drawl grating across his nerves with the glee of a game about to be played. "You've wandered mighty far from the bungalow, Mr. Accountant Man."

"Accountants don't carry veapons," sneered Gertrude. "I say ve lock him up until Mr. Mitchell returns."

Logan risked his version of a charming smile. "I'll admit I'm here on business with Mr. Mitchell. But wouldn't you fine ladies rather have some company to entertain until he gets back? Maybe we could borrow a few of his toys."

Gertrude and Renee exchanged glances, considering the idea. Meanwhile, Logan debated whether to take out the shotgun or the iron maiden. Gertrude was closer but stronger. Renee's shotgun proved the most dangerous threat though.

Renee was the first to answer. "He might be on to somethin' there, Gert."

"Right." Gertrude was a harder sell in the flirtation department. "Get de handcuffs."

With the apparent familiarity of a woman who'd been locked in those handcuffs before, Renee opened a dresser drawer, pulled out a key and unlocked one set of cuffs from the bed. Logan held out his wrists and winked in response to her vampish smile as she hooked the first cuff. The second cuff gave her some trouble. She shifted her gun away from her hand and into the hook of her arm.

It was the chance Logan needed.

In a burst of movement he grabbed the gun and twisted Renee in his arms. He lifted her as a shield at the same time he lifted the gun and took aim at Gertrude. "Drop the gun!"

"Renee!"

When she didn't immediately respond, Logan pulled the trigger, knocking her pistol from her hand.

"Ow!"

"Gert!"

"Back up," Logan warned, edging his way toward the door, dragging Renee with him while Gert massaged her stinging hand. Once he was in the hall, he gave a second command. "Now get over here and lead—"

An explosion of pain ripped through the back of Logan's head. His glasses flew off his face as an icy blackness radiated through his skull. He dropped Renee and the gun and staggered against the wall.

"It's a good thing I came back early to make sure

everything was prepared for Mr. Mitchell and his guest.'' Tanya the Amazon's voice registered behind him.

But when he turned, his legs wobbled beneath him and he crumpled to the floor. In his spinning world he was only vaguely aware of Tanya's dark hands fastening the second manacle around his wrist. "Lock him up downstairs until we find out more about him. I want to know if he's nosy or a thief or after something more.''

Logan felt himself being lifted beneath either arm by Gertrude and a surprisingly strong Renee. His only struggle was to remain conscious as they dragged him down the hall. But even that battle would soon be lost.

Women! he bemoaned silently as his world spun toward oblivion.

And the one he loved the most would be helpless without him.

16

WHERE was Logan?

Grace had been hoping against hope that she'd find him waiting in her bedroom, a computer disk dangling from his fingers and a sly grin of success creasing his handsome mouth.

She'd talked up a storm as they'd neared the estate gates, warning him through her microphone of their imminent arrival almost an hour ago. She'd asked Harris for sixty minutes to prepare herself for their evening together, hoping that would be long enough for Logan to get her some kind of message about his success or failure.

Had he found the hidden computer? Was he safe? Was backup on the way?

Grace studied herself in the dresser mirror, seeing a paper-doll image of a grown woman dressed in a white lace teddy and matching robe, looking for all the world like an innocent lamb being led to the slaughter. Harris wouldn't like the virginal look, she was sure.

Well, not on her, at any rate.

But that was the idea. She'd play his game so far, keep him occupied as Logan had requested. But, ultimately, she hoped she would be a big turn-off and that Harris's interest would wane before he did anything to her too horrible to even consider.

She applied a pale pink lipstick to add to her untouched look and stewed about Logan. If he had found the computer, where was he? If he hadn't...

Grace's heart turned over and her stomach clenched into a knot.

If he hadn't found the computer then she'd have to complete the mission on her own.

And the only reason why Logan couldn't have searched two rooms in the time they'd been gone was if he'd gotten into trouble. "No." She looked at the image in the mirror and told her that wasn't an acceptable explanation. "He's all right. Something's gone wrong, but he's all right. He has to be."

A sharp knock at her door ended her prayers and speculation. Logan would have simply snuck in, so this had to be Harris or one of his women.

"Miss Lockhart?" Ilsa. "It is time. Mr. Mitchell does not like to be kept waiting."

"I'll be right there."

For a woman who usually had so much trouble controlling her blushing, Grace had suddenly grown pale. She pinched some color into her cheeks and headed for the door. At the last second she went back to her attaché and reached inside for her flush-out computer disk.

Slipping it into the pocket of her robe, Grace stood straight. She lifted her chin at a defiant angle and fixed a pouty expression of disdain on her lips.

She was going to complete this mission. She'd find the damn computer herself and corrupt the system. She'd put the cuffs on Harris Mitchell so tight they'd pinch, giving him a small taste of what he'd done to her mother. Once she read him his rights, she'd turn this mansion inside out until she found Logan and knew he was all right.

Because they were partners. He was counting on her to complete the mission and come out of it in one piece.

Roy Silverton hadn't and it had nearly destroyed Logan.

But she would get the job done.

She wouldn't let Logan down.

THE PAINFUL THROBBING in his head was the first indication to Logan that he'd regained consciousness.

He opened his eyes to escape the blackness, but discovered he was locked in a small room, a closet maybe, and that he was trapped in the dark. A pinch at his wrists told him he was still handcuffed.

He breathed deeply, in through his nose and out through his mouth, taking in reviving oxygen and clearing his head before sitting up. He groaned and pressed his hands to his forehead, cursing the dizziness that resulted from changing positions.

A few minutes later his head had cleared enough to start thinking of escape. He checked his watch—11:00 p.m. Grace would be back by now. Hell. She could be with Mitchell by now. Double hell. If he'd been found out, then Grace could be dead.

He pushed aside the flood of white-hot anger that clouded his rational thinking and forced himself to concentrate. Commander Carmody had set them up with thorough fake backgrounds. If Tanya did have him checked out, she'd find an unambitious accountant with an assortment of degrees and a penchant for betting on the races.

She wouldn't find an FBI agent intent on making her pay for whatever harm might come to Grace.

He'd been twenty minutes late and a lifetime too short when he'd gone to back up Roy Silverton.

He'd die before he'd let the same mistake take Grace from him.

Logan quickly took stock of his surroundings. The bitter smells of cinnamon and nutmeg teased his nose, along with the sweet scent of peanut butter. He could hear two women talking. A heavy German accent and a backwoods twang.

He must be in the pantry off the kitchen. How would he get himself out of there? How would he get past Gertrude and Renee and the bodyguards who were surely patrolling the house now?

Logan Pierce wasn't the best in the business for nothing.

He climbed to his feet and felt his way around the pantry shelves. He found what he was searching for and smiled.

From the top shelf he picked up the heaviest can he could find. Then he knocked a second can to the floor, setting off a chain reaction of falling foods, and waited.

Moments later he heard a key in the lock. The door opened. Logan charged.

It was only a matter of seconds before Gertrude was out cold and she and Renee were locked in the pantry in his place. He found his Undercover .38 on the table, checked the cartridge and tucked it into his waistband. While Renee shouted and pounded on the door, Logan emptied the magazine from her Ithaca shotgun and tossed it into the trash.

With his wrists still manacled, he stole through the house, taking the straightest route down the hall and up the stairs toward Mitchell's bedroom.

He ran into Ilsa first. But her killer kick was no match for a man on a mission. He wrapped the chain of the cuffs around her neck and wrestled her to the floor, squeezing her throat until a lack of oxygen rendered her unconscious.

While he searched her for a key to unlock the cuffs, he heard the first screams.

"No! I won't! You can't make me!"

Logan froze. His heart pumped ice in his veins at the terrified sound, pleading for mercy.

Logan frowned. Those weren't Grace's screams. It wasn't even a woman.

"No! What are you doing?"

Harris Mitchell was playing one of his sick, masochistic games.

"Yes!"

That was Grace's triumphant shout. Oh, God, no.

Logan pulled a key from Ilsa's boot and was running, praying. He freed one wrist as he bounded up the stairs two, then three, at a time. With the other cuff still dangling from his wrist he pulled his gun and bolted down the hall, charging straight at Tanya.

She pulled her gun and unfolded herself from her stool. "You can't come in here," she warned, setting her stance and aiming her gun. "Mr. Mitchell!"

Tanya fired. Logan fired. She dodged. One blow to the side of her head and she was knocked out. She crumpled to the floor.

"Grace!"

He shook the knob and pounded on the door.

"Gr—!"

He stepped back as the lock turned, and braced his gun between his hands.

The door swung open.

"Lo—" Grace swallowed his name and stumbled back a step when she saw the gun pointed at her face. "I'm okay." She pushed her palms in the air, warning him of her surrender. "I'm okay."

Stepping into the hallway, she pulled the door closed

and launched herself into his arms the second he lowered the gun. Logan gathered her in, squeezing her roughly, burying his nose in her hair. "Gracie, I'm sorry. I'm so sorry I didn't get here in time."

He ran his free hand up and down her back, along her arms, across her bottom, checking for signs of injury. Dressed in some white scraps of cotton and lace, she felt firm and round and full of life. Everything seemed to be healthy and in one piece. He couldn't find any bruises or marks.

And then he palmed the back of her head, kissing her hard, raining kisses on her cheeks and eyes and anywhere he could reach. And she was kissing him back, clinging to his neck, combing her fingers into his hair. Laughing.

"Oh, Logan, I did it!" She caught his jaw and kissed him full on the mouth. "I did it!" She continued to talk between kisses. "I found your broken glasses...outside Mitchell's door and knew...you were in trouble. I knew I had to finish...the mission. I knew...you'd come...if you could."

The mission? "What are you talking about, baby. Are you okay?"

"I'm fine. Really, I'm fine." As panic fled and sense returned, she pulled away from his arms and latched on to his hand. She found the handcuff. "What happened?" She shook her head and flashed a gorgeous smile. "Never mind. Let me show you."

She pushed open the door and led her inside. Logan caught sight of Harris Mitchell standing next to the bed and raised his gun. "No, Logan, it's okay."

Only at the touch of Grace's hand did he lower his weapon.

Then he got a better look at the bastard. Mitchell had become the victim—whether willing or not—of his own toys. He was handcuffed to a bedpost, dressed in a fur-trimmed gown with something that looked very much like a tail hanging down his back.

"What's *he* doing here?" Mitchell's demand sounded like a spoiled child's shrill demand. "I told you I don't like other men around. If you want another woman, fine. But no—"

"Shut up." That was Grace. Logan looked down to see her plant her fists on her hips and order Mitchell into submission.

"Yes, ma'am." Did that suddenly subdued voice really belong to a notorious crime lord?

Grace flipped out her hand toward Logan with all the snap and polish of a dictator signaling an execution. "Give me your badge."

"Did I miss something here?" asked Logan. He kept his gun in his hand and didn't respond to her request, too confused by what he was witnessing to surrender his defense.

Mitchell laughed. Grace snapped her fingers. Mitchell fell silent. "Your badge, Logan? Please?" she added softly.

Responding to this kinder, gentler version of the Grace he knew, he reached into his back pocket and pulled out the wallet that held his Bureau shield. Grace snatched it from his hand and crossed over to Mitchell. She opened the wallet and shoved the badge in his face.

Mitchell squinted. He looked from the badge to Logan to Grace. The color drained from his face and the bravado faded from his voice as shock set in. "You really are with the FBI. I thought that was part of the game."

Grace threw her shoulders back and puffed out her chest in a gloriously feminine show of pride. "Agent Grace Lockhart, FBI. You, sir, are under arrest for multiple counts of money laundering, extortion, assault…and rude and indecent behavior."

"That's not a crime—"

"Whoa, Gracie." Logan grabbed her elbow and pulled her back a step as her temper flared. He retreated even farther as Mitchell's face ruddied with color.

"You damn little bitch! You can't arrest me in my own—"

"Shut up!"

Logan turned at the sharp tone of Grace's command. He took her by both arms and swiveled her to face him, gentling his voice and trying not to sound too confused about what must have happened during the hour he'd spent unconscious in the pantry. "What happened? Did he hurt you?"

She shook her head and smiled, clearly pleased with herself. "It's a little trick I learned from my mother."

"Your mother?" Had Logan fallen into the Twilight Zone? "How did Mimsey get involved with this?"

Mitchell tried to join the private conversation. "I knew Mimsey once, you know. I could have had the mother and the daughter both."

Grace turned and shook a finger at her captive. "Harris, if you mention my mother's name ever again, your days as a junior Marquis de Sade are over."

Mitchell responded with a steely gaze.

Logan surveyed the room. Every torturous device and sick toy was still in place. But he had a funny feeling that Grace wasn't in any danger. Not really.

"Is something going on that I should know about?" he asked.

"Just wait." She disappeared into the closet.

"Grace?" She reappeared moments later, waving a

computer disk and looking triumphant in her teddy and—
"Riding boots?"

Though he'd been quick to notice the revealing cotton
and lace she wore, he hadn't paid much attention to the
tall leather boots that clung to her thighs.

"It's a long story," she reassured him with a smile.
"The important thing is—after I handcuffed Harris to the
bed—"

Logan waved aside her explanation, demanding that
she make sense. "Wait a minute. How did you get him
cuffed? If there's no room for a badge in that getup
you're wearing, where did you stash your gun?"

She smiled. "I didn't need it. He wanted to play a
game. So I made one up. Once I applied a few of those
tricks from your list, he was incredibly easy to manipu-
late."

That didn't bode well. "A game?"

Now she was the impatient one. "That doesn't matter.
I found another secret room off the back of his closet
when I went searching for a costume. I located the main
terminal and downloaded my program. Commander Carmody should be able to round up every member of
Mitchell's organization now."

"Carmody." Logan swore. "We need to call in
backup."

"Taken care of." Grace's smile was practically contagious. Had she ever looked this happy? This confident?
"I sent him an e-mail. He'll be automatically paged as
soon as the message is received. But I suppose we could
track down a phone if we need to."

She'd done it. She'd actually done it. Grace Lockhart,
frumpy computer nerd without a clue about men or life
as a field agent, had done it.

Logan's trepidation about her safety receded a little.

His chest swelled with pride and he let his smile match hers. "You pulled it off, sweetheart. You got your man."

Grace's smile faltered for an instant, then returned. "I learned from the best." She laid her hand against his cheek. Logan lost himself in her big green eyes and savored the gentle touch. "You trained me well...partner."

"I had amazing material to work with. Partner."

With that he bent and sealed his pride and thanks with a kiss.

The sound of approaching sirens broke their embrace. Grace looked up at Logan. "Can we go home now?" she asked.

Logan picked up her robe and wrapped it around her. It didn't hide much, so he draped his arm around her shoulders and led her out of the room.

Home. It sounded good. But he wondered if he could really ever find his way there.

A COUPLE OF DAYS LATER, Grace was packing up her attaché when Sam Carmody stepped into her office. Automatically, she straightened to attention and smoothed the hem of her mint-green skirt. "Well?" she asked.

"Mitchell's arraignment went just the way we wanted. The federal attorney filed charges of money laundering, extortion and racketeering, and linked him as an accessory to numerous violent crimes. Even if he bargains his way out of some of the charges, he'll be going to prison for a very long time."

"And the others?"

"His female crew has already been arraigned, and the attorney general's office is going to be busy for several months running the trials of every two-bit hood and big-money connection your computer program exposed."

Sam Carmody smiled and extended his hand. "Good work, Lockhart."

Feeling his respect in his smile and praise, she shook his hand. "Thank you, sir."

"Now go take a few days off. You deserve a break."

After Carmody left, Grace wondered exactly what she was supposed to do with herself. More than anything she wanted to call Logan. They'd been separated for debriefing shortly after leaving Mitchell's estate. Then she heard he'd been called in to consult on another assignment, sent out into the field already, and she'd gone home. Alone.

He'd promised to call, but he hadn't. Was he busy? Should she wait? Was it over? Had there ever been anything real between them?

She slipped a file folder into her bag and her fingertips brushed against something else. Something familiar.

She pulled out her steno pad with all the notes she'd taken from Logan. The sexy list. The lies. The words of frustration and hope that she'd poured onto the pages as she learned about herself and men and sex and life.

And love.

The Grace of old would have replaced the steno pad, taken it home and packed it away in a trunk.

But the new Grace smiled. It was a wickedly fun, yet hopeful smile.

Sitting back in her chair she pulled out her mechanical pencil, clicked it twice and started to write.

BY MIDNIGHT that same night, she heard the well-tuned roar of a Harley-Davidson motorcycle pulling into the driveway of her saltbox.

Grace checked her hair in the mirror, then cinched the belt of her fuzzy white robe.

She opened the door before the bell stopped ringing.

For a moment she could only stare up into Logan's flint-colored eyes. She took in the haggard lines of fatigue on his face and smiled. "Hi."

That same gray gaze roamed her face as if reacquainting himself with every eyelash and stray curl of hair. And then that gaze zeroed in on hers. "I got your message. You said something came up with the Mitchell case. Are you all right?"

She invited him inside and shut the door behind her. "Carmody says you're back on assignment already. Don't you get any downtime?"

Logan shrugged, crinkling the leather of his coat and filling her living room with its rich, rugged scent. "Yeah, well, no rest for the weary, hmm?"

His ever-observant eyes took in the crackling fire in the hearth. The two wineglasses set on the mantel.

And the chess board set up on the coffee table between her two couches.

"There's nothing wrong with the Mitchell case, is there." It wasn't a question.

Her heart raced in anticipation of what she must do next.

"No. But I knew you'd ride to my rescue if you thought I was in trouble."

He buried his hands deep in his pockets. His breath seeped out on a weary sigh. "Gracie...I'm—I don't know if I can give you what you need. You deserve someone who can stick around—"

"Shh." She pressed her finger against his lips and shushed him. As long as he loved her, he had everything she needed. She took heart in his vulnerability, knowing their strengths complemented each other. Knowing that, together, they created a stronger whole. "I wanted to show you something."

She crossed to the mantel and picked up her steno pad. "What are you trying to learn this time?"

"Nothing." She turned to him and smiled. "I'm conducting the training this time." His eyes narrowed, questioning her. "I've made a list."

"Of what?"

"The ten reasons why we should be together."

Logan's face paled, then flushed with color. He took a step toward her, then pulled back with a look of distress. "Grace, since I was a little kid, I've never had anybody or anything to call my own. The things I care about get taken away, and it's made me a hard man to live with. You don't want to do this. You'll only wind up getting hurt. And I don't want to be responsible for that."

He was breathing hard by the time he'd finished. Grace waited patiently, her heart breaking for all he had lost. But she couldn't go to him. Not yet.

"Are you done?"

"I guess."

"Then it's your turn to listen to me." He angled his head at the determined tone in her voice. "I want you to learn every item on this list and I want you to believe it. I want you to think, live and breathe the items on this list."

His mouth quirked into half of a smile. "I never said that to you."

"No. But I did it anyway. Here goes.

"Number one. The sex between us is great."

His smile blossomed. "You'll get no argument there."

Good. It was a hopeful start. "Number two. I need someone to watch my back and keep me out of trouble."

He shook his head. "I don't think so. You managed Mitchell fine all by yourself."

She moved a step closer. "That's not true. If you hadn't inspired confidence in me, I'd have tucked my tail between my legs and quit before the job was done. Emotional support is just as vital as physical support."

"Okay, I'll give you that." He unzipped his jacket. Maybe he could feel the temperature in the room starting to rise, too. "What else is on your list?"

"Number three. We make a dynamite investigative team."

"Is this list about work or us?"

Grace swallowed hard. "Is there an *us?*"

Logan shrugged out of his jacket and hung it over the back of a chair. He nodded toward the steno pad. "Finish your list."

"Number four. You like my mother."

"Mimsey's great." He tempered his enthusiastic response. "Do *you* like your mother?"

She smiled. "I'm beginning to. I'm having dinner with her and her fiancé tomorrow night."

"I'll have to congratulate her. Next rule."

"Number five. I like your Harley."

Logan nodded with a smug expression on his face. "All smart women like Harleys."

Grace laughed and stepped closer. "Number six. The sex between us is *really* great."

Now Logan was laughing, too. He moved across the room until only the coffee table separated them. "I guess I'm an excellent teacher."

She gave credit where it was due. "I guess you are." Slowly, she began to circle the table. "Number seven. I didn't really believe in myself until you believed in me."

"Aw, Gracie." He reached out and brushed his fingers across her cheek.

She turned her cheek into the caress and savored the

gentle touch of his calloused hand. Then she turned and pressed a kiss into his palm. "Number eight. You want a place to come home to at night."

He caught her jaw between his hands and angled her face up to his. His eyes were dark now, dark with fire, not with shadows. "What are you saying to me, Gracie?"

She smiled, blinking back the tears that suddenly stung her eyes. "Number nine. I love you."

She tossed the steno pad on the couch.

"And number ten." She took a deep breath. "You love me."

"You *are* a smart lady." Logan lifted her up onto her toes and covered her mouth in a blazing, rapturous, soul-healing kiss.

Grace offered him all that she was, all that she believed, all that she carried in her heart.

"What's under the robe, Gracie?" His lips scudded across her cheek and nipped at her ear.

She had her hands up under his sweater, scorching her fingers on the heat of his muscled back and flanks. "What do you want to find under it?"

"You."

A half hour later they were lying in front of the fire, their naked bodies spooned together beneath a quilt from her couch. As Grace's pulse rate returned to normal, Logan traced lazy circles up and down her arm. She was floating in a sea of blissful warmth, with the fire in front of her and Logan at her back and love in her heart.

"Gracie?"

"Hmm?" Thoroughly loved, she was almost too tired to respond.

"I really am meeting with Carmody tomorrow about a new assignment."

"No." So soon? She rolled over and faced him, raising

her hand to his cheek. "Is it one that will put you in danger?"

"Only if you say no."

Damn it all, the man was grinning. Grace's leap of fear transformed into curiosity.

"Say no to what?"

"Becoming my partner."

"Your partner?"

"In every sense of the word." He scooped her into his arms and rolled onto his back, carrying her with him so that she rested on top. "I do love you, Gracie. I do. There's no one else I'd rather have watching my back. And I can't get enough of watching yours."

Her eyes swam with joyful tears. "I love you, too." She kissed him once. "Yes." She kissed him again. "Yes, I want to be partners in every way. My house is big enough for you to move in. There's room for the Harley in the garage. I keep fresh coff—"

He kissed her then. It was long and sweet and full of promise.

He left her lips to explore that erogenous minefield he'd discovered at the base of her throat. "We make an unbeatable team, Gracie. I've put in a lot of years out in the field. Maybe I'll take fewer assignments—"

She traced his lips with her fingertip. "Just the ones we can work together."

He nipped at her fingers and smiled. "Then I think I'll come back and teach at the Bureau academy. Something tells me I might be pretty good at it."

"As long as you're not teaching Seduction 101 to anyone else."

"No way, sweetheart." He took her breast into his mouth and teased her with his tongue, igniting the passion between them all over again. "I only give private lessons in that department."

Then he rolled her beneath him and taught her about making love all over again.

Blaze

The Trueblood, Texas
tradition continues in...

 HARLEQUIN® *Blaze*™

TRULY, MADLY, DEEPLY
by Vicki Lewis Thompson
August 2002

Ten years ago, Dustin Ramsey and Erica Mann shared their first
sexual experience. It was a disaster. Now Dustin's determined to
find—and seduce—Erica again, to prove to her, and himself, that
he can do better. Much, *much* better. Only, little does he guess
that Erica's got the same agenda....

Don't miss Blaze's next two sizzling Trueblood tales:

EVERY MOVE YOU MAKE by Tori Carrington
September 2002
&
LOVE ON THE ROCKS by Debbi Rawlins
October 2002

Available wherever Harlequin books are sold.

TRUEBLOOD,
TEXAS

HARLEQUIN®
Makes any time special®

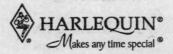

If you enjoyed what you just read,
then we've got an offer you can't resist!

Take 2 bestselling
love stories FREE!

Plus get a FREE surprise gift!

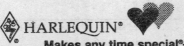